D1074738

The
Daughter
Ship

The Daughter Ship

Boo Trundle

PANTHEON BOOKS NEW YORK

All rights reserved. Published in the United States by Pantheon Books, a division of Penguin Random House LLC, New York, and distributed in Canada by Penguin Random House Canada Limited, Toronto.

Pantheon Books and colophon are registered trademarks of Penguin Random House LLC.

Small portions of this story were previously published in *Seventies Gold* by 3 a.m. analog in 2015.

Library of Congress Cataloging-in-Publication Data
Name: Trundle, Boo, author.
Title: The daughter ship : a novel / Boo Trundle.
Description: First edition. New York : Pantheon Books, 2023
Identifiers: LCCN 2022045467 (print). LCCN 2022045468 (ebook).
ISBN 9780593317297 (hardcover). ISBN 9780593317303 (ebook).
Subjects: LCGFT: Novels.
Classification: LCC PS3620.R859 D38 2023 (print) |
LCC PS3620.R859 (ebook) | DDC 813/.6—dc23/eng/20220926
LC record available at https://lccn.loc.gov/2022045467
LC ebook record available at https://lccn.loc.gov/2022045468

www.pantheonbooks.com

Jacket illustration by Boo Trundle
Jacket design by Jenny Carrow

Printed in the United States of America

First Edition

1st Printing

for viv and ray

Part One

TRUITT

I want to introduce you to my girls. We all live together in a U-boat. Why are we trapped in a German submarine? Because my dad Craig is a World War II buff. We grew up browsing his bookshelves in Virginia Beach. It's a naval town, home to aircraft carriers and battleships. Fighter jets rip the sky above the dunes. Somewhere underwater, and not too deep, is our submarine, a ghost ship, a wreck, a childhood. *Ping.* (That's the sound of the echo sonar, searching for a target.)

I may not be the smartest kid in the submarine, but I'm the loudest and the strongest, and it's up to me to decide what's true. The others have their own idea of true—Smooshed Bug, Star. They have their stories.

Smooshed Bug says, "There's no such thing as true."

"I know what's true," I tell her. "I know what happened."

"True to you," she says, "is not the same as true."

I'll give you a tour of the *Unterseeboot,* and that's the last German word I'll use. Undersea boat. You know the shape, a cigar. I'll start up front: powered torpedo room and crew quarters (bunk beds soldered into the hull), officers' quarters, galley kitchen, radio closet, control room . . . keep coming, follow me through . . . here's the engine room, and then, at the very back, another torpedo room. Two hundred and twenty feet, bow to stern. We're starting this very claustrophobic. Everyone lives on top of each other. There's pressure on every inch of the boat from all that water. *Ping.*

My dad loved to read about Adolf Hitler, Japan, Italy, all that mess. His bookshelf was full of red and black. He also loved boats, cars, tractors, anything with an engine. He spent most of his free time on his back gazing at the underbelly of a car.

Dad's garage was a run-down shack, the only structure left when my parents bought the lakefront property. They built an angular, supermod house but left the doorless shack in the house's shadow with a dirt floor and one broken window, dusty and jagged.

I see myself standing in that dirt in my scouting gear. Khaki shirt, white kneesocks, shorts, and a tidy red scarf. (I've earned twenty-five badges, which isn't easy.) A humid summer night, still not dark, though it should have been. I was waiting to say something to my dad, to get his attention. He was under the car, and he didn't like visitors. Why was I out there? Maybe it was time for dinner.

He held a greasy black wrench in his hand. He was mad. Something was wrong. Maybe he couldn't fit the connecting rod into the crankshaft. He took his wrench and whacked a pipe. Any old car, Dad could get it going. He had a magical ability to fix his special things, and they were always breaking.

There were three radios lined up next to each other on a workbench inside the garage. He also had an extra refrigerator out there, where he kept his beer. He tuned all his radios to the same station, a talk show. Dad yelled at callers, every single one, as he worked. "Goddamn idiot!" I agreed with his disagreeing. I hated what Dad hated, including Mom.

He didn't look up, even after I called out to him, so I went inside the house, where it wasn't time for dinner. Mom was upstairs, writhing on the bedroom floor. I didn't like that, whatever it was, maybe excess energy in her body, an overload to the power station. I wanted nothing to do with it.

Dad stuck his name on everything we shouldn't touch. He had a plastic labeling gun, very high-tech. He typed out his initials on stiff pieces of tape so there was no mistaking what was his. Band-Aid box, camera case, glass bottles of Coke. He even labeled his pencils. He moved the tape down as he sharpened them.

As soon as I was old enough, I climbed onto a chair, broke into his briefcase, and chewed through his pack of Juicy Fruit gum. His ten-speed bike had a leather tool case, a fitted satchel with snaps that attached under the seat. There was tape on the satchel, tape on the seat, tape on the handlebars. Plus, the seat was too tall for my legs. I rode it anyway. Fell, got hurt. Did it again.

If there had been someone to see me try and fail, some kind of witness, it might have gone better. A watcher. A scout for the scout. (There never is one, you know.) What would that other scout have seen? Me, the girls, all of us. Being pulled toward a fan in socks on a well-oiled floor.

STAR

I never was a whore. I did work as a stripper at a place called Eddie's Topless. This was in 1996, when I was twenty-three. The best thing about a job in a titty bar is that you get to make up a fake name. I went with *Star*.

Eddie's Topless took up the first floor of a stucco Tudor house out in Queens, New York, close to LaGuardia Airport.

It was bottom rung, seedy. Let's go back there, to a May afternoon. The bar was mostly empty, as usual. I went onstage barefoot in a frilly vintage nightgown and slowly pulled it over my
head. Underneath, I was already down to my thong. I only had
one. It was made of black cotton, stretched and faded. I played
a horny, depressive housewife. Natalie, the bartender/manager,
found this act amusing.

Two guys walked in and sat at a front table. When I came
down from the stage, a wooden platform covered with filthy red
carpeting, Natalie dragged me over.

"Can Star join you?"

The men looked up. Boys, really. Like me, they were in their
early twenties.

"Hi, Star," said one of them. "I love your fake name."

Fake name? Ha. What was my real name then? *Katchie.*

"Are you okay?" asked Natalie.

"Oh yeah," I said. "It's just . . . I know these guys."

But they didn't know each other. Or they weren't supposed
to. One was my older brother Gordon; the other was Max, my
best friend in New York City.

"Cute friends," said Natalie. "Friends still have to buy drinks."

Gordon wiped his forehead with the sleeve of his button-
down shirt. Natalie moved off, and Gordon looked like he
might cry. I dropped into a chair.

"What the hell are you doing here?"

"You have to come home. I'm not leaving here without you."

"This is stupid," I said. "Max, you shouldn't have brought
him here."

"Come back to Virginia Beach with me," said Gordon. "Dad
says he'll pay for film school."

"I didn't know you applied to film school," said Max.

"I'm not doing this."

I ran off, upstairs. The dressing room smelled like cockroach spray. I pulled off my blond wig and stared at myself in the mirror. My short brown hair was self-cut, chaotic. My face looked fat and puffy. The face of a girl who lives in a submarine. We kept going down, and then we would go deeper from there, and farther into the black, cold, unknowable places. This required us to submerge with our main vents open. The seawater rushed into the ballast tanks, allowing us to sink, sink. To resurface, we would have to push the water back out of our holes.

Ascent. It takes a lot of force and power. Better to stay on the surface in the first place, like my friends from Brown. These girls—they were my first friends in New York—all managed to live periscope deep. They shared taxis, found promising internships, and lived in doorman buildings. I was at Eddie's with my ass in the air.

SMOOSHED BUG

"Star, come back! You're in a dark place."

Star jolts upright. Bursts of violet, red, yellow, and orange light explode from the top of her head, and from her hands and feet. She's spinning and rocketing like a firecracker. Even her lady parts go up in flames. When she's done burning, all that's left is a lightbulb that hangs in the galley kitchen of the submarine. Star can talk through it when she's needed, if she's needed. I'll decide.

"Relax," I say. "Sit down."

Truitt sits his butt down at the navigator's desk. It's in the middle of the passage, screwed to the floor, a table with folding leaves.

"I want to tell you a story."

"No, Bug. No story." Star is talking to me, but she is still in the lightbulb. I can barely hear her. "Your stories suck."

"This is a good one, I promise."

"Is it 'Jack in the Beanstalk'?" asks Truitt. He has his sextant and his gyroscope lined up over his nautical charts, which is silly. Our steel coffin hasn't budged in years.

"No," I tell him. "It's not 'Jack and the Beanstalk.' Haven't you heard that one enough?"

"Then it's a memory. Not a story. Why don't you call it what it is? It's one of your precious memories and you want to tell us all about it again and again."

I hate to annoy Truitt. But I have to talk. And talk and talk. There's nothing else to do. The submarine is hot and smelly. Green mold on the sliced bread. Rotten lemons with white sores on the rind. Sheets that were wet with sweat then dried again. Wool blankets that smell like feet. And NOT MUCH AIR.

I stand in the galley kitchen. Space is tight; there's no natural light. I'm wearing dirty polyester separates from the Sears catalog. Star is thirteen, Truitt is fifteen, and I'm only eight, but I'm the leader. Truitt is afraid of me. He has to take care of me; he can't hurt me. He wouldn't dare.

"It's a love story," I say. "Because I loved Millie."

"Tell it, then," says Star. Her bulb is out. She'll light up again when a man comes around.

"I won't stop you," says Truitt.

All right. I've always loved horses. The plastic kind. Our next-door neighbor Millie collected them. Pinto, bronco, mustang, colt. Lined up on top of her dresser like they were about to run away. I escaped to her house all the time, whenever I could.

We spent hours on her living room floor making houses out of playing cards. My houses always fell down, right before I finished them. If I tried to stop building, Millie bit me.

I was there with her when a bad man called the house. Millie answered the phone. The prank caller said, "How old are you?"

Millie answered, "Seven and a half."

The caller said, "I want to lick between your legs."

Millie hung up and told me what happened. Since she told me right away, it felt like this bad thing had happened to me, too. Her mom was at the store.

Millie shrugged and said, "Let's take the raft out."

I knew this wasn't allowed, and on top of that a bad idea, but I followed Millie down to the lake and her family's inflatable rubber raft. Float Lake was muddy, low tide, black and slurpy. We dropped the raft over the side of the bulkhead and climbed down the dock's wooden ladder. To steady the raft, I carefully placed my hand against the dock piling. It was covered with barnacles.

"I don't want to go out in the boat," I said. "I'm not allowed."

"Too late now," said Millie, and pushed us off in the shallow water. I started to cry.

"You're such a damn baby."

I jumped from the boat into the mud and scrambled up the barnacle-covered wall, then ran home with shredded hands and feet. Blood everywhere. I needed stitches, lots, to pull everything back together. This was back when stitches didn't go away on their own. A doctor had to pull them out.

"That's enough story time." Truitt drops down from the ladder. "THE END!"

He puts his hand over my mouth to prove his point.

"Do you want to show us your scars?"

I sit down to take off my socks. He shouts, "I don't want to see your stupid scars!"

Then he climbs the tower ladder again and wedges himself into an upper rung. The submarine shudders and we hear, off in the far underwater, a muffled explosion.

"Torpedo!" says Truitt, very serious, concerned. "The submariners are awake."

This is the cue for Star to start fingering herself, absentmindedly. You know where. The lightbulb flickers.

TRUITT

When I listen to Smooshed Bug's story, I picture Katchie the way she is now, five feet nine, with a size ten shoe, a loud white lady with a Prada purse. Oh, and she calls herself *Katherine*. With this stature, she could have been a brave little girl. But she was scared, weak, and ineffective. She had a tiny little heart and a growing head. Her feet were feathery, her voice a gurgle. When she scrambled up those barnacles, she knew what would happen.

"I don't want to see your stupid scars!" I tell Bug.

Katchie loved Millie a hundred thousand years ago. Then she grew up and married Phil. She had no problem attaching

him to her body. He bit into her belly shortly after they met.
He latched on. His body fused with hers. This is what happens
when a barnacle stops swimming around.

It's hard to say bad things about our husband Phil. Everyone
loves him. He's handsome and rich; he's nice and laid-back.
In fact, he's perfect. But what about that time he shrunk Em's
favorite sweater? Was that perfect? Then he put the sweater on
Emily's teddy bear and tried to make her laugh. Em didn't laugh.
Neither did Katherine. It wasn't funny.

He lost the children's jackets. He misplaced shoes and hats.
He burned pasta, which isn't easy. He lost the shopping lists
after he got in the car to go to the store. He disappeared for days
and days and left the mundane tasks to Katherine. She didn't
complain. She felt so pointless, a casualty of the passage of time.
She went back to the grocery store, back to the pharmacy, back
to the preschool, back to the mall. Back and back and back and
back. She filled the tank with gas.

Emily was a sucker. All day and all night, she sucked on the
corner of her blanket. She made it stink. Her sweet little mouth,
innocent spit. Katherine had to wash the blanket constantly.
Along with all the other clothes.

"Read the tags before you throw stuff in the dryer. It's
important to me!"

"It fits Teddyman now."

Phil tried to make a joke of it.

"Teddyman has a new sweater!"

Barnacles produce a sticky stuff in their ovaries. A cement.
They secrete it through their antennae. It's hard to see these
antennae, but every woman has them, trust me. It's my job to
know these things.

"Don't help me, Phil. Don't do the laundry. If you can't read a fucking tag."

Em's blankie was like a shriveled squirrel carcass on a state highway. Her dry saliva smelled dead. This was a surprise to Katherine, because she loved everything about her children. To her, even their sweat was sweet. Their shits, adorable. Not Phil's. His shit stank. And he wouldn't read tags. On clothes. When he washed them. That's how he ruined everything.

KATHERINE

The only thing I know for sure, other than the fact that I still exist, is that I gave birth to Emily and Zack. There was nothing there, no breath of body, no firing of cells. Phil and I conjured them out of thin air. Then we raised them through puberty and into their teens. You don't get an Oscar for that. You get jack squat.

When they were little, and I was away from them, they missed me more than anyone has ever missed me before or will ever miss me again. Parts of their souls turned off. Terror oozed from their questions if I called.

"Do you have your plane ticket already to fly home?"

"Is your stomach okay?"

"Will we be awake when you get to the house?"

"What if there's a fire at your hotel?"

Zack gave me detailed reports of his life without me. He held his breath on the phone when he talked. This made him sound like a dying man who wants to get his last words in. Emily offered summaries of nightmares, fresh every day. An alien who paralyzed children with its tears. A terrorist at school who put a bomb up the teacher's skirt. The relief and joy on their faces when they saw me come through the door! It was enough to pop their cheeks. They bubbled and chattered, lighting up in my presence. Love!

But what else did they know? They were four, seven. To them, I was perfect. Phil was perfect, too, in his distant, never-home, upstairs-on-a-conference-call way. Phil and I made these people, and we had the advantage. We couldn't get rid of it.

STAR

From Eddie's, the titty bar in Queens, I took a car service straight over to see my boyfriend Ian. He let me in the apartment's service door, which opened up to what we called his "bunk room."

"Keep your voice down," he said, getting back into his bottom bunk. He made those beds. To save space, I guess. It was tight for two. "Maggie and the baby are sleeping."

I was very drunk. My words were sliding.

"Make me pregnant," I said. "Please get me pregnant."

Ian pulled back. "What?"

"Mothers aren't sluts. Only daughters."

"Come on, Katchie."

"Women with children don't kill themselves."

He held me after that. Stroked my hair. "That's not true anyway."

I woke up the next morning in Ian's bunk. He was sitting at his desk, messing around with an old typewriter. Someone was cooking food in the kitchen. It smelled like bacon.

I sat up slowly. I had a terrible brain-ache. Ian turned to face me.

"So," he said. "You want a baby?"

"What?"

"You don't remember telling me that last night?"

"I don't want a baby."

"I hope you didn't forget all the fun stuff that happened after."

He smiled, and it came back to me. Ian was good with his fingers. Magical, even. But here was Maggie, suddenly standing at the bedroom door. "Ian, come help me in the kitchen."

I dropped my head back to the pillow. I got up after a while and joined Ian at the table in the kitchen. Maggie was washing dishes in the sink.

"Hi, Katchie. Did Ian tell you we're gonna move away from here?" She was talking over her shoulder. "Maybe next year."

Ian didn't say anything. His daughter Siobhan was sitting next to him in her high chair, playing with her Cheerios.

"New York's too toxic," said Maggie. "Especially for girls." She glanced at me. "You look horrible. Are you okay?"

"Not really," I said.

"We'll take her to Ireland," said Ian. "Raise her there. With my people."

"Yeah," I said. "My brother wants me to go back to Virginia Beach. But I can't. I have too much going on here."

"You do?" said Maggie. "What do you have going on?"

"My film work."

"When was the last time you worked on a film that Ian wasn't involved in? And when was the last time he had a paying job?"

"Hey," said Ian. "Take it easy, Mags."

Maggie unlatched Siobhan, lifted her out of the high chair,

and carried her up to Maggie's part of their renovated loft. Ian had his little bunk room in the back. He took a joint out of his shirt pocket and lit it.

"You should grow your hair," he said. "Stop wearing shirts and pants from the men's department."

"Says the man who's married to a famous feminist."

He closed the door to the kitchen, then took a huge hit off the joint.

"Maggie doesn't have a dick. She never will." He slipped his hand under my shirt. "And she can't have mine."

I climbed right on top of him in the kitchen chair. I loved him so much. And he was ugly, that was the strange thing. Well, no, *ugly* isn't fair. He was forty-three, beat-up and craggy, missing some teeth. Too old for me, but he had a lot of charm. I heard a door slam. Maggie had taken the baby and the stroller. She had gone out.

KATHERINE

In one version of "Jack and the Beanstalk," the giant's wife tricks her husband because she's in love with a boy named Jack. A scoundrel. The giant walks in on the affair, and the wife hides Jack in a bucket, then in the stove. All over and anywhere, she hides her lies. But the giant smells the boy, smells his warm blood.

"Try being nice to me for an entire day," I told Phil.

Or no, I didn't tell him that. I tried to be nice to him instead. That's something I learned in one of my twelve-step programs. Keep the focus on yourself. Don't try to change him. You want your partner to be nice to you? Be nice to yourself.

I started at 9:00 a.m. on a Saturday because the weekends, when Phil was home, were my hardest days. I was crying and begging in the kitchen by noon. Then I pulled myself together and made lunch for everyone. Phil says *sing* and the harp begins to sing. He says *lay* and the hen makes gold, right out of my ass. There are at least thirty ways to tell this story.

The wife lies right to her husband's face and tells the giant that what he's smelling is just an old dead cow. Just a cut steak, a bone-in rib eye from the supermarket. Not a live child at all. And that dumb giant believes her.

"Go ahead, Phil," said Dr. Goodman. "Tell me what happened last week."

"I called home from Chicago. I was spending a few days there for work. Emily answered on Katherine's cell phone. She told me that Zack was running around the room. She laughed and told me that no one was looking after him."

"Zack's a loose cannon," I said, interrupting. "You know he's only eighteen months old." Dr. Goodman nodded. "And Emily's only four. She was feeding him Oreo cookies."

"I think I have the floor," said Phil.

"Go ahead, Phil," said Dr. Goodman.

Phil cleared his throat. "I said, 'Emily, where is your mom?' She said, 'Mommy can't come to the phone.' 'Why not?' 'Mommy's lying on the floor. She's all sweaty.' I said, 'I'll call back later,' and then I didn't have a chance to call. I was presenting at a dinner and . . .'"

Phil faded out there. He trailed off midsentence and sat blank-faced on the couch.

"What was wrong with you?" Dr. Goodman turned to me with deep care and concern, for which I paid.

"I had a crazy stomach flu," I said. "It came out of nowhere and completely knocked me out. I woke up at four a.m. in my bed. Zack and Emily were both in the crib, fast asleep. I barely remember putting him there. Emily must have climbed in later. Oreos everywhere."

I looked at Phil.

"What did you want me to do? Fly home from Chicago?"

"You don't love me."

Phil raised his voice and leaned forward.

"How in the world can you say that?"

His face darkened with a signature look. It started between his heavy black eyebrows.

"How can you think I don't love you? You don't really believe that."

"You could have called someone to check in on me. At the very least."

"It all worked out. No one was hurt."

"I—I was hurt," I stuttered. "I'm hurt."

"Jesus," said Phil. "You don't even make sense."

This was years ago. We still see Dr. Goodman. I don't think he works with many other couples. I think mostly he defends foster children in family court. I found him through a friend. Dr. Goodman couldn't remember the friend who recommended him. Or maybe he lied. For legal reasons.

Phil and I must be doing all right, because we fuck on a regular basis and it's decent, we do an okay job with it. I admit that I need, like, and sometimes love having sex. But also, fucking confuses me. Giants eat humans. They also make mistakes. They fall asleep when they should be awake. They get greedy, count their gold, lock up their magic.

TRUITT

Smooshed Bug is angry this morning. Very upset. Star finds her
in the head. Bug is crying—a soft, rhythmic weeping. Star waits
awhile outside the steel door and lets her whimper. She knows
what's going on. Bug's sitting on the can, letting Phil's semen
drip out of her, minnow by minnow. Bug doesn't like having
spunk in her snatch. Star knocks.

"Bug! What's up? What's wrong?"

"Nothing. Just cleaning up a little."

"I'm sorry I had sex with Phil," Star tells her. "But you know,
he is Katherine's husband. It's my job. My duty."

"I don't want to talk about it."

Bug unlatches the door to the head and comes out.

"You're not gonna flush?"

"She can't." I lurk in the dark gangway.

"We can't just let it pile up in there."

"We have to. We've dropped down too deep. Too much pressure from the water now. I can open the valve, but our sewage
won't go anywhere. Might even spray back into the submarine."

"Gross," says Star.

"You're one to talk about gross," says Bug.

"I have to fuck Phil. It's what married people do."

Bug sounds faint, prissy. "I never want to have sex with him
again. He doesn't love me."

"Oh, Bug," says Star. "Who cares about Phil? I love you."

"He hurts me on purpose."

Bug will go on forever if you let her.

"Shut up, Bug!"

Star flashes me a look.

"What was it about last night that got you so upset?" she asks.

"I asked him to touch me after you two had sex with him."

"I didn't have sex with him! That was Star."

"I said to Phil, 'Will you hold me? Even though you hate me?'" (More weeping—Bug can really drown in it.) "Phil said, '*Get off me!*' He was mean about it."

"I don't know why you had to accuse him of hating you. You know he doesn't like that."

Bug shakes her head. "We have to get out of here. We need to leave the submarine."

I hate to admit it, but Bug is right. If I don't get this boat off the bottom of the lake, Katherine will take this twenty-year marriage and blow it to bits. It's true that Phil can be mean. But without him, we won't survive.

"He does hate me." Bug sniffles.

"Then why would you ask him to hold you?"

He goes away every week for work. But he always comes home. Then he goes away, but again he comes home. The sound of gravel beneath the wheels of the airport taxi: It's a turn-on for Star. Phil puts down his suitcase and climbs into bed, then gets under Katherine with his greasy tools. He stares at the black gaskets as the oil drips down.

Later, after, he sits at the kitchen table with his computer and Katherine fights for his attention. Star is long gone. Katherine acts out people, conversations, arguments. This is the lady with waist-length hair who runs the dry cleaner's. This is the upholsterer with gold teeth who's looking for nude models to paint. This is the man in vintage tennis clothes who crowded Katherine at the cash register.

Phil stands up, goes to the kitchen sink, and runs the hot

water. He's trying to wash his hands, and he can't hear her voice over the sound of the faucet. He nods, pretend-listens, laughs to keep her fooled. His hands are greasy and stained with black from digging around inside her body. Grease is black; it's cold, unburned oil. It doesn't wash out. Not really. It just fades into the skin. Why bother washing?

SMOOSHED BUG

Mom dropped me and Gordon at the country club and went to run errands. I had a private tennis lesson. I'd brought my bathing suit and racket in a clear vinyl tote. I fainted in the ladies' locker room after the lesson, when I was taking off my tennis shorts and my underpants to put on my suit. What did I see? I don't remember. Maybe something scary. The good part of fainting is that you're still alive after. I went out to the pool.

Anne Burroway was waiting for me by the diving board. Anne's family lived in a pointy white house with wings like a bird. It stood directly across from ours on Float Lake. Anne's words came out funny and thick, as if her tongue were numbed. She had stringy blond hair in an outdated pageboy, Coke-bottle glasses, and an overbite. This was her last summer at home. Her dad shipped her off to a special school.

It started to rain. Huge plopping drops. Everyone ran to the snack bar together. I shivered in my wet suit and stared through the screened windows at the pavement around the edges of the pool. The concrete was changing colors.

A boy named Dickie Mueller took Anne's cheeseburger and spat on it when she was off looking for ketchup. Then he put the bun back on. When Anne returned, he and his friends exploded with laughter.

I let Anne go ahead and eat the burger. Dickie was the meanest boy. Later, after it stopped raining, Anne and I wandered out to the golf course to see what was going on with the boys. Dickie threw a water balloon from the bushes behind the sand trap.

"Slut!" he shouted. "In your face!"

He and his friends wore corduroy shorts and striped tube socks because the country club had a policy about wearing socks with your shoes. Jews couldn't be members, or Blacks, or Catholics. My grandfather Walt was a founding member. That means he wasn't any of these things.

My mom came to get me and Gordon, and I told her what Dickie called me.

"You're a liar," she said. "If there's one kind of person I can't respect, it's a liar."

STAR

Gordon gave up on me at Eddie's Topless when I fled to the dressing room. But he didn't leave New York. He showed up the next day at Max's art studio, where I was staying for free. It was in a dilapidated warehouse on a cobblestone street in Brooklyn near the river. I had views of the crotch of the Manhattan Bridge.

"Come on," said Gordon. "Let's pack your stuff."

"What stuff?" I asked.

"I don't know. Your stuff."

"I don't have any stuff. What I do have is in storage."

"Then you do have stuff."

The building was a factory once. Button press, assembly line for roller skates, molders of zippers, makers of gadgets. In the nineties it offered raw space to painters and sculptors. I wasn't supposed to be living there. Gordon nudged a pile of empty soda bottles, beer cans, and KFC bags with his foot.

"Jesus, Katchie. Look at yourself."

I tried to see what he saw, starting with my shoes, Converse sneakers, the same kind I'd worn since seventh grade. Gordon still wore the same clothes, too. Dockers, a flannel shirt, slip-on loafers.

"You're an alcoholic," said Gordon. "Maybe worse."

Gordon is named after James Gordon Wood, a Confederate general. We were raised to view J. G. Wood as the hero in our family tree.

He pointed to my face.

"There's a science experiment on your lip."

I hated that herpes sore. It never went away.

"Do you even have a toilet?"

I nodded. With a very cold seat in the winter months. I also had a small sink. But no shower or tub. And no hot water. I showered twice a week at Max's apartment in Tribeca.

"Please come home with me. You can't think this is much of a life."

"I can't go home. I'm making a film."

Gordon walked over to a big wooden table, the only proper furniture in the room. He inspected the pile of plastic videocassettes. They had pothead titles like *Nude Blue Star* and *Periodical*.

"*Frenchie Kisses?*" He turned it over in his hands. "Is that one of your films?"

"It's a rough cut."

"What's it about?"

"Unprotected sex. It's a fake public service announcement. I submitted it to CalArts. They didn't like it. I'm naked in most of it."

"Maybe you need a plan B."

I had used my stripping money to buy a fifteen-hundred-dollar video camera. It was just a handicam, nothing near professional quality, but I loved it. Natalie said no one who worked at Eddie's had ever invested money in the future. This made me feel good, but I didn't believe her.

"I have a life here," I told Gordon. "And a boyfriend."

"He'll understand."

Gordon sat down on my bed, a Boy Scout sleeping bag on an old mattress. The sleeping bag was printed with campfires and slingshots, flags and fishing poles. I got it from a dumpster.

"What makes you think I need help?"

"I'm going to pray for your mattress."

"Pray for whatever you want," I told him. "I'm not going home."

DEAD GIRL REGISTER: HETTIE WOOD

My name is Hettie and I lived in North Carolina with a soldier husband named James Gordon Wood. I was fourteen when we met, seventeen when we married. He was my brother's best friend from military school, and he was a *dragoon*. This meant he could fight two ways: on the ground or on a horse. He had swords.

Other details? He was very short, maybe five feet, two inches, but I was barely five feet myself. Everyone was short in 1860. J.G. liked to drink, play cards, smoke, and eat fatty foods. In other words, he was a United States human.

More about me, how I felt: ashamed of my body, overate and underate, wanted to be alone, wanted to be protected, clung to lovers and friends, helpless, sexually submissive, submissive overall, abandoned, lonely, overwhelmed, betrayed, unable to take action, stuck in my dark thoughts. And constipated all the time. Then came the piles. It's all I could think about. That and God. I was spiritual.

Consider the qualities of a Star. Dazzling, adventurous, shining, connective. And very far away. By the time you see her, so much time has passed, she doesn't exist anymore. Because of distance and the speed of light.

The army sent J.G. to the Washington Territory, and I went along. A year in a bumpy wagon. Hot nights on blankets under the stars. He got me with child. I gave birth to my fine first boy, Ballard, at Fort Walla Walla with whiskey on a bearskin rug.

The midwife must have been a member of the Coeur d'Alene, Spokane, or Palouse tribes. When I told the story, after we got back to Tarboro, I made the midwife Apache. Because I liked attention, and people were more afraid of the Apache. I called Native Americans "Injuns." J.G., my husband, killed them from his horse with a pistol. We didn't think of them as people.

Confusion is a form of fear. If you're scared of everyone and everything, just existing means you're brave. We try not to use limited words like *brave*. Because all words are limited. But we use what we have.

My father Moses was a state senator, an abolitionist; therefore, he lost his seat. I also considered myself an abolitionist. And a Christian. But J.G. and I had a slave girl who helped us, name of Ellen. We rented her from her owner. We called her a "servant."

KATCHIE

In the third grade, I fantasized about Dickie Mueller every night before I fell asleep. I was serious about Jesus at the time. It was a personal thing, not something my family pushed on me. They rarely went to church. But I knew about Jesus. I didn't have a firm grasp on his teachings. I knew he had more power than my dad, tape gun and all.

I also got the idea that Jesus and boys didn't mix, so I apologized to Jesus, over and over, for being so excited about Dickie Mueller. It came to where I had to make a choice. Dickie or Jesus, otherwise known as the Lord. The Lord went.

That year in school, because of Dickie, I felt I could do the thing I had to do, which was the third grade. There were other girls he might love instead of me. I knew this. What Dickie loved was his shell necklace. We called them "puka beads," but they were shells. Or they looked like shells. Most kids could only afford plastic pukas. Dickie's were definitely real.

"What do you think?" he said. "That puka beads grow on trees?"

I found my own shells. My family took picnics to a bay

beach. You could only get there by boat, and my father had a boat. It was DAD'S BOAT, not some little inflatable raft. It was an old fishing boat, pretty and dainty and wooden. He named it *The Sinker.*

The shells I found there were bigger than pukas, and lumpy. I thought maybe I could make a necklace out of them with a needle and thread, because the shells had little holes in them. But not all of the shells had holes. And not all the holes were in the right place.

Gordon and I spent all day Sunday trying to string the shells together, and we finally got it done. Monday morning when we put on the necklaces, the smell was worse than raw fish. I guess there had been live animals in the shells when we pulled them out of the water. We were supposed to kill the animals, boil them or spear them or suffocate them. You drive the creatures out before you string the shells together. We didn't know that. I wore the necklace anyway. God, it stunk. I only wore it that one time.

Dickie's authentic puka necklace broke during math, while everyone was sitting at their desks. The shells scattered all over the floor, and Dickie cried his eyes out. Red face, snot, all of it. Usually, Brian Braxton was the boy who did all the crying. He'd cry over a broken pencil. I'd never seen Dickie fall apart like that.

I leaned down and grabbed one of the scattered shells, stuck it in the pocket of my denim skirt. Took it out later, had a closer look. Plastic! Dickie's puka shells never had anything living in them at all.

Stop loving him, I told myself. *He's a fake.*

As if talking to myself ever did any good.

KATHERINE

When the kids were young (toddlers, babies), I leaned hard on Dr. Goodman. He took personal calls between my weekly sessions.

"I can't stop watching autopsy dramas," I told him. "I'm crying a lot and I can't sleep."

"Anything out of the ordinary going on?"

"Phil's on a work trip for three weeks."

"Is that unusual?"

"I need a day off. Away from the kids."

"Try backing off on the autopsy shows."

I sent twenty-five texts and seventeen voice mails to Phil's cell. He ignored them. He often went from one meeting to another, and there was a difference in time zones and sometimes his phone battery died and also sometimes it didn't ring.

"Maybe call his parents," said Dr. Goodman. "They live nearby. Isn't that right?"

Phil's parents, Nick and Helen, came over to help. Nick took me to get groceries. He insisted on going to a superstore so he could get bulk pricing on paper towels. We spent at least an hour filling our carts, then came to rest in front of a gift kiosk and its display of waxy potted plants. I pinched the pink leaves of one, and they tore off in my hand.

"Oops."

"What are you doing?" asked Nick.

"I thought it was plastic."

"Now you have to buy it."

"No, I don't."

"Why did you touch it?"

"I thought it was fake."

"Phil can afford it." Nick put the plant into my basket, and I started to cry. Nick didn't notice, or if he noticed, he didn't let on.

"Got everything you need?"

I nodded.

"Let's go pay."

When we got back to my house and pulled into the driveway, Helen was waiting on the sidewalk. She was wearing the same oversize black sunglasses that Nick had on. She was pissed.

"Your son won't get out of the car."

Emily ran out of the house in her pajamas and threw herself at my knees.

"Mommy! Mommy! Mommy!"

I dragged Emily with me to the minivan. Zack was in the driver's seat clutching the steering wheel. He didn't answer me when I said his name.

"Let him play," I said to Helen, who was crowding in behind me.

Emily was tugging on my skirt. "I missed you, Mommy." I swept her up and carried her into the house. Helen was on my tail.

"Kids die in hot cars every day," she said. "I looked for your keys. Did you take them with you? I searched the whole house. I don't know how you find anything here. It's total chaos."

I ripped open a box of fruit chews, tiny doll-size bunches of bananas and grapes. Emily took the candy from my hand. I tried to put her down, but she squirmed and kicked in protest. I pretended I was about to drop her, and she landed her feet on the floor.

"You shouldn't scare her like that," said Helen.

"Emily, go tell Zack he can have fruit chews if he comes inside."

"Zackie doesn't like fruit chews."

"Go get him!" I shouted.

Helen gave me a look. "We'll head out."

"I thought you were going to stay until dinner."

"We were. But I feel like there's tension."

Nick came into the kitchen with more grocery bags. He was whistling. He saw Helen's face and he stopped. I left them there, unloading groceries, and tried to lure Zack out of the mini-van. Just as I got him out, Nick and Helen drove away in their matching sunglasses. I lost my hold, and Zack fell to the paved driveway and started to scream. I lifted him up, and he wrapped his legs around my middle and burrowed his head against my neck. We moved across the yard that way. Zack was an extension of my body, a swollen tick.

DEAD GIRL AS HETTIE

The war was upon us! The United States split in two as North and South, and we were South. J.G. went to Virginia to walk into bullets and seek promotion. The place was noisy, dusty, and crawling with whores. I wrote him long letters about my body problems. Pregnancy made the piles so much worse. By then, I was carrying our second son, James. My husband was in camps all over Northern Virginia, training boys for the army, for the Confederacy. The forests caught fire. Men and trees burned alongside. A death was a point for the other team.

For my husband—and this was true for all of the soldiers—
the odds were against survival. Corpses piled up like logs against
a rickety woodshed, offal and body parts. Skeletons marched in
bare feet, left foul wet stools on the road. Stale biscuits and water
make bad decisions, so it was impossible to plan. My husband
slept with his boots on.

I sent a man to help. His name was Edward. He cooked
and kept camp. Edward peddled his services on the side and
earned enough to buy new clothes at a shop in Richmond. J.G.
whipped him around the shoulders and head with a stick for
that. I was at camp for a visit with my husband, and I saw him
attack Edward. I pretended to myself that I didn't know it would
happen.

Snow on the ground, no blanket or fire. The piles of shit in
camp and sleeping in it, waking in it, trailing it around. Advance,
retreat. Advance, retreat. On starving horses. Until there was
nowhere to retreat to. No one was paid. Deserters were shot.

KATCHIE

Max had a party. Gordon was still in New York, lurking around,
waiting for me to change my mind. I took him with me to
Max's, but I ditched him at the door. Then I locked myself in
the master bathroom with Presley, a guy I knew from Brown.
After a while, Presley claimed he was out of coke. He did have
two beers. He kept me in the bathroom, pressed up against the
sink.

I started to rant about my boyfriend Ian and my role in
his "open marriage." His wife Maggie had a boyfriend, too, I

explained. A drummer in a rock band who was always away on tour. I'd never met him. I said, "I think I'm a voluntary sex slave."

"Slavery isn't voluntary," said Presley.

"They have a baby," I added. "Siobhan. She's not even two."

To me, at the time, a baby was as precious as a backpack full of potatoes. But I didn't wish her any harm. I said, "She won't remember any of this."

Presley made a face. "What kind of people do you hang around with?"

Coming from Presley, the son of an indicted Wall Street criminal.

"They aren't Rhodes scholars, thank God!"

"I don't know any Rhodes scholars. I know people who applied. Do you know Jamison Brickford?"

"Fuck off, Presley."

I broke out of the bathroom and bumped into Lori Glass. Pencil skirt, knee-high boots, frilly white blouse with a tuxedo collar. We were roommates at Brown our senior year; we moved to New York together. Lori didn't like Ian. She didn't approve of the topless dancing, either. She said I drank too much, and she didn't like people who did drugs.

She dropped me, and then I stopped hearing from my other college friends. They'd only been putting up with me because they felt better about their own choices when they saw mine. They were all going to end up working at Christie's and Sotheby's and PBS or going to law school. I was going to die in a gully by the landing strip at LaGuardia.

Lori looked at my track pants. "Is that hip-hop?"

Across the room, Max had his red parrot, Shmoo, perched

on his shoulder. I took care of Shmoo once, for fifty bucks, while Max was in St. Barts. I walked around the East Village with Shmoo on my shoulder. We watched TV together. Then I had a dream that Shmoo had a hard-on, an erect little bird penis, and I was jacking him off. After that, I didn't let him out of the cage.

That night at Max's party, I saw everything around me like it was under glass. The entire loft apartment was a hologram, and the hologram was inside another hologram, and it was all lit up with currents of electricity, shimmering and translucent, but wildly powerful, endlessly charged. Lori Glass was wearing her body the same way I was wearing my tracksuit. Everyone was. Casings for electricity, sleeves for light. My brother and Max, making out in the corner, were glowing orange and red.

What was stopping me from going home, refueling, provisioning, making repairs? The universe had sent me an escort, Gordon. He still lived with my parents in Virginia Beach. Maybe he was better equipped for survival than I was. I had always assumed the opposite.

But how would I stand my mother's bad breath? And also, she torpedoed the toilet and didn't care who knew. I hadn't forgotten that she was addicted to laxatives, which explains some things but not everything. Her shits were wild and out of control. Her shits were like avalanches bearing down on a ski lodge full of people eating chili.

At the breakfast table growing up, Gordon and I would be sitting there munching on our Cap'n Crunch—Mom just standing there drinking her coffee—and she would suddenly flee from the kitchen in pain. The bathroom was right off the kitchen. We could hear the battle going on in there, the groaning and weeping; loud, epic farting noises. Gastric explosions. We had no idea what was going on. Well, we had an idea. But we didn't know what to do with it.

I grabbed Gordon's car keys from his coat, which was in Max's room. I also emptied Max's wallet, in the drawer where he always left it. Three hundred and twenty-four dollars. Enough.

TRUITT

If Star could keep to herself, and STOP FUCKING PHIL, maybe we could channel her energy, charge our battery cells with it. Get the basic systems running again. As it is, the batteries are dead weight. The heaviest useless thing on the boat.

Here she comes now, humming snatches of a Bob Dylan song. She makes her way into the control room and sits down across from me. The stale air smells of men and diesel fuel. She leans back against the periscope shaft and takes a bite of a French baguette. It's hard as a rock. God knows where she found it. I grab her baguette and hit her over the head with it. It breaks, and wheat dust scatters through the air like snowflakes.

"I thought we had an agreement, Star!"

"What kind of agreement?"

"You implied that you would stop."

"I'm not becoming a nun."

"You're our best chance of getting up to the surface," I tell her. "We have to get up there soon."

"I don't want to go to the surface."

"You'd rather suffocate?"

Star has spent many a night in the torpedo room, which also

functions as the crew's sleeping hatch. In a U-boat, this is the
same space. The submariner who fires off a torpedo instantly
creates more room in his living quarters. A bunk opens up.

Star grabs the bigger half of the broken baguette and takes
another bite.

"Where the hell would we go?" she says. "Even if we could
get to the surface?"

She's thinking, though, considering the possibility. Twenty
men fore, eighteen aft. She has no bed of her own. *Ping.*

"It's fine down here," she muses. "The sex is good."

"Are you sure?"

Smooshed Bug emerges from the darkness. She has the radio
headset on sideways, one ear covered with a headphone, the
other exposed. Before I can confiscate the headset, Star steps
closer to me and pulls up her torn blue dress. She's wearing frilly
underpants, childish cotton things printed with purple hippos.

"Are these slutty?" she asks.

"They could be."

"At least they're clean."

She's been wearing them since 1987. They come up to her
waist and the elastic is loose, worn-out.

"There's blood on them."

"There isn't," she says.

The blood is way in the back, past the crotch.

"Look."

I show her.

"New blood is red. Old blood is brown."

"Whatever," she grumbles. "Dead Girl says you're wrong
about everything."

"Dead Girl? Who's that?"

"Forget it."

I don't feel like looking at her anymore.

"I'm going up."

Going up to the conning tower just means climbing to the top rung of the ladder and crouching there in the dark. The hatch can't be opened, not underwater. I remember sticking my head out of the tower hatch and taking that first gulp of air. As if I had never taken a breath before. When was the last time we surfaced?

SMOOSHED BUG

Summer or winter, every day when Dad came home from work, he made himself a drink. He wore a gray suit from Brooks Brothers, a white button-down shirt from Jos. A. Bank, a red tie, and a pair of blue cotton boxers with a flap. After the first drink, he went up and changed into his casual clothes, starched jeans and an Izod. Then he went and messed around with a hammer in the garage.

At dinner, I sat on his lap. Both his hands were up the back of my shirt and he wrote on my skin with his finger. He spelled out words with his fingertip and I tried to guess the word before it was finished. Z-E-B-R-A. M-O-O-N. When I got the word right, I won. Especially if I guessed the word before he finished spelling it out. What did I win? Nothing tangible. He told me I was smart.

He sometimes kept his hands under my shirt when the game was over. I stayed on his lap—where else would I go? He scratched my back, only my back. Sometimes the sides, a little.

Gordon and my mom were sitting right there, too. Everyone eating dinner. Just a game, what should we call it? The game that gave birth to Star.

KATCHIE

I had crabs. As I drove south from New York City to Virginia Beach in Gordon's car, with the cash I stole from Max, they were crawling up the back of my neck. They had escaped from my pubic hair and were ranging freely wherever they liked. I don't know exactly where I got them. I probably got them from my pot dealer.

It's easy to get rid of crabs, but you do need hot water and common sense. I lacked both in New York City, so I still had crabs when I arrived in Virginia Beach at midnight in my brother's car. Crotch crabs may feed on your blood, but they don't have giant blue claws, and they don't bite your toes as you walk into the ocean.

The old Cadillac wanted to take me home, like a horse in a spaghetti Western. I took it to the address for Gordon's friend Nance instead. She lived in a small brick ranch house a block from the beach. I parked in front and stretched out across the front seat. I needed a minute to calm my nerves.

Early the next morning, a woman came knocking on the car window. She was tall, muscular, a fit forty in a tank top and army pants, long black hair. Nance Custis. She's actually Phil's aunt. She introduced me to Phil—I'll get to that later. At this point in the story, it's May 1996. I hadn't met Phil. Not yet.

Nance said, "You're Katchie?"

I straightened my shirt. "Yes."

"What are you doing? Did you sleep out here? Why didn't you come in? Your brother says you're quitting drugs. Good for you."

Her house was dark inside, a little musty and mildewed. She pointed to her couch.

"Have a seat. I'll make us some food."

I closed my eyes and didn't wake up until later that afternoon when Nance came home from work. But she left again right away for a spiritual group she was leading. I wandered around and inspected the framed aphorisms on the walls, the giant LP collection in crates, her shelves full of self-help books. A pizza arrived as I stood there trying to figure out what to do next. I'll never forget that pizza.

When it got dark, I drove past my parents' house. Then I cruised their neighborhood, Duchess Dunes, which was built around the shores of Float Lake. All the homes fronted either the lake or the canal, which led out to a bay, and then the ocean. The water in Float Lake was flat, brown, and stagnant. It had a dead feeling. Tall pines stood in every yard. Knotty, thin-limbed, sappy. Spanish moss hung from the oaks.

I hid the car up the street and cased my parents' house on foot from the road. The earth was soft under my feet, sandy soil covered with a layer of brittle pine needles. Through the window, I could see the top of my dad's head above his reading chair. My mother's bedroom flickered with blue light off the TV.

I crept down to our dock and walked to its edge. I got hit

right away with a blobby dark thrum. Maybe it was the slap of the water against the bulkhead. Or maybe it was the glassy twinkle of the lake itself.

"What are you doing here?" He was standing behind me on the dock.

"Hi, Dad."

We didn't hug or move closer to each other.

"Gordon said you didn't want to see us."

"He called you?"

"We gave him the money to go up there and get you."

"I've been gotten. But you lost Gordon."

"He'll be home in a week. Two weeks tops."

We both knew he was staying up there with Max. My parents never talked about Gordon's personal life.

"You should be living here with us," my dad said. "Not with some hippie landscaper your brother used to work for. What's her name again?"

"Nance."

He made a disgusted noise with his mouth. "What's the point in coming home if you don't want to see your family?"

"I'm going through something."

"Come inside and have a drink."

I didn't want a drink. What I wanted was a tiny guillotine that would chop off extremities. I could guillotine my hands and feet. Or start with one of my fingers. The head goes last because you need more sophisticated equipment.

"No thanks," I told my dad. "I've been drinking too much. Way too much. I'm quitting."

"If you're not going to stay with us," Dad said, "you'd better not . . . you . . . well . . ."

"What?"

"I don't mean to say you're not welcome. You are. For now. Right now, you're welcome. But the invitation's not open-ended."

TRUITT

Star waited by the lake for a long time after Dad went inside. She wanted something that she didn't get. This is the key to how and why relationships work. One side wants to give up electrons. The other likes to receive them.

Take a battery, for example. There's a positive charge and a negative charge. They work together; they're a team. Electrodes in a battery are never, ever, NEVER EVER EVER made of the same materials, or the same metal.

I won't admit this to Star, but I sometimes long for love. I get pulled in by seamen, too. They sneak up on me. Sweaty men with brown teeth and something they call "needs." They often haven't showered or seen the sunlight for days.

A blown fuse, Star sat by Float Lake. The burnt-out feeling was so familiar that she barely noticed. Float Lake water is piss-warm like amniotic fluid. Broken oyster shells and slurping mud. Fish? I never saw any. I have seen water moccasins at dawn and dusk, sliding across the surface. The water is brownish yellow, also a little green, but a gassy green, oily. In the winter it never freezes.

"Go back to the submarine," I told her. "Dad hates you. He's hated you for a long time. You know that."

KATHERINE

Let's talk about the mother's disappointment when her son Jack came home with a handful of magic beans. She hit her little boy.

"Take that!" she said. "And that!"

She hit her son. What do you expect? They were poor, and all they had was a fucking cow, and he went and traded it for a handful of beans. Magic beans!

Phil came home from the airport. The kids and I were hanging out on the floor in the playroom, working on a puzzle, a barnyard scene.

"That's cute," said Phil. "Are you guys having fun?"

"It's not a realistic pig," I said. "Real pigs aren't pink. They're black and brown, giant and hairy. They have whiskers in their ears like old men. They're oddly sexual."

"Jesus, Katherine."

"Kids, I'm going to talk to Daddy for a minute."

I led Phil to the screened-in porch at the back of the house. From there, our baby birches looked like adornments at a mini golf course. Two years later it seemed like they'd been there forever. Birches are thirsty trees. They need a lot of babying.

"What's wrong with you?" Phil asked.

"I've been hearing those voices again."

"Don't think of them as voices," said Phil. "They're just dark thoughts."

I put my nose up to the screen, and the tiny squares came into sharp focus. Everything beyond it was a shadowy green blur. I could smell the aluminum: rusty, dirty, earthy. I remembered the taste of window screen from when I was a child, because I ran my tongue over the screens sometimes. I touched the screen with the tip of my tongue.

"Stop that," said Phil. "You need help."

"Oh, please. *You* need help. All I ever do is get help."

I reached up and twisted an earring, then the other one. They were big diamond studs. Phil gave them to me for Christmas. I return about 90 percent of his gifts. I didn't really love the studs. But I kept them and wore them.

"You should go somewhere," he said. "A hospital inpatient thing or something. A guy who works for me went to one when he was anorexic."

"Yeah, I go off to the funny farm. And I come home to two dead children."

My tears started pouring out all over the place. Phil put his arms around me.

"I'll take some time off from work. I'll chip in more at home."

But I didn't want him to. He traveled so much that when he was home, he had no skills, no competency. He couldn't even wash peanut butter off a spoon. Zack was almost four; we hadn't finished potty training. He was taking forever. Maybe he liked the feel of shit in a sealed diaper, heating up. Or he didn't want to take time away from toys and fun to sit on the john and wait. His shits were man-size already. And Phil was absentminded at home, preoccupied with his company, NetWorth. I worried if something happened to me, if I wasn't there, he'd leave Zack in diapers until the third grade.

"You're okay." Phil pulled me in. Hands up my shirt.

STAR

When I turned thirteen, my legs grew six inches in a week. My new body busted through my dance tights and backless sweatshirt. I even outgrew the scrunchie in my hair. My period came at the end of the summer while I was sunbathing on the boathouse, which was made of corrugated metal. I spread my beach towel on the flat black roof; the tar stained it. I went in after a while to use the bathroom. I got the news in my purple bikini bottoms.

I carried a book and a bottle of Diet Coke back to the boathouse and climbed the splintery green stairs. Slathered my body with baby oil and lay there for hours, listening to the sound of the water as it slapped against the metal. The current was sweet and steady. If a boat went by in the canal, the wake from the motor would hurry the slapping. Then the waves would go back to a slow smack.

My purple bikini clung tight to my new boobs. I walked around the yard while Dad mowed the lawn. He wrapped his head in a bandanna, a replica of the Confederate flag. He and I vibrated in a mutual magnetism. The electrons were pouring from his mouth, his ears, his nostrils, his torpedo. It was my job to catch them, because electrons flow only if they have somewhere to go. The electrons have to keep moving in a continuous stream. One hundred thousand nautical miles, a pipeline of veins and arteries. My heart.

Slap slap, the sound of the waves against the boathouse. Slap slap, the brown lake with its brackish water. Oyster shells in the muddy bottom. At the bottom, the very, very bottom. I burned, then blistered, then peeled in the rough sun. My skin fell off in chunks. Dad had patched the boathouse roof with tar and shingles. It melted in the heat. I trailed the gooey black stuff into the house on my bare feet.

The next day, we rode bikes to the beach. It was hard to find parking on weekends. Dad had a fun metal basket attached to his handlebars. It was just big enough to hold a small cooler of beer.

It was the Sunday before school started, eighth grade. At the end of the summer, Dad was always very brown because he was olive-toned and he tanned well. There were little creases under his breasts where the skin was still white. Places that stayed in shadow even when the sun was bright.

I saw a girl my age standing in the ocean, alone out there. I had an idea of who the girl was, but I didn't know her. There were no waves that day. It was especially calm. I waded out to where the girl was waiting, her face half submerged.

I said, "Aren't you going to be at my school next year?"

The girl nodded. Gordon was standing on the beach, watching us, threatening to come out there and interrupt. I glared at him. He kicked some sand and walked up the beach.

"Ow! A crab got me!" I knew it was a crab, even though I couldn't see down through the water, which was brown like always. It had something to do with the trenches and currents near the mouth of the Chesapeake Bay. Sea lice, sea nettles, moon jellies, lady crabs, sand fiddlers, blue claws. I couldn't see them, but I knew they were there.

"A crab got you?" The girl started to laugh.

"Isn't your name Sheila?" She nodded and stood up straight in the water. It wasn't very deep; she must have been crouching before she stood. She was tall and very developed, much bustier than I was. I knew right then and there that she was going to be my best friend. Maybe because it was just the two of us out there in the water, and the universe had given us this chance. It only takes a second to fall in love.

TRUITT

I made it twenty hours at Nance's house before I went back to see my parents. I locked up Bug and Star before I got in the car. There was a pressure-resistant hatch on either side of the control room. With the hatches shut, there was no way for them to make contact.

It happened to be Sunday night, hamburgers, *Sixty Minutes* into *Murder, She Wrote.*

"Sit down and have a drink," said Mom. "Your brother usually comes on Sundays. Who knows when on earth he'll come back from New York."

"I'm not drinking anymore."

"Anymore meaning never again?"

"I'm an alcoholic."

"No, you're not."

"Don't ask me to prove it."

Mom thought she knew how to drink, and that she drank like a lady. She thought if you drank like a lady, then you weren't alcoholic. When I drank, I went black in my mind and lost huge chunks of time. Where was I? What did I say? What did I do? When I drank, I had no off switch. I woke up naked with guys I'd just met, then kept them around to justify the original blackout sex. When I drank, I squatted in the street, peed in the gutter. I barfed between garbage cans then went back into the bar and ordered another pint.

Mom stayed home and measured out her wine in a measuring cup before pouring it into the glass. She always forgot, after two cups, to measure. Then she drank the whole box.

"Where's Dad?" I asked her.

"I don't want to talk about it."

Our house on Float Lake was cutting-edge when it was built in 1975. Giant plate-glass windows, raw white cedar siding. The entrance hall went up three stories like a gym or a museum. The rest of the rooms were arranged around the perimeter in a border of squares. A huge sculpture hung from the high ceiling; it was made out of steel car bumpers.

While my parents were overseeing the construction, we stayed in my grandparents' beach cottage. Walt and Kitty, my mom's parents, lived in the city of Norfolk, but they always kept a cottage at the beach. Except during World War II, when German U-boats were picking off the cargo ships and merchant vessels in the Atlantic. Right off the shore on Sixty-ninth Street. They sold their cottage then. They bought another one later.

My dad's mom died in 1974, right before the builders finished the new house. He drove down to Georgia in a rented truck and brought his mother's dishwasher back up to his new house in Virginia. The fucking thing never worked properly. Dad fought with it for fifteen years. Some men do that, repair old things, and keep repairing them, when the old things continue to break down. A different kind of man goes out and buys a new one. Dad hated that dishwasher, even when it was working. Hate made him happy.

All the appliances in our house were constantly breaking. Was this the power of negative thinking? Maybe, but they were also old. The hot-water heater, the washer and dryer, the oven, the dishwasher, the septic tank, the central air-conditioning, and the forced-air heating system, at the heart of which was an oil-burning furnace. We weren't allowed to touch the thermostat. My room was cold. We fixed everything with rubber bands.

"Are you sure I can't get you a beer or a glass of wine?" Mom asked. She was headed out to the garage, to the "booze fridge."

"I told you. I'm not drinking anymore."

"That's fine," she said. "But don't call yourself an alcoholic. That's ridiculous."

Over the years, the house fell into disrepair. But the décor hadn't changed. Same old furry shag carpet, same chipped glass tabletops. Moody seascapes from the Boardwalk Art Show. Lots of mystery paperbacks. Mom tore out the pages as she read.

SMOOSHED BUG

My heart lies sideways in my chest. It would grow if I grew, but I never grow. Still, my veins and arteries, laid out in a straight line, would stretch for one hundred thousand miles. That kind of pipeline could carry a person far away. Even farther than Camp Riverbow, which is in West Virginia.

Dr. Goodman is obsessed with the love letters I received at camp. Most of them were sent my first couple of years, before I turned thirteen. Dad illustrated them with drawings of batteries. Diagrams that showed the positive node and the negative node, with arrows and numbers to show how low Dad's battery was running, with me away at camp, and no one to snuggle with. *Dear Anode,* he wrote. *Dear Cathode,* I wrote back.

I was never homesick during those summers. I never missed Float Lake. If I could describe the yellow water, the poison of it, the way it spoke at night when I went out in the yard. I wasn't the only smooshed bug. There were hundreds of us. Truitt took every chatty girl down to the edge of the lake and threw her in. None of these girls could swim. They sank straight to the bottom and died. Pressed down there in the mud. Pretending to sleep.

TRUITT

I know there are dead girls down there and I feel responsible for them. No commander is proud of his casualties. If I pulled even one of the girls out, let her rise to the surface, I'd have to keep her in a huge jar like a creepy Victorian naturalist. In formaldehyde with blackened eyelids and wispy hair, shriveled hands and feet, cotton-stuffed and shrunken. Dead body parts have always fetched money.

Say you come across a decapitated head, right after its owner has met her end at the local guillotine. You can rig this severed head up to copper wires and run a current through the nerves and muscles. You can make her eyes open. You can get her mouth to smile. Sure you can, if you have a positive charge. What? Electricity works in the body? Yes, it does, unless it kills you first. If you're still alive, anything is possible.

DEAD GIRL REGISTER: AVERY WILCOX

Katchie agreed to take a walk with her mother, on the condition that she could wear something from her childhood room. Kate was using the room as a walk-in closet. Every surface was covered with new clothes, price tags still attached. The dresser drawers were full of sweaters and nightgowns. Also old things, like ski pants and cheerleading shoes, taffeta gowns from Katchie's debutante ball. The closet bulged with suit sets in all colors. The bed was piled high with blouses, belts, and bell-bottoms.

Katchie emerged from the chaos wearing a long gold lamé dress.

"I forgot I had that!" Kate was waiting on the front steps of the house in her walking gear: Reeboks, baggy shorts, a headband, and a chunky wood safari-themed necklace beaded with carved animals.

Katchie sucked in the wet, dense air. It was dusk. There was no one around. Everyone was inside waiting for *Jeopardy!* Katchie's childhood friends were grown and gone. They owned condos in mulched complexes near the mall.

A mosquito truck drove by and sprayed a mist, which left a chemical smell. The bugs got louder. Katchie lifted her forearm to her mouth and kissed it, making a line along the inside of her wrist. Kate could guess what her daughter's skin tasted like, based on the taste of her own. Everything she ever was. It all lived on inside her daughter.

"Stop it!" Kate grabbed her daughter's arm and pulled it away from her face. They walked by a gap in the trees and gazed upon the Float Lake shoreline with its perimeter of aging but splendid 1970s houses. The biggest was Sheila's house, the Wilcox mansion.

"Why stay with this stranger, Nance?" asked Kate. "Sheila didn't want you?"

"Sheila's away at rehab."

"Again?"

Katchie and Kate stared out at the lake. They held the same exact thought in their heads for that split second. Sheila's oldest sister Avery was water-skiing and crashed into a moored sailboat, hit her head, and sank to the bottom of Float Lake. Sheila's mother witnessed the accident. She was outside watering the lawn, and she swam out into the lake and dove to find her child.

Float Lake is sludgy. Visibility is nil. Jackie, Sheila's mother, dove and dove, fueled by maternal adrenaline. She found her daughter and dragged her to shore. Avery was sixteen. She wasn't wearing a life vest. It was 1987.

Avery was released from the problem of living. Her mom was forced to continue without her. She had two other, younger daughters, Elaine and Sheila. But children are not interchangeable. Jackie Wilcox lost one.

Consider the possibility that *child* and *adult* are meaningless words. Everyone pretends that wisdom rolls forward, expanding as the limbs get longer. It can also go the other way. We get dead and born again and get dead and born again a million times each day.

Katchie thought about Avery every single time she went water-skiing in high school. Sheila's eating disorder was bad then, too. She would barf in the water while she waited for Katchie to circle around and get her in the boat. Katchie would see flotillas of Pizza Hut cheese here and there as they motored around. Sheila knew that Katchie saw the floating cheese. Katchie's seeing it, Sheila's knowing she saw it, the girls' not talking about it, this was intimacy. And food for the crabs.

TRUITT

On the very day that our stay with Nance expired, Sheila returned from rehab. Nance had a three-night limit, nothing personal. Sheila was thrilled to set Katchie up with a room. She lived with her parents and had a whole wing of the mansion to herself. Katchie and Sheila sat together in their private living quarters for hours at a time. They flipped through magazines, smoked cigarettes, watched *Oprah,* and, of course, they talked.

Katchie wanted to run back to her "real life" with Ian in New York City, but he wasn't returning her calls. Ian was enlightened, in his way. He also had a reputation as a womanizer. Had he moved on?

"Good riddance," said Sheila. "He's a toothless old man. And married."

"Your sister Elaine's with an older man. You said she's happy."

"She's a bitch."

"You used to love her."

"Wendell probably stuck his tongue in her mouth, too."

Wendell was Sheila's stepfather. He'd been married to her mother Jackie forever.

"Why do we have to talk about this?"

"I'm healing," said Sheila. "You're helping me heal. By letting me talk about it."

"You don't look like you're healing." Because she was still overweight, and a chain smoker, a diet soda drinker. And she kept going back to rehab.

"How would you know what healing looks like, Katchie?"

"Fuck healing."

"Let's take my mom's new Mercedes and do something stupid and crazy. Let's go to the mall and get facials."

"That's not stupid. Or crazy."

"I'll pay for you to get a makeover and buy you some pretty clothes."

"Oh. And then I can get a job in marketing."

"What's wrong with that?"

"Let's overeat. That's stupid."

Sheila took Katchie to AA meetings every day. If you make it to ninety days without a drink or a drug, they give you a green coin. Sheila had a jewelry box full of them. But she'd only been sober for three weeks. She had a hard time sticking with it, and no wonder. She was the girl in high school who passed out in the bathroom at the party, blocking the door. Wait, no, that was Katchie. Wait, no, that was Sheila. They were best friends.

The men and women at the AA meetings hung around in the parking lot afterward and offered Katchie cigarettes, hugs, encouraging words. They weren't people she had ever seen before. Virginia Beach was bigger than Mom and Dad's country club scene. Who knew?

The house on Float Lake is gone now. Mom and Dad were forced to sell it when they finally divorced. When the buyers tore down the house, they razed everything in the yard. Laid waste to all kinds of trees and flowering bushes: red cedar, live oak, longleaf pine, slippery elm, flowering dogwood, American holly. Even the bamboo, which Dad made the mistake of planting. He thought it would cut down on mosquitoes.

Bamboo grows quickly, and it became his nemesis. He tried to cut it, and it grew back stronger, taller, thicker, greener. Came back overnight, it seemed, three feet every day. In time, the bamboo destabilized the foundation of both the house and the run-down garage; its rhizomes spread into the sandy soil underneath.

But the living room was still there in 1996, with a glass coffee table, an orange sofa, a fireplace. And Mom. Katchie stopped by one night after an AA meeting and found her in Gordon's room, sitting on the side of the bed, talking on the phone. She was in just her bra and her high-waisted, see-through underpants. Her pubic hair was smooshed up under them like a burglar with nylons over his head.

"Where's Dad?"

"He's got dinner plans with Mrs. Pringle."

Mrs. Pringle was Dad's girlfriend. Even I knew that.

"Jesus, Mom, how do you put up with this?"

"I've got my friends."

Ernest and Julio. If you get that little joke, you know that I'm calling Mom a wino. This is disrespectful and mean. What kind of person doesn't love her own mother? A boy like me with a twisted heart! It lies in a slanting position near the middle of my chest toward the front. It's wider at the top than at the bottom. The wider end points toward my right shoulder. The narrower end points downward, toward the front of my chest and to the left. The lower end is the part that beats.

Actually, there's nothing wrong with me. All of this is healthy and normal. According to cardiologists, it's exactly how I should feel. My heart is perfect. Electrical system healthy.

Then what about the black smoke that sometimes comes bursting out? The gushing oil, the fiery explosions? We must accept that escape from a submarine is next to impossible.

Do you think I forgot?

DEAD GIRL REGISTER: OLIVE WOOD

Here's how General J. G. Wood died. His last charge took him to the top of Seminary Ridge. This was at Gettysburg, the famous bloodbath. The battlefield was hilly and broad. Wood's orders came at dusk after a hard day of fighting. He was outmanned.

When he and his men reached the seminary, he told them to burn everything in sight, the abolitionists' books especially. General Wood was wild and hungry, his face black, his boots in tatters. Thirsty as hell. Night fell; it was silent. Animals, birds, bugs—every living creature had fled.

He was damned, this man.

The sky exploded at dawn. The Yanks opened up with shells and solid shot. Pieces of metal and stone fired the air all around. We're talking a couple of miles that they hurled those things and hit J. G. Wood, who was evil and also the grandfather of my children. He was standing at the edge of the trees. He took a piece to his thigh.

Hi, my name is Olive. I married Ballard, the older son of the dragoon. This swearing, gambling, slave-whipping book burner was my husband's father.

Hettie heard that her husband was injured. She waited at Good Springs. Nothing else to do. Her brother arrived on horseback (this was Hettie's only surviving brother; he died a month later). He told Hettie that J.G. was headed home to Tarboro in a medic's wagon to rest and heal. Wood never got home. An artery broke along the way. He bled out.

"If your father had lived," Hettie told Ballard, my husband, "we would have won the Battle of Gettysburg. If we had won Gettysburg, we would have won the war. Robert E. Lee said so himself."

The everlasting IF. Hettie fed it to her two sons for breakfast. She found Ballard a job sorting mail at the depot in Tarboro. A year later, his younger brother James started at the same position and no disgrace. It was railroad work killed a man.

Ballard gave me two babies, Walter and Harriet. They arrived in 1886. That such a nervous oyster of a girl could survive giving birth to twins surprised everyone. None more than me. But Ballard came down with Americanitis, or DRUNK ALL THE TIME. He gave it to James. Then it was piecework on the rails for them both.

Look at it this way. Glory has hooks in it. As does shame. Because honor is relative and an empty game besides. J. G. Wood probably saw this himself as he was bleeding out on the dirt floor of a storeroom in Staunton, Virginia. He wrapped a self-made tourniquet around his thigh, tightened it with a hairbrush. His heart sped, beating wild and fast and frantic. It flooded his system with the blood that was left.

The doctor rushed in and sawed off the leg. It was too late for his heart. Too late for God. Too late for his children, because it was too late for him to change his mind about the slaves. Not that he would have.

TRUITT

How long have we been down here? I can't remember the last time I tried to fix anything. I used to run a maintenance check every day. When I finally dragged myself around the boat this morning, I discovered that both of the periscopes are corroded, stuck in place.

I look for Bug to tell her the news and I find her in the bow, in the bunk room. She's lying on her side, pretending to eat beans from an empty can.

"What's that?" she asks.

"Duct tape."

"What are you going to do with it?"

"Fix the broken shelf in the radio room."

"What broken shelf?" Bug jumps up to get close to me.

"Doesn't matter. Tell me a story. Tell me your best one. A long one."

"Really?" Bug hops up and down three times on her right foot. Then she does the same on her left. It's a thing she does. Keeping it even.

SMOOSHED BUG

Forget about Dickie Mueller. By the ninth grade, I was in love with Jeff, who was two years older than me. I met him at the country club. He was a caddie, not a member. He'd wait for me by the backboard. A caravan of bikes went by, girls with blond ponytails and colorful chewing gum.

"Watch and learn," said Jeff, relaxed but intentional. He went after the girls. I threw down my tennis racket and ran after him. He wanted me to.

"Come on! Hurry!"

He talked the whole time while we ran, like he didn't care what he was saying. We lost track of the girls on a crowded beach. Hot sand, radios, greasy skin, and beer. People burning all around.

I took Jeff home to Dad's garage. He wouldn't come into the house. I showed him Dad's things, the fridge full of beer, the calendar with naked ladies, the jars of screws and nails, the radios. I turned one on and fiddled with the knobs.

"This is our song," I said. I'd change the station back after he left. I wasn't allowed to touch the radios. Wasn't even supposed to be in the garage.

"There's not one song that makes me think of you," said Jeff.

"Not one?"

He shook his head.

"I have fifty," I said. "For you."

It didn't matter. He loved me. I knew it. He wasn't committed, but he didn't go anywhere, he didn't leave. I bounced out of the garage in my bathing suit, and I ran into a shard of chopped bamboo that was growing out of the sandy soil. I had a huge gash on the front of my shin. Jeff did the unthinkable and came inside the house. Because it was a Sunday, my dad was there.

I said, "Dad, I've got this cut on my leg; it's bad."

My dad looked at my wound and looked at my wound. Then he offered to get me a Band-Aid. He was protective of the Band-Aids, which he kept locked away in his "office" upstairs. It wasn't much of an office—a wooden desktop wedged into the gap between two shelves in the linen closet.

It was my mom's job to keep the house stocked with basics

like toilet paper, Scotch tape, and soap, but . . . the bread in the bread drawer had green fuzz on it. The fruit in the fruit basket had flies dancing around. There were weevils in the flour and the oatmeal. The communal Band-Aid box was empty. We stole them from Dad when we needed them.

Dad came out of the linen closet. I pretended I didn't know that he kept the Band-Aids in his briefcase. He brought out a bottle of hydrogen peroxide, too, which I had truthfully never seen. I wonder where he hid it.

STAR

Jeff put his mouth to my nipples when I was fifteen. I thought he was nursing, drinking milk. I wasn't dumb. I was getting straight As. I was reading Dostoyevsky. But I did think my breasts were made of milk. I was afraid that when Jeff finished, my new tits would be flat and empty, permanently drained. I swear I wasn't dumb.

Dad's ten-speed had already deflowered me. Jeff didn't know that. He told me if we didn't have sex, he was going to break up with me.

"That's selfish," I said. "If there's one thing I can't respect, it's selfishness."

A week after he dumped me, Jeff had a new girlfriend. She went to the public high school, so I didn't know her. But I knew her name. Jeff was getting it. There was no doubt in my mind, and besides, he told me so.

I said, "Fine, Jeff. If it's that important, I'll have sex with you, too."

Jeff came right back. I told you he loved me. I was old enough to drive by then, and my father let me use the '70 Chevelle. It was broken, leaking oil. "If the engine light comes on," Dad warned me, "pull over right away. No matter what no matter where."

This was the car I drove to school. I took it to see Jeff in Norfolk one night. The car overheated and I didn't see the engine light. Or if I did see it, I kept going, thought I could make it home. We drove through black smoke. We were high and drunk and we weren't thinking. The blackest smoke I ever saw.

We finally pulled over to the side of the road, but it was too late. I didn't have the courage to walk to a gas station and call my dad. Jeff and I climbed into the backseat.

That's the night I let him put it in all the way. It's not like he'd never messed around at the opening. We moved back and forth for a while, me on top. Then his face got scary and we were finished. I kissed him and told him I loved him. I did it because I wanted to. And I think no one will dispute that the absence of blood was due to an accident on my dad's bike. How hard is it for a kid to pump up a bicycle tire? My bike was often out of commission. I was always trying to ride my dad's.

It was dawn when the state trooper found us and rapped on the window with the butt of his Maglite. The engine was cold by then, still charred but no longer smoking. Nothing could be done for it.

Dad's too old now to work on cars. Besides, engines have changed. Cars are digital and computerized; they have plastic parts. They still drink oil and gas, smells Dad loves. The Chevelle was a huge loss. Dad had spent a lot of time under the hood of that baby. It meant he would have to get a new garage car, something to tinker with. It didn't have to be a hot rod. It just needed to have over 100,000 miles. Emotional wheelhouse. Steel machine, a puzzle. Everything had its place. When you hit it with a wrench, it didn't cry.

SMOOSHED BUG

The next day was Sunday. (Hamburger night. *Murder, She Wrote.*) My whole family, including my grandmother Kitty, was gathered around the TV set. I freshened up Kitty's scotch.

It was late May, and warm, but not hot enough for mosquitoes. I went down to the backyard, stood on the dock. I thought I heard that when a virgin had sex for the first time, there was blood, a little or a lot. Red. Or brown. Or something.

Oh darn. I knew there wouldn't be blood. In that way you can know something and not know something at the same time. As I stood there, something slipped over the side and into the lake with barely a splash. Sank straight to the bottom. Into the yellow water and drowned for good. Always, we're old enough for everything.

STAR

The control room's a mess. Pipes are exposed, rusty, coming apart. The ventilators creak, blocked with grease. The electrical wires cross each other in a jumbled nest of red and green. Wheels, manometers, scopes, and gauges sit cold and unused. Truitt has pulled everything apart. He's trying to make repairs.

"I think that's the best we've ever done with that story," I tell Bug. "You added some good details. Like *Murder, She Wrote.* Hilarious."

"Thanks. I like talking about Kitty."

We all loved my grandmother, even Truitt.

"When you tell about Jeff, the first time he put it in. That's good. No turning back after that!"

"Shut up, you slut." Truitt rips off a piece of duct tape; it makes a loud scraping noise. He has a menacing look on his face, like he's about to spit water out of his mouth. He checks the length of the tape. Satisfied, he stands there with the strip in his hand.

"You really loved Jeff," says Bug. She's totally relaxed, flipping through the ship's log on the chart table. She's not actually absorbing the data; she's turning the pages mechanically. Keeping her fingers busy. Bug never sees trouble coming.

"I still love Jeff!" I say. "Love never dies."

"Where the hell do you come up with these things?"

Truitt sticks a tiny edge of the duct tape, ever so carefully, onto the handle of the periscope. The tape strip dangles there like a noose.

"Of course love dies. And, Bug, I've been telling you to shut up for days. You've been running your mouth more than ever."

Bug wraps her arms around Truitt's waist.

"Up," she says. Truitt drops his roll of tape and scoops her into his arms. He carries her around the periscope in a circle. She nestles her head into his chest. God, they're a pair.

KATHERINE

Giants eat little girls for breakfast. And some girls put themselves on the table. They throw the magic beans into the garden and trade themselves for a golden harp. I know I'm getting the story mixed up here. I'm butchering it. Is this my way of saying that some little girls are very bad, very naughty? I'm told they are.

Last year, Phil and I decided to go on more dates, to venture out to restaurants in the city. We drove into New York to see a comedy show near Times Square. Phil was crowding me on the sidewalk as we walked, edging me to the inside so he could protect me. I pushed my way back to the outside, near the curb, and a cyclist whooshed by in the bike lane.

Phil yelled, "Watch out!" and blocked me, stopped me, shoved me.

I said, "Don't do that!"

He said, "I meant well."

How can humans be trusted? We can't be trusted. The blood in our circulatory system is always under pressure. Thrombus, blood clot, clot of blood.

"I come into the city all the time," I said. "I've never been hit by a bike."

Phil's face scrunched up and turned red. His temples got veiny. He closed in on me with his scowl.

"You're the most controlling person I've ever met."

"I'm never going to fuck you again."

"What? What are you talking about?"

The heart keeps pumping through any kind of cut or laceration. And blood carries waste. It gets rid of things. Five liters in the body. Drain it down, four, three, two, one. Then you're dead.

"Don't ever touch me again."

"You love being touched."

"You won't change. You won't compromise. You won't adjust. That's how I know you don't love me."

"Not everyone can constantly work on self-transformation. Some people have jobs."

We were standing on a crowded street, a Saturday night in October, right after all the theaters had let out. No one paid attention to us at all, facing off, screaming. I reached into my purse and touched my bottle of Xanax. My gyno prescribed it.

I had no plan to take pills. But I did like having them. More than that, I liked keeping them a secret from Phil. He told me that if I ever drank again, or got hooked on pills, or any mood changer, he'd leave me. He paid for my therapy, yoga training, massages, acupuncture, art explorations, life coaching. He was never stingy with the babysitting funds. He never questioned what I did with my time.

My time, my time. Magnetism, like electricity, is invisible. If the currents run in the same direction, they attract each other. If they run in opposite directions, they repel each other. *Circuit* means circle. A family is a haunting.

STAR

I come across Bug while she's writing in the ship's log. A wild script, scritchy-scratchy, like a crab had a seizure in our inkwell.

She's wearing the radio headset and she listens intently. Is she transcribing? Writing down orders? I look over her shoulder.

truitt must get boat working. must reach surface. no air. phil in rage. wants sex.

"Bug," I whisper, surrounding her with warmth and light. She drops her pen and leaps from her seat. The radio headset clatters to the floor and I pick it up. I hear a familiar voice coming through.

"You found Dead Girl," I say.

"No, I didn't," says Bug. "She found me."

Dead Girl takes a body and appears in the control room. She sits on the edge of the tiny linoleum counter and dangles her legs. She's wearing a black crinoline dress and a petticoat, lace-up boots, and stiff white stockings. Of course, she doesn't have a real body. She did have one, a long time ago. And now she's attached to the outcome. Of her body. What I mean is, *Katherine.* Dead Girl hangs around Katherine. She's not a ghost. She's family.

"I'm glad you're here," I tell her. "I want to run something by you."

She says *Go ahead* with her eyes. I put on the headphones. We can't take a chance that Truitt will hear us.

"I've been thinking."

"Don't do that," says Bug.

"Maybe we're dead."

Dead Girl comes into the headphones and her body dissolves, just disappears. The dress. The boots. Poof.

"Go on." I want to say her voice is loud, but a loud voice is jarring and unpleasant. Dead Girl's voice is symphonic, excited, expansive. *Loud* is the wrong word.

"Maybe we die and get born again," I say.

"Yes!" she sings back. "You're exactly right."

"If we were dead, we'd know it," says Bug.

"Don't stop. Keep going, Star."

"Every night when Katherine goes to sleep, we die and are born again. And then, in bigger ways, we die every day and are born again. And then, in even bigger ways, because we learn to think about life differently, Katherine dies, too. She dies while she's still alive. Always already dead. If we stay awake. If we are willing and open. If we can be brave."

"You may be dead," says Bug. "I'm not."

Truitt pops through the hatch and grabs the radio headset. He doesn't lag behind us for long, no matter what we're doing. He's a scout. Always on high alert.

"What's going on in here? This radio hasn't worked in years."

Smooshed Bug starts to giggle. Truitt lunges and takes her by both wrists. Bug doesn't struggle. She stopped fighting him long ago. Actually, I don't think she ever resisted him. She's too tiny. And I don't have a body. Or if I have one, I'm not in it. I'm no help.

"If you loved Jeff so much," says Truitt, "why did you dump him? Why did you cheat on him all the time?"

I want to fizzle out and leave, but I'm worried for Bug. Truitt has been carrying that roll of duct tape on his tool belt. He touches it now like a gun in a holster.

"*Cheat*'s not even a word," I tell him. "*Dump* isn't a real thing that people do. It's a made-up word. *Dump* doesn't happen."

"Last time I checked, it does," says Truitt. "You don't know how to love. You don't know the first thing about love."

Truitt tries the headphones, puts them on his ears. But Dead Girl won't say anything to Truitt. After a while, he throws them on the steel floor.

Bug jumps up. "I didn't do anything!"

Truitt slaps a strip of duct tape over Bug's mouth. Her eyes go wide with terror. He pushes her up against the periscope housing and tapes her to it, rounding the pillar slowly, adding a layer of tape with every rotation.

Hello, my name is Star. I die for love.

KATCHIE

I took a hot shower at Sheila's house and dosed my crabs yet another time with the special shampoo. Sheila wasn't worried about her bed or her couch being infested. She wasn't fastidious or paranoid about bugs. She was a smoker, a TV enthusiast, a Metallica fan.

After that fourth try, the crabs were finally gone, zapped, ridded. It had been a long time since I'd felt this clean. My hair, my skin, my piss, blood, spit and shit, dreams and blinks, yawns and stretches. Everything was flowing, clear, unpolluted. After smoking pot all day and drinking every night for years, it was delicious to be sleeping at night. Ten hours. Up in the morning. Powdered donuts for breakfast. Simple.

Sheila got me a job working with her at her mom's convenience store, Quickie Mart. Jackie owned three of them. She let her husband Wendell run them. But he rarely stopped by. The overall pattern of the job was this: I stocked the shelves. Then I sat around and ate hot dogs and listened to Sheila talk about her healing process.

"I want to introduce you to someone." I looked around. The store was empty.

"Meet Mickie. My inner child."

"Who?"

"Mickie's been getting in the way of my happiness. She's been stuck back there where I first got fucked-up, when I was a little girl. She loves you and she wants to say hi."

"Mickie wants to talk to me?"

"Don't give me shit about this. It's over your head."

"I met you when we were kids, Sheila. I already know Mickie."

"Mickie's younger than thirteen, Katchie. And she thinks you don't like her. She's about to cry."

I gave Sheila a sideways hug. "Where did you learn how to do this?"

"In my last rehab. We did a lot of psychodrama. Inner-child work."

"Oh," I said, "California."

That night I plopped down beside Sheila on the couch. She was watching sitcom reruns.

She said, "I can't stand it anymore."

"Can't stand what?"

"I wish Mom would leave Wendell. She believes me. What I told her. And she's going to leave him. We're going to take him to court."

"When?"

"When she has time to talk to her lawyer. Wendell could go to jail. I was only in fifth grade when it started."

TRUITT

Sheila and her mom boated around Float Lake with Wendell on hot days. The three of them went out to dinner when Jackie felt like treating. Would Sheila really send Wendell to jail after he had shown up for her high school graduation, her swim meets, and her family sessions at several rehabs?

Stop. Halt. Pay attention. If Wendell had stuck his tongue in his ten-year-old stepdaughter's mouth—if this were true, and if Sheila had really told her mother, why didn't Jackie do anything about it? Jackie was the one with money. She could have kicked Wendell to the curb. On the contrary, the Fourth of July was coming up, and they were all three going to South Carolina for the week. To a beach house.

We simply can't be sure what Sheila said was true. Her step-father was a sloppy drunk who breathed down the neck of any girl or woman who would let him. And we do hear about grown men putting their sexual organs into small people. You know. Children. But it's impossible to believe that kind of thing.

A therapist can easily plant memories in a girl's mind to keep her on the hook for more sessions. Sheila's mother Jackie could afford whatever issue Sheila came up with. She could build a mansion for inner-child Mickie to live in all by herself. A mansion with an indoor pool. It was cheaper than divorcing Wendell.

I persuaded Katchie to move out of Sheila's house when the talk got too heavy. I get goose bumps thinking about how much power I used to have. Now all I can rustle up in Katherine is a sense of confusion. On a bad day, I'm stuck behind a barbed-wire fence, growling dogs, bars on the windows, asylum setting, crazy women clawing the windows, meat-grinding machines set up around a pile of burnt bodies that look like roasted marshmallows.

On a good day, Katherine listens to me. I may have finally convinced her to stop going to AA meetings. She's been going to one or two every week for twenty-two years. Sheila has been her AA sponsor since 1996, and they still talk all the time. All these years Sheila has stuck around. I don't even try to push her out of our life anymore. She can keep Katherine away from the booze, but she's no help at all with the deep despair.

Dr. Goodman tries to help with the despair. That's his current focus. I'd like to get rid of Dr. Goodman.

DEAD GIRL AS OLIVE

The newspaper forgot to mention that my husband Ballard was drunk when he died. He took two journalists to lunch. Rode in from Lenoir, met them in Tarboro, was showing off, fell to his death after too much whiskey. That's how the writer of his obituary happened to see the accident.

> June 23, 1895: Mr. Robert Ballard Wood, passenger agent of the Chester and Lenoir narrow gauge road, was killed at Lincolnton Thursday by falling underneath the passen-

ger coach of a mixed train in an attempt to board it while the train was moving off. He caught the rod with his left hand but failed to catch the coach with his right. His body swung around between the coach and the car ahead, his foot slipped and he fell onto the rail directly in front of the wheels of the passenger coach. He was dragged along the rail for about 150 feet, when the wheels passed over his body, mangling it most horribly. Both legs were broken all to pieces, his body cut in two, and the top and back of his skull torn off. He was a son of the late General J. G. Wood.

KATHERINE

I was rushing to get Zack to a playdate with a shy second grader. This boy's mother was pushing a friendship on us. Zack would try kids like this for a month and then never speak to them again. A Public Enemy song came on in the car. It reminded me of Matt, my college boyfriend. How we sat around together all the time and listened to music. I would draw and write. He would stare off into space. He could see notes in the air; he was a musical genius. Or I thought he was.

Zack caught my face in the rearview mirror. "Why are you crying?"

"This song reminds me of my old life, and my old friends. Sometimes I miss them."

These friends aren't the same people anymore. Lawyers, tech writers, sales and marketing of whatever. They're busy and fulfilled. Or at least busy. Matt makes background noises for films and commercials. Glasses clinking in a restaurant, slamming car doors, rain. If these sounds weren't added, you'd miss them. But you don't notice when they're there.

I didn't explain this to Zack. I simply turned off the radio. A few minutes later, we got to his friend's house and I walked him to the door.

"I hate it when you cry, Mom."

"Music does that to me sometimes."

"Then don't listen to music."

When I got home and walked into the house, the first thing to hit me was the smell of old wood. Old, like a wagon after the hay. Still. Solid. Sunlit. Waiting for me. I put down my purse and went into the kitchen. The wood on the floor there was darker. Polished, new, a softer wood, scratched to hell by our metal chairs.

I missed my two children when they were gone, but when they were home, I wished them gone again. They made a little mess in every room and demanded that I act happy, human, willing, able.

I went upstairs and straightened Em's room, working around all the pink, glittery, feather-coated crap. Back then it was fair-ies, sequins, and Disney posters. Without the clutter, it would have felt like Emily didn't exist at all. Zack's room never needed help. He kept it neat. Also, he didn't spend much time in there. He liked to be out and around in the yard and house, where other people could see him. Swinging his bat. His décor was navy blue and spare. The knob on his sock drawer was missing.

For the first few years of school, Emily sang on her way home from the bus stop. When she turned the corner, always, she was singing. By fourth grade, she would be crying, running in a full sprint. I watched from my perch in my bedroom window, clutching my cell phone. It was almost 3:00 p.m. She was due home from school any minute.

Was she banned from a table at lunch and then, turning with her lunch box, banned from another? Did a girl spit on her coat, thrown to the side during a game? Did another girl pick it up from the ground with a long stick and hold it in the air, as if to say, *This coat is contaminated*? Did everyone laugh? Everyone wasn't everyone. It was everyone to Emily. Her friends, who became her tormenters. Ella, Bridget, Lily, Sophia S., and Sophia B.

I tried to check in with Phil, but I went directly to voice mail. I sent him a text: *Nervous about Emily*. Phil saw my text; he started to write something; I saw the little bubbles on my phone screen. But then the bubbles disappeared. Nothing.

I called him again, and again, until he finally answered.

"I'm on a phone meeting," he said. "What's up?"

"I'm waiting for Emily. I'm freaking out."

"Is she home yet?"

"I'm so scared. Things have been going badly."

"She'll be fine." I could hear him tapping on his keyboard. "What did you do today?"

"I was working on my film. I have this old video footage of a horse that I want to use. It's so old it's barely there. I need to have it transferred."

Phil didn't answer. He was thinking about his email, probably. He writes a lot of them. He sits very straight at his laptop and types with proper ergonomic angles.

"I drew horses for a year straight when I was ten."

Phil's head actually gets bigger when he's typing on his computer.

"Anyone can draw a horse," I said. "And a witch. You do it with circles. But I can't draw wild horses swimming in the ocean."

"Can we talk about this when I get home?"

If there's one thing I don't respect, it's selfishness.

"Phil?"

"Yes."

"You can also draw mice with circles. But I don't like mice."

Down on Prospect Street, Emily appeared around the corner. She was running. Her pink backpack was full and swinging wildly, like it might pull her to the ground.

KATCHIE

Mom picked me up in her Toyota sports car. She was gripping the leather steering wheel. Her chewed-down nails looked more chewed than mine. Shrunken and white-haired, my apple-doll grandma was sitting in the passenger seat. I leaned in to give her a kiss. Like kissing a turtle. That wasn't Kitty's fault.

"Kitty wants to go to the club," said my mom. After we gave the car to the valet in front of the club, she said, "Take that awful thing off."

I pulled the Quickie smock over my head. Underneath, I was wearing a sundress I took from the closet in Sheila's sister's room. I'd had it on for days. Mom slapped me with a wet kiss on pointed toes. I'm a lot taller than she is. A lot.

"Well," she said. "It only took forty days to get you home."

Forty days. I was well on my way to a purple AA coin.

Kitty ordered a big fat scotch as soon as we sat down. I

answered all of Mom's questions from the fictional point of view
of Lori Glass. At that time, the mid- to late '90s, Lori was working in public relations at Channel 13. She lived on the Upper
East Side. Her boyfriend was a first-year lawyer.

Everything in the dining room that day at the club smelled
like crab. You pry the shell off and the gook is exposed. Mustard-
colored stuff that must be crab shit. You don't eat that part unless
you do it by mistake. It's called "picking a crab" when you sit
down and rip it to bits. You have to work hard for the white
meat in the claws. The dark meat is in the body. We ate lunch.

Later, in the hot, humid country club parking lot, Mom and
Kitty and I walked by my dad's car. "Wait, is Dad here?"

"Oh, yes, that's right, I think he is."

Mom helped Kitty move along through the parked cars.

"What's he doing?"

"He's playing golf with his girlfriend. She's quite the golfer."

"Why don't you get a divorce?"

"We can't afford it. And maybe Dad doesn't want to marry
Mrs. Pringle."

"Does she have a first name?"

"Not to me."

"Lawd ha' mercy, sakes alive," said Kitty with her deep southern accent. She said this so often, it was almost a tic. It was nice
to see my grandmother, but she bristled when we touched on
topics that upset or disturbed her. Mrs. Pringle, for example,
or anything "unladylike." But then she would let loose with an
ignorant opinion, which she would deliver as God's truth. "The
redbirds should fly with the redbirds and the bluebirds should fly
with the bluebirds."

More likely, she opened her mouth to gulp more air. As if

the air were suddenly failing her. She would shake her head very subtly, almost imperceptibly. As if she wanted to put her hand up and say, *STOP!* But she never did that. She just folded her chin down to her neck and paused. Blinked heavily, with a protracted squeeze of her eyes, like blinking took a huge amount of effort.

Why not discuss our difference of opinion on the matter?

No, never. That would be unladylike.

A racist, then. I turned against all women at the same time.

DEAD GIRL

No doubt it's a surprising fact that Katherine carries dead girls inside her. That her blood is yellow and warm. That Float Lake water runs in her veins and arteries, reeking of crab and chicken flesh. We will now consider a little more in detail how alive and dead can circulate in the same system.

The progression is this: Katherine is still alive.

Or maybe the progression is: She's still here.

Every minute of every day, thump thump thump. If she doesn't die, if she decides to live, one million barrels will pump through her heart. One million barrels! Enough to fill two oil supertankers. Blood! Not oil. All of you, pumping away, your fatty hearts. They're slightly yellow, at least on the surface. And happy enough, until the giants drag them out of the lake and throw them in a bucket.

When Katherine is sleeping, dawnish hours, 5:00 a.m., Phil gets up to piss. His limbs are heavy and he's only half awake. He's a big man, no fault of his own, tall and weighty. He comes back from his piss and climbs into bed, which shakes the mattress.

Early morning, before sunrise, when scary things happen. Phil's a thick person with arms like cannons. He rattles the bed, and then Katherine is fully awake but still lying there. He rolls over to take her in his arms.

Giants have feelings. They do their best. When there are no fresh bad children around, they like crabs for lunch and dinner. They throw the frantic creatures into boiling water. Giants get away with this, because they are so much bigger. They can do whatever they want. The crabs turn orange. Even their claws. They can't stay blue.

Is it Phil's fault that he needs to piss? That he wants to have sex with his wife? She hates him for waking her up. She fills the king-size bed—no—she fills the entire bedroom with her unspoken rage.

Let's consider *fault*. Let's consider *blame*. The giants send their sunburned children to dangle a string over the side of the bulk-head into the lake. The string has a rotten, raw chicken wing tied to the end of it. That piece of raw chicken might have been lying on the sandy floor of Dad's garage for days, covered with green flies. Also attached is a lead weight, small, the size of a walnut, a sinker.

The giant children use nets to catch the crabs. They dump all the crabs into a metal bucket with just a few inches of water in it. The crabs try to tear one another to pieces. Claws waving wild, they wrestle until one lucky crab gets to the top of the pile and climbs over the side of the bucket. He drops into the grass, scrambles to the edge of the bulkhead, and flings himself into the lake.

Katchie lies on her stomach, peering into the lake, her net poised for capture. She sees the crab go over the edge, and she dives in after him. There's something on her mind. It's too big for her body. Her body stays put, right where she is. Crabbing off the bulkhead in her family's backyard. Virginia Beach, 1980. It's a brave and crafty crab.

KATHERINE

"I'm not going to AA meetings anymore," I said to Nance on the phone.

"Does Sheila know?"

"I don't need to tell Sheila. I'm not going to drink or take drugs. I'm just tired of meetings."

"Maybe you can go see Pastor Jerry."

"The priest at the Greek church? Phil's not religious anymore. His parents can't even drag him over there. They take the kids on Easter."

"You've given up on your therapist. You've given up on AA. Just go see Jerry. For me."

That's how I found myself in Pastor Jerry's office, surrounded by paintings of Jesus. I told him that I was starting to feel obsessed with Lori Glass, my old friend from Brown.

"Why's that?" he asked.

"Lori's a big Hollywood producer. She went to the Academy Awards. I saw this on Facebook."

"You're imagining your friend's life," said Jerry. "So is she, in a different way. We all do this together."

"No. She really went. She wore a Chanel dress."

"Human beings are completely wrong about everything; that's why we suffer."

A woman was poor and hopeless. Things hadn't turned out for her. All she had was a failing farm, a simple cottage, and a son, Jack. She didn't even know why she gave birth to him. He was useless. Until he stumbled into magic. She threw his damn beans in the garden, and they grew into a ladder to a different world. Jack climbed all the way up above the clouds. He was a bad person, but he ended up rich. He lied and stole from the giant. He seduced the giant's wife. He took everything from the giant, even his life. The giant *died*.

"Are you okay, Katherine?" asked Pastor Jerry.

"Yes, why?"

Jerry looked at the clock on his desk.

"It's been five minutes since you said anything."

"I'm taking a little break from having sex with my husband. And the fact that I'm taking a break. This is causing stress in the marriage."

"How long has it been? Since you had sex?"

"A hundred years."

He stared.

"Three months."

"Why do you feel you need to stop having sex with your husband?"

"He's mad at me all the time. I mean, ALL the time. And he doesn't love me."

Pastor Jerry nodded with a smug look on his face. I could see the Bible opening up in his mind with flipping pages, like the beginning of a show on public television.

"I know the Bible has a lot to say about love," I told him. "But I don't want to hear it. No offense to Jesus. Otherwise known as the Lord."

Pastor Jerry didn't laugh or even smile. I told Nance later that I was pretty sure he hated my guts. She said, "Ministers don't hate, or hold grudges. Difficult people are their job."

Jerry was a man of God. And what was I? A difficult person? I thought of my many therapists: Sara, Barb, Garth, Judy, Randall, Jenny, Jennifer, Jen, Chris, Marla, Darla, Duane, Dr. Goodman. Enough to fill a party bus. No wonder friends like Lori Glass think I'm nuts. She said it many times behind my back in the '90s. She said it to my face more recently. Our families happened to vacation at the same Colorado ski resort. Lori asked me over hot chocolate how my mental illness was going and I said, "Fine. How's yours?"

Maybe that's why I mentioned Lori to Pastor Jerry. Lori has her accomplishments, but I get credit for still being alive, not to mention the fact that I have two kids, and the skill set to pack them up and get them out on a ski slope with all the proper gear. At least I can ski.

KATCHIE

I stood on the dock. I wiped my hands on my shorts. My fingers were sweaty, my face sticky. The air was humid, bug music everywhere. I was home now. And so was my dad. He stood on the deck, watching me. His entire body radiated anger. Rage was expected and usual. I stood there, too, paralyzed in my own submissive smolder. Nothing better to do. Really, what the hell did anyone have to do? It was the Fourth of July, a holiday.

A jet ski buzzed by on the lake, close to the shore. My dad hated jet skis almost as much as he hated dogs, particularly Dobermans and German shepherds. Maybe it was love, not hate. Maybe it was both for him. He also hated the neighbor's cat, who scratched up the top of his convertible and devoured her own babies. And he hated the neighbor. No love there. Or maybe he fucked her sometimes. I don't know what went on in the '80s.

Dad told me often how much he hated his life situation, which was servitude to the dollar, and choicelessness, something he may have chosen. Dad didn't see it that way. He hated the young guy on the jet ski more than he hated the actual jet ski, despite its horrible buzzing noise, and the fumes and the spray. But he hated that, too.

I knew his grudges better than I knew my own. *Garrumbuzzzgrrr*. The jet ski made wide circles in the center of the lake, then looped down to the far end and lunged back again to the other side with a tail of white spray.

I like things juicy, always have. Sometimes juicy means painful. Juicy means alive. And things were starting to feel awful dry. I let Dad stare at me with hatred on his face. I was his, after all. His to hate.

He went around the back of the house to the garage. The jet skier buzzed by and sprayed our dock with a whoop and a cry. Dad screeched out of the driveway in the Mercedes. Maybe he was angry because he had to wear a black suit on the Fourth of July. He was taking Kitty and my mom to a funeral. Some ancient cousin had sandpapered herself into eternity.

I found my mom upstairs in her dressing room getting ready. Her skin was getting blotchy as she aged. Her nose, in particular, was very red. She used powder over the foundation. Eye shadow, mascara, lipstick. She moved on to the hair spray. Tease,

tease, a good long tease to the short, wavy, frosted hair. Fix the whole thing in place.

She was in her high-waist underpants and her see-through bra, with Band-Aids in place over her nipples. Maybe so her nipples wouldn't show through her blouse or dress. She always did this with Band-Aids. As a kid, I thought her nipples were bleeding. Later, I thought they were losing milk. I wish I'd never seen them at all.

Mom hurried out of the room and I was alone in the mirror. I looked better after two months off the sauce and other drugs. My hair was growing out; I had lost the bloat, lost some weight. I had a tan. No scabs or sores. Mom came back, looking for something. Maybe a lipstick or an earring.

"What do you want?" she asked. Not meanly. She wasn't being mean. She isn't mean. She's nice. No, she's not nice.

"What do you need?"

"Nothing."

STAR

Truitt marches around, pretends to take charge of the submarine. I've locked myself in the bow compartment with the hatch sealed, but I can still hear him through the public address system. He barks into the microphone.

"Wind's from the southwest," he says, "ten knots. Visibility high. Barometer: nine oh eight."

The loudspeaker booms through the boat, and I can picture Bug taped to the periscope. She's been there for months. Or has it been years? I hear her crying and whimpering at night, or what we call the night. We have lights in the sub, but who knows if it's daytime or nighttime? I make it up. The illusion of time. Down in the cold water, in the black deep, HOW CAN WE KNOW?

Truitt won't shut up in there.

"Clear the bridge. Prepare to dive!"

I took the pledge. Finally. I did it for Bug. No more submariners. Used to be, if I found one asleep in the corner, I would fuck his brains out. Oh, don't worry, it was always the commanding officer. Every time. I might imagine it was someone else, but, open my eyes, come into my body, and it was always Phil. Strong, tall, handsome. He makes all the money. But also, he does reject and hurt me. I'm not pretending he doesn't.

The commanding officer has a bunk toward the front of the boat. He only comes back to the stern when he wants to lie down with me. Usually in the morning, before the alarm.

"No, hon. I don't want to be touched. I've been trying to tell you. Don't touch me anymore."

Let's call Katherine the ocean. Let's call time irrelevant. Let's put the submarine in her body. Now fill it with horny men. They do have sonar. A way of seeing in the dark, in the blood, a swishing tide. If a torpedo doesn't hit, if it misses . . .

Part Two

KATHERINE

Margaret, a friend from AA, came over to have coffee. She followed me into the kitchen and we sat down for a chat. I was distracted by her haircut. It was a squish bob, or a square blob. She wanted to talk about Zack and Emily, about how they would be affected if I started to drink again, and whatever other trouble I might get into as a result.

"We haven't seen you in a while."

"I'm not drinking," I said. "I'm taking a break from meetings. From therapy. From all that effort. I need to rest."

"Have you considered going away to get some help?"

"Yes," I said. "I've been looking at a place called Hope Haven."

"Where's that?"

"Phoenix."

"A place where you can deal with your deeper issues?"

"It's a rehab. For things like codependency and, I don't know, general craziness."

"What's going on, then? Depression? Anxiety? Infidelity?"

"Listen," I said. "Phil has deeper issues, too. He stores them in his testicles. His feelings come out when he orgasms. Little minnows."

"Of course he has issues," said Margaret. "We all do."

"Right. But some people are *worse*. I'm a *worse*. Off I go to the loony bin."

"Is there some kind of crisis? I mean, what's going on?"

"I don't fuck him anymore."

"You like having sex with Phil," Margaret said. "That's what you used to say."

"Yeah, well, there's more to a marriage than the in and out."

"How long has it been?"

"Too long."

"So what? I know couples who go for years—"

"Phil won't put up with that. That's not how he rolls. He's threatening to go to a prostitute."

"He wouldn't."

"Zero humidity in Phoenix. Phil's the one who ruined our marriage."

"My experience with relapsing addicts is that there's some truth they're not facing."

"Your experience with relapsing addicts," I mimicked. "I haven't relapsed."

"The relapse happens before the relapse. We all think you're in that place right now."

We all? WE ALL? My AA home group at the Episcopal church. They meet every Friday night in the basement room at 7:15. Women are too, too dumb. When the engine light goes on, you have to pull over. The smoke is dense, thick, black. It's hard to ignore.

"Thanks, Margaret."

"You look tired, Katherine."

I knew I looked like shit. But there's never a right time to say that to a person. There's never a good-enough reason. The relapse before the relapse before the relapse before the relapse. Willing to be willing to be willing to be willing.

KATCHIE

A few days after the Fourth, Nance had a sweat lodge cere-mony in her backyard. Her "New Age" friends were there. We squeezed into a four-person tent, seven people in all. I had only met the tall guy with a goatee. I think he was Nance's boyfriend at the time. She smudged us all with smoke from a burning bundle of sage, which she waved around in the air. Then she poured water from a watering can onto the hot rocks in the middle of the tent.

"Don't touch these," she said. The air in the tent was smoky, steamy. Nance had plaited her hair into tiny beaded cornrows. We were all on top of one another. Did I mention we were naked? I reached out and grabbed Nance's leg, near the ankle. She took no notice. She was busy leading her ritual. She called on all the elders in the various directions, north, south, east, and west. Soon everyone was chanting.

Lam lam lam Lam lam lam Lam
Lam lam lam Lam lam lam Lam

Sweat was dripping down into my eyes. My butt was slipping around on the tent floor. The air smelled funky, human, and damp. Nance twisted her ankle out of my hands and turned to face me. Her teeth glowed white.

"Relax," she said. "Close your eyes and let yourself see things. In your mind."

She crawled over to another corner of the tent. When I closed my eyes, I saw the usual black void in my own head. I stared into it for a while. Nothing new. Maybe it wasn't exactly black, more like black light, or a greasy ultraviolet black, like a puddle of oil on pavement.

A shape formed in this textured darkness and came toward me. A small woman, maybe forty-five years old, was walking along a wooden sidewalk of a town, one block of storefronts on rickety wooden buildings. She wore lace-up boots and a long black dress with a full skirt. A horse and cart went by. The road was muddy. The woman said hello to the man driving the cart. Then she grabbed her middle, screamed, doubled over, and squatted down in front of the general store.

"Seeing something?" said Nance. "Hold this little baby for me."

She put a wadded-up towel in my arms and moved off. I kept my eyes closed and held on to the little baby. It was crying. I was afraid I might squeeze it too hard, accidentally smother it, kill it somehow.

One of the men in the tent was watching me . . . the man with the goatee. He wanted to take the baby. What was his name? He was Nance's boyfriend. I could see his shriveled penis between his legs. *I should kill him,* I thought. But I didn't have a knife or a gun. I only had the baby. I loved the baby. You can't not love a baby. I love every baby. And yet, it's easy to suffocate a baby. It's never on purpose.

Nance came around. "Why are you staring at Tony?"

"He shouldn't be here."

"Why not?"

"He's dangerous."

"Focus on your own quest," said Nance. "Close your eyes."

The woman in the black dress was sitting next to me in the tent, fussing with the baby in my arms. She had wide-set blue eyes exactly like my mom's. Eyes that pull apart sideways a little more than most. She looked like an exotic deep-sea creature with toggled features that make it easier to see in the dark. A pretty sea creature with a straight part and a tight bun.

"Here's what we do with babies," she said. "We feed them. See? Babies have sweet little heart-shaped mouths. We give them a warm liquid. We change their nappies. We carry them in our swelling, growing bodies. We share ourselves. We feed these babies from our nipples and we keep them alive with the nutrients in our blood."

What have you done today, Tony?

He was close, so close that our feet and ankles were entangled. He was also big, and hairy in all the wrong places. I hate seeing penises when they aren't erect. Unattractive mice with bald heads: mice who have eaten away a part of themselves. I held the towel to my chest.

Now it was Nance sitting next to me.

"Stop looking at Tony. Go inside your own head."

I saw myself standing on the dock, looking out across the lake with my dad behind me. We hadn't had one real conversation since I had moved home. I lifted up out of my body and found myself looking down on the same scene, the dock, and my dad. From the aerial view, Float Lake is a smashed oval, the shape of a hard-boiled egg, with a couple of bites taken out. Or a blood cell about to split in two.

The land around our house was called Cabin Point. Probably a long-ago slave cabin that got hung on to. Someone engraved *Cabin Point* on the brick wall that ran along the front edge of the property. Ivy had grown over the wall by the time my parents bought it; no one called it anything. The cabin became Dad's garage.

He kept everything important out there in mason jars that

lined the tilted, uneven shelves. He had rigged up all kinds of haphazard storage systems. Shelves attached with bungee cords to ladders propped against rusted refrigerators. And a faded American flag hung from the ceiling, left over from when he was in the marines. There was a window, but the glass was so dirty, I couldn't see through it.

I was trying now. To do that. To see through this crusty glass from the inside. To see out.

"Why are you crying?" asked Nance.

"I'm not crying." I pulled the baby tight into my breasts. It started getting hot. Like it was on fire.

The woman in the old-fashioned clothes spoke to me. "I was just walking along the streets of Tarboro in my lace-up boots, my black crinoline dress. I spent the morning posing for a daguerreotype. I was headed home to prepare a lesson for the students I took in as boarders at Good Springs to pay the bills. The lesson was on prunes and porridge, on regularity. I was thinking it over, walking through the dusty road, Main Street, and *you* dropped out of a hole between my legs."

"Give me the baby," said Nance.

"I can't. She's sick."

"I know," said Nance. "She's got a fever. She's not going to make it."

"No, no, no, no!"

The air in the tent smelled like crabs. I had to get out of there. I opened the flap with shaking hands. Someone reached out and zipped it up behind me, and good for them. I looked at the wadded-up towel once I got into the house. It wasn't a baby. It was a towel, an old ratty one at that. I threw it on the floor.

STAR

I climb through a circular hatch and find Truitt in the control room. He's wearing a heavy-duty black raincoat. He's got the string of the hood pulled tight. I can barely see his angry face, his nose, eyes, and mouth. His pale legs stick out from under the coat. There are puddles around him on the steel floor. He's wearing rubber boots.

"How did you get so wet?"

"I have my ways."

"It's time to set Bug free. And take the tape off her mouth."

"No."

Smooshed Bug begs with her wide-open eyes. She makes noises behind the shiny silver tape and squirms. She's not physically strong. She's a string-bean girl. Healthy, but skeletal.

"We're running out of air," I tell him.

"If I can find a few good battery cells, I can bridge the plates."

"Set her free," I say. "This isn't right."

Truitt grabs me by the shoulders and gets me in a headlock. He digs his fat Eagle Scout ring into my scalp. I can't feel that shit anymore, thank God.

"Forget it," he says when I don't react. "I have better things to do."

He starts peeling off his wet clothes and hangs them from rods and machinery corners. He struggles with his boots. When he gets them off, he turns them upside down, and water pours out. The control room smells like dead fish. Corroded pipes and wires hang from the ceiling. Truitt shivers, naked, all bones.

"How can I help you?" he says. "I suppose you want to talk about your feelings."

"I only have one feeling," I tell him. "And I have it all the time. I feel *confused*."

"You don't act confused."

"Take the tape off her mouth."

"No."

I follow Truitt into the bunk room, where he starts digging through a mountain of blankets and oily rags, searching for dry clothes. I stare at the cage, where we keep our two mice. When the air gets dangerous to humans, meaning not enough oxygen, the mice will presumably keel over and die. The last time I checked, they were little gray lumps, lying limp in their cage on the crackly old newspaper. Now they are gone.

KATHERINE

I took my clothes off and walked around the house. Both kids were sleeping over with friends. Phil was in Singapore. One a.m. All the lights on. If the neighbors looked into the windows, they would have to accept what they saw. I used to love drawing horses.

The shower in the master bathroom is a coffin, upright, with nozzles and excellent water pressure. It has a glass door set in stainless steel. I think the tiles and the tub, the hardware and faucets and handles, and the shower door are from the 1940s. The steel door frame has an engraving from a foundry in Newark.

Dead people have touched all my bathroom equipment. I feel safe in that knowledge, and I feel safe in our big old colonial house with the hardwood floors. I drifted from room to room, up and down the stairs between the second and third floors. If I wanted to get my body wet, I had a choice between the shower or a trip to the soaking tub, which is on the third floor, a completely different country. Wives have died there; husbands have died there. I don't know when the house was built. Nineteen thirty-four?

That's what it said in the real estate listing, but downstairs in the library (that's how it was labeled on the official floor plan), in the fireplace, there's a piece of black steel molding that says *Newark 1912.* Maybe that's when the house was built.

I stepped into the shower. I was thinking about Emily. Her birthday was coming up. Sweet sixteen. She wanted to spend it with friends, and Tucker, her boyfriend in the twelfth grade. I wasn't upset about this. She doesn't owe us anything. She's a young woman with a fertility of her own, and a boyfriend, moods, makeup. If she smoked pot with Tucker and they burned out the engine, or if she felt angry at him and didn't know why, or if sex burned with Tucker . . . well . . . sometimes it burns.

When Emily got too upset, when she was little, I sometimes made her take a shower. It calmed her down. What I mean by *too upset* is having a panic attack. She would cry so hard she lost her place in reality. Then she would say that she couldn't breathe. That night, on the eve of the eve of her sixteenth birthday, I found myself in the same position. Crouched on the floor of the shower, hot water running down. No breath, blood racing, heart exploding in my chest.

TRUITT

The water in Jersey is hard. That's what I've heard, and I won't argue. It's so full of minerals that it leaves a weird brown residue around the mouth of the toilet bowl. It's orichalc, I think, a mysterious, ancient ore that everyone has forgotten about.

I considered asking Katherine to chip away at this crust with a butter knife; then I thought better of it. Orichalc. Somewhere between a metal and an ore. Not to be compared with oil, but yes, similar to oil. It was melted down, like nickel or gold. A melting process, a ritual. A precious molten metal.

I've been thinking about the engine. Some sludge is normal. But maybe we have too much. The only way to tell for sure is to take it apart. But you should never disassemble any more than you have to. And it's very hard work in the dark.

If she's sweating, if she's hungry, if she's eating, if she's full, if she's empty, she's in a body. Her body is inherited. An oil leak would be a basic engine problem, and would produce excessive smoke that is gray, not black.

She has her clothes off. She roams around naked. She knows what's coming. She's trying to pretend she's better than me, stronger. I work my way between the pipes. Nuts missing. Bolts rusted, cracked, or gone. Under the water, I question the machinery. There's no one to answer, but you have to inquire. That's what troubleshooting is all about. I haven't got much to work with. Not to mention no crew!

Star begs for Katherine. *Leave her alone.* But I pin them both down. So they know who's in command. Above and below. Katherine struggles to fend off her own pinching fingers. Soap, shampoo, hair. She keeps her fingers busy. But then, under the water, she surrenders in a rush of shame. Pleasure, relief, release, homecoming.

Our past, our past, our oily past. The derrick, the wells, the underground pockets called "traps." Pump pump. Open-heart surgery is a technique for repairing a damaged heart. The surgeon first opens the patient's chest. All things are liquid, solid, or gas. Oil. Oil. Family. Unburned oil gets dirtier and dirtier. It doesn't go away unless you burn it.

Oil has been found that is light yellow and almost as clear as water. Oil has also been found that is black and thick. Oil is heavier than air, but lighter than water. Straight from Katherine's body like a spoonful of crab salad. It has to do with the physical versus the nonphysical. We are the dead. There are no losses.

DEAD GIRL REGISTER: HARRIET WOOD

Hi, my name is Harriet. Olive was my mother. A flu took her when we were eleven. Grandmother Hettie sent my brother Walt to live with Uncle James in Norfolk. She kept me in North Carolina for herself. Folks started to think she was my mother, instead of my grandmother. I never corrected them. Mother. Grandmother. She was wicked and crazy. Separating twins? She was obsessed with poo, my poo. Nothing else mattered.

Walt wrote to me, told me he cried for me every night when he went to bed. He did his best to please Uncle James, Aunt Margaret, and cousin James. We called this cousin "Jimbo." Walt had skinny arms and legs like a bird, wide green eyes like my own. When we stayed with them in Norfolk, Walt took me downtown and bought me candy and ice cream.

People shared beds. It was a different time. Me in the cold bed with my grandmother sleeping. Big people are so very dumb. Small people don't always realize this. We know about our bodies as soon as we are born into them. We know what's supposed to happen.

Grandma Hettie had no patience for feelings. All she wanted to know was did I empty myself daily. I cried when she gave me the castor oil or made me eat prunes. I cried when she gave me water treatments. Up at night again sobbing. She pinched me under the covers. *Hush!*

We still lived at Good Springs, in the house where Hettie was born in 1842. It was her family's "estate," or manse. The house was four over four; the rooms were small, maybe ten feet by eight feet with slanted floors. It wasn't a plantation, not even close. Just a small farm.

Cousin Jimbo went to France when he was seventeen. He wrecked a motorcycle, hit his head. *Dazed and bruised,* he wrote, *but otherwise fine.* Except he had a tiny, invisible rip, a weakened place in his brain that broke free one night while he was sleeping. This was on the transatlantic steamer. The crew dropped his body overboard. It's not like they could keep it in the icebox with the hard cheese. Overboard. That was the protocol.

I got it into my head that Jimbo was still alive when they tossed him off the side of the boat. What does a ship doctor know about the difference between alive and dead? They thought he was dead. Maybe he was dead. Maybe he wasn't. They threw him overboard. That much is true. Alive, sinking, lungs filling with salt water. Scrambling, limbs flailing in the cold sea.

After the funeral, the no-body funeral, Uncle James thought he saw Jimbo out at the corner, and ran to greet him. Not a ghost, exactly. More of a wish.

"He was your first cousin," Walt told me. "You couldn't have married him."

"Doesn't matter," I said. "I loved him."

"I loved him, too."

"That's different."

KATCHIE

After the sweat lodge, I left desperate messages for Nance on her answering machine. It took two weeks, but she finally called me back.

"I'm sorry," she said. "I didn't want to interfere with your process."

"What process? I can't live with my parents anymore."

"I'd bring you to my place, but my nephew's coming down from New York."

"I thought you didn't like houseguests."

"Phil is my oldest brother's son. He's not a houseguest."

"I'm feeling really fucked-up," I told her.

She said, "How about I come over?"

"Now?"

"Yeah."

"Right now I'm kind of busy."

"Doing what?"

"Planning my suicide."

"I wouldn't do that," she said.

"Why not?"

"You've got lessons to learn about love. If you take your own life, you unlearn them. Then you'd have to get reborn and do this same life all over again. Every single damn thing."

Nance has always gone in for dime-store philosophy. She calms me down, though. She showed up at my parents' house twenty minutes later. I took her through the dining room to the kitchen, and she noticed my dad's well-stocked bar.

"Can I make a drink?"

"Whatever you want."

"You're sure? I don't want to make it hard for you. To not drink."

"I'm not tempted." This was true. I was going to an Alcoholics Anonymous meeting almost every day. Nance stood there for quite a while and considered my dad's abundant bar. She was wearing overalls, beads, and Birkenstocks.

"Forget it. I don't need to drink," she said. "Show me around?"

We wandered into the den, where Dad kept his Nazi book collection.

She grabbed my hand. "I'm concerned."

I didn't like the weirdo museum, either. I hated this room. I started to walk out, but Nance pulled me back.

"Gordon says nice things about your dad."

"Dad doesn't live here anymore, not really," I told her. "He spends most of his time at his girlfriend's house. My mom hides in the dark, watching TV with my grandmother."

"Was he born during World War Two?"

"No. In the thirties."

"So he was a kid during the war."

We passed through the living room on our tour and I looked out the window at the lake. Black under a half-moon.

"This is a nice room," said Nance. It didn't get much foot traffic from day to day, but it was easily the most beautiful place in the house. An entire wall of windows faced the lake, the pines, the open sky. My parents dedicated the other walls to family photos, and Nance was standing there in front of them. The centerpiece was of course a photo of "the General" in full Confederate uniform. He was a tiny man with dark hair, dark eyes, and a triangular beard. His wife Hettie, also petite, stands beside him in the photo.

"That's her. The ghost," I said, pointing to the photo. I had been freaking out about this since it happened, but now the incident felt matter-of-fact. "That's the one I saw in the sweat lodge."

"We're reincarnated over and over with the same people," said Nance. "Through many lifetimes. Our father in one lifetime may be our son in the next."

If Nance was right, and I'm not saying she was, then I had people around me who had been around me for many lifetimes. My mother and father very possibly wanted to kill me for misdeeds from other centuries. They had no idea, of course, which made them even more dangerous. But they loved me, because they said so.

"All right, all right," I said. "That's enough hocus-pocus for one night."

DEAD GIRL

"I like your drawing," I tell Smooshed Bug.

She covers it with her hands. "Don't look."

I had discovered her in the control room taped to the periscope shaft. Completely immobile. Her mouth sealed, her eyes. The duct tape was gluey and getting old, stuck in her hair. God knows how long she'd been like that. Time moves unevenly underwater; it's hard to track. I unwrapped the poor thing and sat her down at the navigator's desk. Gave her more crayons there than you can possibly dream of . . . and all the good colors. Bug went right to work. Muttered something about horses, and swimming with circles in the dark.

"That looks like a heart," I finally say. She is drawing fast and wild with great concentration.

"Oh, this isn't a heart, dummy. It's the place in the body where babies grow."

"Babies grow farther down."

"Not this one." Bug tries to crumple up the drawing, but I slide it out of her hands.

"I know where babies grow," says Bug. "Usually."

"Then why did you draw this baby inside a heart?"

"I just had the idea. That's all."

"Do you mind if I add to it?"

I keep going, scribbling, elaborating, adorning the heart-womb. I can't stop. I use every crayon in the box. I tape sheets of construction paper together and I plaster them around the control room. The drawing covers every wall then stretches into the galley kitchen. I transform the submarine into a temple, awash with pulsing linings, tissue, veins and arteries, rivers of glittery silver and gold.

The human heart. It's shaped like a fist. It wants to be a tube, a long snakelike thing that stretches out, relaxed, taking up room, like a doorstop you might use in the winter to keep the draft from coming under the door, a nylon stocking stuffed with cotton, the shape of an arm or a leg. But it's not an arm or a leg! It's a heart, a vital organ. It has to fit into the body cavity with all the other vital organs, even though it can be argued that the heart is the most vital. It folds back in on itself to make room for others.

Bug sits on the floor and watches me work.

"The heart is generous. And a good citizen," I tell her.

"Cool," she says when I finish.

We clean up the mess, share some vanilla wafers and drink some milk. That's how you wrap up a morning at church school. Bug has already forgotten about being taped to the periscope. *Ping.*

KATCHIE

I went to see the opera with Nance. Her nephew Phil had reserved seats for us, right up front. He came in from the back and leapt onto the stage. *"Figaro, Figaro, Figaro."* Singing, singing. All face and mouth, campy eyes. At intermission, Nance stayed in her seat.

"I'm not going out in this energy."

"Phil's great," I said.

"Too bad this is his last performance."

"Why? He's amazing."

"He's not good enough. He's not making it. His mentor did this as a favor. Phil came down from New York City on his own dime."

"He's hot." I found Phil mesmerizing from the moment I saw him. And I have always hated opera.

"He's the understudy to the understudy," said Nance. "For a regional show."

Afterward, we took Phil to the Barnacle, a bar with porthole windows, fishing nets on the walls, rotted buoys lying around. I ordered a ginger ale.

"You don't drink?" asked Phil.

"Not right now."

He put his arm around an antique wooden mermaid, salvaged from the bow of a wrecked ship. Kissed her. I laughed, and he gave me a look. His brown eyes were shining. I felt lit up and fearless. My herpes sore had healed. My hair was clean and soft and no longer crawling with crabs. I had been swimming in the ocean every day and I wasn't bloated from beer and drugs. My skin wasn't patchy and scabby. I'm not trying to sound like Rocky, or Cinderella. I'm just pointing out that Phil and I were meant to be together, at least back then we were.

"Don't even think about it," said Nance, later, when Phil went off to piss.

"Are you serious?"

"He's about to move to California. He's starting a business with his brother. Something on this new World Wide Web thing. Don't pounce."

Phil's skin was smooth, olive-toned. He had moles on his

face and his neck. He also had his mentor's hotel room in downtown Norfolk for one night. That's where he took me.

From the window, I could see the entire harbor, dotted with
destroyers, tugboats, aircraft carriers, pleasure vessels. I sat down
on the bed. I could hardly breathe. I acted relaxed, however,
aloof and indifferent. I had been mastering this since Dickie
Mueller broke his puka necklace.

I said, "Mr. Brown Eyes."

"I'm sick of them."

"Get new ones. But I might not want you without them."

"I'll keep these, then."

"Your stage makeup makes them evil. You scare me."

"What are your life goals?"

"You're cruel to ask," I said. *My goal is to live,* I thought. *Give
me something to live for.*

He kissed my neck, moving around me, and said, "You'll be
okay."

"How do you know?"

He pulled my shirt up over my head.

"You're tough."

"I'm not tough. I'm nothing."

"We all have to live with that."

He unzipped my pants and I wiggled out of my jeans. While
we kissed, he reached down and put his hand between my legs.
And then we were swimming into the flood. Anxious guards
shot flares above our heads, until the flames fell and set fire to
the water. Blankets were thrown to smother the flames, but
then the blankets caught fire, and Phil and I were rolling around
in them. I was left on my side, staring at the television screen.
The picture was unusually blue.

Phil ordered from room service. I wasn't hungry, didn't want anything. He turned on the news and ate his club sandwich. I lay stiff and silent beside him. Then I started to cry. He touched my nipple with a waffle chip.

"Feeling sad?"

I held out my hand and looked at it. Ten fingers. Ten stubby, chewed-off nails.

"When do you go back to New York?"

"Tomorrow."

I sat up straight and pulled my hair behind my ears. It was getting longer, and growing brown in increments. Phil went to the window. He was comfortable being naked. He had a strong, lean body. I went over to him, still crying. He held me, stroked my face, led me back to bed.

I woke up an hour or two later. My head on his chest. It was dark, 3:00 a.m., but there was light reflected into the room from the tankers and battleships in the harbor.

"Are you awake?" I asked.

"Do I want to be?"

"Do you know the best way to defend yourself against a rapist?"

"Do you?"

"The trick is to play along," I said. "When a rapist forces himself on you, you act like you're into it. And he's like, *Wow, I'm not as gross as I thought. She likes me! Even with all my zits and my birth defect.*"

"What birth defect?"

"I don't know. Cleft palate."

"Your fantasy rapist has a cleft palate?"

"It's not a fantasy."

"What's your point, Katchie?"

"The rapist gets all relaxed; he's trying to rape some girl, and she plays along. He's like, *Wow, this is great; she's actually into me,* and then he relaxes. He lets down his guard."

Phil had his eyes closed.

"WHAM!" I said. "She knees the rapist in the groin. She gets him right in the balls, slams him with her knee, as hard as she can."

Phil got up and fumbled around. He was looking for something on the dresser in the dark.

"What are you doing?" I asked.

"I'm worried about my balls."

"She runs away after she kicks him."

Ping.

KATHERINE

I took myself to a cardiologist in the city. Nick and Helen recommended him. Helen's heart is fine, but Nick has arrhythmia. They go to all their medical appointments together.

Dr. Sander saw patients in a shabby office in the basement of a brownstone on the Upper East Side. There were file cabinets everywhere, as if he and his staff had not discovered computers. Maybe Dr. Sander had a thriving practice in the 1980s. Now he needed to sell himself to a hospital empire quickly or retire. I trusted him more for this reason.

He fiddled around with me for a few minutes, feeling my pulse. He listened to my chest and checked my blood pressure. We were using his "casual acquaintance" instruments. He was completely bald. He took bald to its highest degree. His white doctor's coat had a little ketchup stain at the bottom of the sleeve.

"Your numbers check out fine. And everything sounds good."

"Then why do I feel like I can't breathe?" His stethoscope had left a circle of cold skin between my breasts. "And my heart bothers me every day."

"Bothers you how?"

"Hurts. Burns. Itches."

"Your heart itches?"

"It feels like there's something inside of it. It hurts in all these different places at once."

I spread my fingers out across my chest.

"Except more than five places." I held three fingers of my other hand beneath my heart to demonstrate. "Eight places."

The doctor said, "The only way to look inside your heart is to use sound."

"Sonar?"

"We call it ultrasound. Echocardiography. EKG. Lie down here on the table. On your side. Let's hook you up."

TRUITT

"Bug!" I scream. "BUG! Come out."

You can't imagine how well Bug can hide. Like she was born to be invisible. And yet, all I have to do is ask. She slithers out, ducks under the hatch opening, and stands before me in the control room. She's wearing a visor and cutoff shorts—red, white, and blue, printed with the Budweiser emblem. I shout out loud when I see her face.

"Jesus, Bug, take that thing out of your mouth!"

She looks surprised, like she has no idea what I'm talking about. I grab hold of the squirming, wet mouse. Holding it gently in my hands, I carry it to the bunk room and put it back into its cage. Which one is it? Bug and Star gave them names, but I never paid attention. *Innie*, I think. *Innie* and *Outie.*

Mice don't deserve names. They're born and they die every day, some in the field and some in the house. Some can be high-stepping, can think very well of themselves. Others despise their very cells and atoms, even though they have no idea that cells and atoms exist.

Smooshed Bug waits in the shadows, pale and quiet. She opens her mouth, and a second mouse squeaks and squirms at the back of her throat. This one is bloody.

"For fuck's sake!" She snaps her lips shut. I throw her to the ground and pry open her jaw. I yank the furry little monster to safety. When I put him in the cage, he runs over to his mate. *Outie,* I think.

I look back at Bug, and she's asleep. I cover her with a blanket black with soot, oil, and body dust. I sit down next to her to wait. Nothing to say until she wakes.

KATCHIE

Early on a hot August morning, eighty-nine days into my sober life, Gordon barged into my room at my parents' house.

"Wake up."

"What are you doing here?"

"Emergency return," he said. "But Max and I are still going strong." He never did move back to New York City after that. Max dumped him on the phone a week later.

"What's the emergency?"

"It's bad," said Gordon. "Dad's leaving Mom for Mrs. Pringle."

"Do we have to get involved?" I asked.

Gordon gave me a look. "Oh, we're involved."

Dad was waiting for us at a restaurant on Chick's Beach. He was full of excuses.

"Your mom won't stay on her medication. I can't keep paying for her pills. And those pills are not the ones her psychiatrist prescribed anyway. They're painkillers she got for her migraines. Or her bum shoulder. Or her restless leg. She shops doctors. She buys pills off her friends who have surgeries or dental procedures."

The waitress had a red apron with crab claws on it. She had freckles and plump arms. She recommended the clam chowder. "It's the white kind."

Dad ordered a Bloody Mary.

"I don't have feelings for your mom," he said. "Not anymore."

I opened a package of oyster crackers and dumped them onto the table.

"She's lost her looks," he added.

So have you, I wanted to say. But I didn't. It wasn't as true about my dad. Was he as handsome as my mom always said he was? She had convinced me that he was some kind of god, a giant among men. I couldn't tell if I was feeling my feelings or hers.

Her version of their marriage was that she loved him and he didn't love her back. Beneath that narrative was a subtext, never veiled. That something was terribly wrong with both him and his undersea boat. In other words, my parents never fucked.

His version of their marriage was that he never realized he had a choice about how he would live his life. That he felt pressure to get married, get a job, and raise his kids, when he would have been happier somewhere else. I picture him in a shack in the woods or living as a hobo riding trains.

My mom hadn't asked to be born, same as me. But she was here and so was my dad, and so was Mrs. Pringle, for that matter. We all had to keep going.

"No one looks the same forever," said Gordon.

Dad's brown eyes flashed black. "Would you let me finish?"

"Sure," said Gordon, adjusting. "Sorry."

Dad's face was red and twisted, furious, fuming, strangled. He took it out on appliances. He reeled back and crushed the kitchen cabinets. He closed the doors so hard, they fell from the hinges.

TRUITT

It would be great if you could always tell something's wrong by looking at it. Sometimes you have to take the engine apart to get in there and really see what's going on. My dad would try from the top first, tinker around under the hood. The hood on those old cars was extremely heavy. If you were small or infirm, if you had arms like a bird, you wouldn't be able to lift it. Dad's arms were tree trunks.

He sometimes hung a naked lightbulb from the Peugeot hood while he worked on the engine. He bought the Peugeot during the oil crisis of '73 because it ran on diesel. Dad thought it would save him money and time in gas lines. He had to go out to the freezing garage every winter morning and start it to get it warm; sometimes he'd let it run while he took a shower.

One morning the lamp fell into the engine, the bulb broke, and the car caught fire. Dad ran back out in his bathrobe and tried to put the flames out with a wet towel. The fire trucks came, sirens and hoses, all in the early morning, before school. Mom stood and watched, drinking a cup of coffee. The firemen saved the garage, but not the car. Dad later decided it was the damn battery. It kept fizzling out during the night.

The same exact lightbulb hung from the ceiling at our old farmhouse in Gloucester. My parents called it "the Stable." I guess it was an old stable. Mom and Dad turned it into a makeshift country house. There was a huge magnolia tree in the front. You could climb all the way to the top. The Stable was on some land—I don't know, maybe ten acres—and also it fronted a river, the Ware Neck River, which flows into the Chesapeake Bay. To get to the river, you had to walk through a daffodil field. At some point, we were there at the Stable when the daffodils were in full bloom, which means it was probably cold.

I remember being cold, always, when we spent the weekend in Gloucester. It's possible that the house had no heat. We slept on cots and on very old, busted mattresses. We slept under scratchy army blankets, two or three. The sheets stayed cold all night. Star slept in one of the stable bays with Gordon. Dad came in and got into her bed. He didn't care that Gordon was there. Everyone knew Star was the best snuggler in the family.

"The good news is," Dad would say, "everyone's going out for ice cream."

Pause. Gordon and I jumped up and down. A trip to the ice-cream store meant we got to ride in Dad's GTO convertible with the top down. It made your hair feel different.

"The bad news is, Katchie can't come."

Pause. Then laughter—Dad's and then Gordon's and then my mom's if she overheard.

Dad loved a good joke. He loved to tell stories about the times Bug was hurt or panicked. When she put her hand in the cup of hot coffee. That kind of thing.

Once, she accidentally stepped onto the elevator at the Watergate Hotel in Washington, D.C. We were there as tourists. The doors opened and Bug got on. The doors shut. She was alone, separated from the family. Bug was about four. Dad loved to imitate the sound of the elevator going down the shaft, the sound of Bug's terrified screaming. It was one of his favorite jokes, a story. He was so good at telling stories, so funny. Really.

KATHERINE

It started in the shower, with breathlessness and tears. And then I was fighting for air. The claws had my heart again, ripping it to pieces. Blood was bursting out of the arteries and veins, breaking the chambers, tearing across the membranes, through the lesions and busted tissue that Dr. Sander had failed to detect. I couldn't prove it. But I could feel it. The light in the shower dimmed, and I crashed out through the glass door.

The shampoo was still in my hair and my eyes stung. I didn't grab a towel. The edges of my vision were blurry and I could barely see. I threw myself on our bed. I pinched myself a few times, not too hard. Then a little faster, in a rhythm. Harder. My hair cold and wet on my shoulders. The sheets wet now, too. Everything cold. I moved over to the other side of the bed. No, it smelled like Phil. His deodorant and his dandruff shampoo. He was always so clean. How long was it now? Since we'd had sex?

My wet body had soaked the duvet. Left a scar like something from a crime scene. I decided to lie there and wait until my heart stopped exploding. I put both hands over it to slow the beating. Phil was at work. A hundred years.

TRUITT

Dr. Sander smiled and patted Katherine's knee.

"I can't find anything wrong. You can get dressed."

When he left the office, I balled up the paper gown and threw it in the trash with his gloves. Probably they weren't even rubber, which comes from a nice little rubber tree. Probably they were synthetic rubber, which comes from oil. Oil means wet from dying. Oil means I bored in with a bit, looking for dead wet things. The dead things flow from our heart.

Remember the girls in the lake, the corpses? These dead girls get pressed down and pressed down by more mud and sand, which sink on top of the other corpses. All this pressing down forms layers. Like a tall stack of jelly sandwiches, the girls at the bottom are squashed by the weight of the girls on top. Some of the jelly is squeezed out. That's the shame.

People know its value. They'll do anything to drill down

and hit a big well of shame. They tap and they tap until, by accident or on purpose, they've got a gusher. Oil underground, like blood in the body, is under tremendous pressure. It shoots up in the air as a blowout, the uncontrolled release of a mixture of oil, sand, gas, mud, and water. Once a gusher catches fire, it's very hard to put out, because the fire is constantly fed with oil from below.

And though it can be changed from one form to another, oil can never be replaced. What's deluded is how people act like it wants to be drilled. Like oil has been waiting down there for millions of years, waiting for us to want it, to need it, to find it and drill for it, to pump it out. Oil, it dreams of extraction. EKG. What a joke.

KATCHIE

"Dad, I feel like you hate Mom."

"Well, I sure as hell don't love her. I'm not sure I ever did."

"Let's take it easy on Mom," said Gordon.

We were still with Dad, at the restaurant on the beach. From the window, I could see the entire Atlantic Ocean, waves and whitecaps, rolling swells.

"You kids don't know how to let a man speak. I'm going to go home and tell your mom the news. As soon as we're done here."

We walked together to the parking lot. My dad had a big wet spot on the back of his shirt. He was wearing tube socks and running sneakers, cutoff jean shorts. I was dressed the same. We were the same. We were twins. We were the same person.

"We'll give you some time," said Gordon. "To talk to her. Before we go home."

"I don't need more than twenty minutes."

When Gordon and I got home, Dad had just left, and Mom was sitting at the kitchen table, reading a paperback mystery. Gordon rushed in for a hug, but she wouldn't get out of her chair.

"Leave me alone."

"Mom," I said. "Are you seeing anyone?"

"How do you mean?"

"Like a counselor or a psychiatrist. Dad said you've been taking antidepressants."

"I'm not depressed. I married a scumbag."

"What are you cooking?" Gordon looked under the lid of a pot.

"Steamed shrimp."

No wonder the house smelled like a vagina.

"Lunch?"

Mom shrugged.

"The water in the pot is almost boiled off."

Mom got up and walked unsteadily toward the kitchen door. "I'm not hungry anyway."

Her words ran together. She had taken a pill.

"Don't look at me like that, Katchie."

"Like what?"

"Like you want to kill me."

DEAD GIRL AS HARRIET

Hettie came into money, a Confederate war widow's pension. She took me to Europe for an education. In Lucerne, I fell into the company of a Mr. David LaRoche, whose family hailed from Charlottesville, near the University of Virginia. The LaRoches knew all about my grandfather the General. They knew more about his campaigns in the Shenandoah than Grandmother Hettie did.

David took me walking down by the lake. A lake that looks like an ocean. Nothing like Float Lake, which is technically a saltwater creek. David and I liked to lie on our backs in the cold grass and look at the sky. He said new telescopes were showing astronomers things that no one had ever imagined. He worked at an observatory; it was his dream to find his own star.

I said, "Maybe you can name a star after my cousin who died."

David knew exactly who I meant. I talked about my family all the time.

"A star named Jimbo?"

"Not Jimbo, silly. James."

"Unlikely."

"Then maybe you can name a star after me."

Grandmother wanted me to marry David. I wasn't sure.

"I can't keep you forever," she said. "Good Springs has a note on it."

We sailed back to the States and stopped over in Norfolk with Walt and my aunt and uncle. Hettie took sick there, out of the blue, but she was old and she didn't have much fight left. I woke up next to a corpse. The newspaper obituary said that

Mrs. General J. G. Wood had taken her last breath in bed with her daughter. But Grandmother never had a daughter. They were talking about me.

Everyone forgot my mother Olive after she died. She wasn't one of them, not really. My father Ballard found her in Lenoir, at the end of the railway line. Dreams of love live and die; some are smaller than the head of a pin. The veins and arteries empty into the ocean, bringing mud and sediment. Black thoughts ooze from the rock and sand, bubble up through the mud.

I married David. The presents were numerous and handsome, and the wedding brilliant.

Walt gave me away. The cow he traded for a handful of magic beans. The best milker in the parish.

KATHERINE

I woke up naked in a damp bed. The sunlight drew me over to the window. I stood there wrapped in my comforter. The house across the street is almost an exact replica of ours. It was built at the same time by the same developers with the same basic footprint and details. Dormer windows, black shutters, Dutch roof, three stories. The Oates owned it; they were honorary grandparents to Zack, who spent every day in our front yard up until when he was nine or ten years old. He set up home base near the trunk of the magnolia. I could see him out there like a miniature ghost with his bat and ball. My lovable boy. In those days, I strapped on a catcher's mask and a padded vest and squatted in the grass. Even then the ball stung my hand through the padded glove. Now he stays until dark to practice with the varsity team. I can no longer catch him.

I grabbed my cell phone from the bedside table and called Phil. He was on a treadmill at the hotel gym somewhere in Asia.

"I don't want to live anymore."

"It's almost Emily's birthday. This would be an awkward time for you to commit suicide."

"I can't do this anymore. I don't want to be here."

"I thought you said Emily wanted to bake a cake with you."

"I can't do it."

"You can't do what?"

"Life."

"You wake up. You brush your teeth. Put on a clean shirt. Do the easy things first."

"Can I ask you a question?"

"I'm sorry. I'm in the middle of my workout. After this, I'm going to take a shower and head to the airport. I'll call you from the taxi."

To inquire is to keep the fire going, to be curious about the people you love. They look sad when you go away. They cry when they can't see your face. While my husband was at work, I took his extra briefcase down from the top shelf in the hall closet and opened it up. Inside? A long life of hating. That's not what I was looking for. I went back to the closet, reached up to the shelf. Another briefcase, pulled it down. Inside? A long life of loving. Back to the shelf. Another case, locked, but I know how to pick.

Inside? Sex with me, his wife, and no one else. A lifetime of it. And a letter to his lawyer about our finances and the ramifications of divorce. Phil had decided against divorce. For the time being. He hadn't mentioned anything to me. That's how snooping becomes self-knowledge.

TRUITT

Katherine stood at the counter in her kitchen cracking eggs into a mixing bowl. This was her dream kitchen, except Katherine never dreamed of kitchens. She dreamed of making films. Still, she oversaw the kitchen renovation and she picked out everything with thought and care. The cabinets, the flooring, and the countertop, which is a made-up synthetic stone. It's a combination of concrete and quartz, which sounds magical, and it is, in the sense that you can throw your keys on the counter and it doesn't scratch. Maybe the quartz is mined; it must be. Mined and then crushed up and then mixed in with the wet concrete and then poured into a mold. Countertop mold. Standard sizing.

Emily stood in the kitchen next to her mom, leaning over a cookbook, reading the recipe. Katherine never baked unless Emily was involved. Katherine's cell phone buzzed and vibrated beside the cookbook on the counter. Emily looked at it.

"It's Aunt Sheila."

Katherine took the phone into the dining room. The table was covered with folded laundry. She had a hard time getting the clothes from the baskets into drawers. It felt like her kids changed clothes six times a day.

"What's up?" said Sheila. "I saw your text."

"I'm a horrible mother."

"No, you're not."

"I'm barely here. I'm barely able to hang on to my body."

"Don't be hard on yourself."

"I'm distracted by emotional pain. I know that sounds stupid."

"You're not always in pain."

"How can I be a good mom when I can't even put clean clothes into drawers? And it's Emily's birthday and I didn't plan a party for her."

"You told me she didn't want a party. Besides, it's not what you do. It's who you are."

"What does that mean?"

"You parent from who you are. You're a good person. You can't change that."

Katherine outsourced. She got advice. She figured it out, bored the whole time, but she did it. It was a process. She had to drive all over New Jersey going to granite yards. She wandered around huge dusty warehouses in Secaucus near the Meadowlands and the hidden Teterboro Airport, where the New Jersey billionaires land their private planes. The warehouses held rows and rows of granite slabs, heavy sheets of rock, presented like index cards in a giant's file box.

She flipped through the giant marble slabs with the help of a bored, muscle-bound warehouse guy. She was looking for perfect slabs, or maybe she wanted imperfection. White marble not popular anymore. Black marble, either. Then she settled on Caesarstone.

"Mom!" Emily called out from the other room. "Are we gonna do this?"

Katherine finished her call with Sheila and went back to the kitchen. A stiff smile. Do the easy things first.

"Where were we?" Katherine turned on the electric hand mixer, jammed it down into the bowl of cake batter. Then she accidentally pulled up on it too early and spun gobs of yellow cake batter out onto the wall and windows.

"Mom!" Emily screamed. "What the fuck?"

KATCHIE

I was in the Float Lake attic looking through my mother's discarded clothes. I had stripped down to my bra and underwear.

"There you are," said Gordon. "I've been looking all over for you. What are you doing?"

"Trying things on. Stuff I can wear in New York."

"Max won't take you back," he said.

"I know. He sent me a letter. He won't take you back, either."

"Why do you want to go back there? It smells like piss, it's noisy as hell, and it makes your nostrils black. Everything's so expensive."

"I've got things to do."

"I'll take your word for it."

"And I've got an opportunity there. A guy thing."

"The toothless Irishman?"

"No, someone else. His name is Phil."

"Nance's nephew. She's annoyed about that."

Gordon pulled a beat-up box out from a dark corner of the attic.

"Here," he said. "Greatest hits."

A bell-bottomed jumper. A Nancy Reagan knockoff suit, tiny, with a pencil skirt and puffed sleeves. A shiny tunic dress with shoulder pads. Balloon-leg black silk pants with an elastic waist. A sweater made of little ribbons, all woven together.

The clothes had the odor of old fabric. Dry, stale, arm-pitted, crotched, skin-touched, worn.

"I hate them both."

"Who?"

"Mom and Dad."

"Hate is a negative emotion."

"No, it's not," said Katchie. "Hate is a transformer."

"Is hate maybe the backside of love? Do you maybe love Mom and Dad as much as you hate them?"

I went around the house, room by room, and collected my dad's things. Off the hanger. Out of the drawer. Out from under the bed. I cleared the picture frames from his desk and walls. Men with horn-rimmed glasses and women with cheesy, fat arms in flared dresses. I took his Confederate head scarves, and his biographies of the Desert Fox, *The Goebbels Diaries,* picture atlases of the world's great battlefields.

I only needed one pile of photos to get it started. Mom and Gordon watched from the living room window. They were drinking and taking pills. Mom was plastered. Gordon was right behind her. I made a nice safe pile in the driveway where it snaked behind the house.

Sheila came over and stood with me in the driveway. I poked at the fire with a broom.

"Is that soot in your cleavage?"

I tried to wipe it away. It smeared across my chest like war paint. I was still in my bra and panties; it was almost dusk. Ninety-nine degrees and 200 percent humidity.

"This fire is pathetic."

"Gordon and I had it going pretty good an hour ago. We poured gas on it."

I took a rake and shoved a few photos back into the flames. They had fallen to the edge of the fire. I dropped to the ground and lay on my back, letting the smoke fill my nostrils.

"You're not going to burn up," she said. "If that's what you're hoping."

"I don't care." I rolled over in the soot and pebbles and ashes. A second later, I got a huge splash of cold water in my face. I barely reacted. Sheila was standing over me with the garden hose. She was wearing flip-flops, and two of her toes were swollen, blue-black and bruised.

"Jesus, what happened?"

"Wendell dropped a beer on my foot. It was an accident."

"You should press charges."

"Is that your idea of a joke?"

I got up, brushed off some pine needles. "Look at me, Sheila. Whatever I say, I hope you can let it go. I need more photos for the fire."

Sheila followed me inside and we went upstairs, into my dad's office. We stood and looked out at Float Lake. When it was glassy and empty of boats, it looked like a giant puddle of oil. At night it was a spot of blood on a pricked finger.

Gordon appeared in the doorway drinking a glass of booze. I didn't want any. Was this healing?

"Don't burn the General."

"Look at this," I said, and handed him a framed photo I took from the wall. Gordon is sitting on Mom's lap like a little baby, but he's at least six or seven. She's resting her chin on his head. He's wearing shiny patent-leather shoes and a plaid coat. He has a little upturned nose.

I'm around four and I'm sprawled out at the base of Mom's chair with my legs spread. I'm wearing a blue dress. You can clearly see that I'm not wearing underpants. My brown hair is messy, unwashed, and very blond at the ends.

"I was cute," he said.

"You can see my cunt."

"Don't call it a cunt," said Sheila. "Not on a little girl. Jesus."

TRUITT

Middle of the night somewhere in the Atlantic at 115 feet. All very quiet in sonar; then I hear what sounds like a faint baby crying. It gets louder and changes to what sounds like a woman being brutally murdered. Screams and shrieks; then it stops.

Bug wakes up. "What kind of fish was that?"

I shrug. "Want a soda? Orange Fanta?"

"Sure." We sit together in a bunk. Bug pulls the covers up to her chin. I'm hoping if I don't mention the mice, Bug will forget I pulled them out of her mouth.

"It's so dark in here. We need Star. Where is she?"

The sailors are all gone. They must have left with Star. Or maybe they left first. Maybe she went after them. Plenty of bunks to choose from. All the torpedoes shot off. So quiet now.

"How did you get the tape off your mouth?" This question

had been tugging at my brain since Bug fell asleep. And when was that? A thousand years ago. A second ago. Next week.

"A friend helped me."

I nod. There's someone else on the submarine. Someone not Star. I've known this myself for a while now. At times, I felt very close to getting the engines running. But now my head is muddled, foggy. The lack of air. Maybe that.

"Here." Bug hands me the ship's log. She writes new notes on top of things she wrote before. It's impossible to make sense of the jumble of cursive writing in different colors of ink. She points to a passage. I can't make it out. Something to do with horses swimming in the ocean at night.

"What's this?"

"Instructions for whoever lives in the submarine after us."

"What makes you think we're getting off this thing?"

"I'm telling them how to draw a horse. Here's how you do it. You make circles. Three circles for the head. Two bigger circles for the body. Little circles for the joints in the legs."

"Draw whatever you want."

"Do you believe in horses?"

"Yes. But I've never seen one. I can believe in things I don't see."

"Then you can believe in Dead Girl," says Bug. Then she throws her hand over her mouth and her eyes get a hollow, frightened look. She's almost a cartoon of herself.

"Oh, stop it. Relax. I heard Dead Girl talking. A voice in your head, starts as a buzzing. Is that how she does it?"

Bug nods. "Sometimes."

"Yeah, yeah, I've heard her. She's been commanding us to surface."

Bug looks through the periscope, nothing more than a rusted cylinder at this point. Surveying the imaginary horizon, she says, "We can't stay away from Phil forever. He really wants to have sex. And he's coming back tonight. From Japan."

"I've told you Mom doesn't like sluts. She doesn't deal kindly with sluts."

Bug presses the entire weight of her head against the periscope lens.

"Children have sex with other children," she says. "And with adults. That's a fact. Adults have sex with children. Please accept this as true. And if you don't accept it as true, then accept that there is no true."

"I'd have to see it to believe it."

"We both know about wild horses, that they swim together in the ocean. But we've never seen them."

I reach into my tool belt and pull out a greasy wrench.

"Life on a submarine is not a pleasure cruise."

"Maybe," she says. "But I want to love and be loved. For real."

I hit the side of the periscope above Bug's head. She jerks back and covers her ears.

"You said so yourself." She's crying loudly now. She can get it going in two seconds flat. "That you can believe in things you can't see," she blubbers. "You just said it two seconds ago."

I hold the wrench over her head and shout. She needs to hear this.

"We're never getting divorced!"

KATHERINE

We went to a Yankees game with the kids. This is one of the few outings we all enjoy. It was sweet of Phil to arrange tickets. We had expensive seats, right up front. Metal chairs so hot. In the third inning, a bat broke and part of it flew into the stands. I tried to shield Zack, but it hit him straight on. I pulled him close, thinking he'd be covered with blood and his brains bashed in. He squirmed away. "Mom, I'm fine!"

Angels caught the bat. With their wings. Those must be the same angels who took care of me when I was young, rolling around drunk and in a blackout. I couldn't remember things. Or trust myself or control myself. Maybe it was an angel who came and took alcohol away. It was a boy angel. Everyone I have ever loved is an angel forever.

A wooden bat came hurtling through the air, over the net and the fence, and hit my precious boy in the head. There was no bump, no bruise, no blood. Everyone else accepted this miracle. But I couldn't let it go. I was unsettled in my head.

We were driving home on the Jersey Turnpike.

"What's your divorce lawyer's name?" I asked Phil. "Did you hire a shark?"

"I don't think it's a good idea to talk about this."

Zack and I were in the backseat. Emily was driving.

"The kids don't mind," I said. "I'm sure they know you want to leave me. Or to kick me out. More accurately."

We were driving past Secaucus. What can I say to describe Secaucus? To ground this story, bring you into our Mercedes SUV? There are wetlands and condos along the side of the road, swans, geese, a NJ Transit station, white concrete, big, and toxic sludge. The sun never fully shines along this stretch of highway. If it's not cloudy, it's raining. The roads brave enough to pass through this area flood all the time and suffer from potholes. Pussy willows. Forsaken sheets of plastic.

All that was already gone by the time Phil responded.

"When's your intake call with that place you were looking at online? What's it called again? Hope Haven?"

"It was this morning. I skipped it."

Emily turned on the radio.

"If anyone asks for a divorce," I said, "it's going to be me."

I couldn't stop what was coming out of my mouth.

"I think that's enough," said Phil. "Don't you think that's enough?"

We were driving past the immigration prison, across the highway from Newark Airport. What I can say about the prison, to offer a description, is razor wire, brown sculpted stone, windowless windows. A surveillance tower with nobody in it. Prisons don't need those towers anymore, due to technology. But they aren't going to tear them down.

"Is a rehab in Arizona really what I need?"

Zack reached out and grabbed my hand. I was stunned almost, to feel his touch, to see him alive. After the bat hit him, head-on, flying through the air like that.

"I want you at home," he said. "If you want to be home."

"I feel weird and unwanted."

Emily cleared her throat. This kind of thing made her uncomfortable. She flipped her lovely brown hair and fiddled with the radio. I had hair like hers when I was her age. I dyed it black, chopped it short.

"Do you feel like using again?" asked Zack.

"No. I'm fine. That's all behind me now."

"But what about meetings? Why aren't you going anymore?"

I thought of Sheila, who had been sponsoring me for what felt like my entire life. And all the men and women I sat with in thousands of meetings over the years. These AA people were reaching their hands out for me, not exactly to catch me. People aren't strong enough for that. Who can catch a falling body? Maybe they can catch a baby or a small child. Not a grown-up, and not from the air. But still. They reach.

"I feel good. I'm solid."

"Mom," said Emily. "We know it's a disease. That it can come back like cancer. We're not stupid. And we know you've been struggling."

"Guess what, Mom."

"What?"

"Emily and I were up in the attic. She found Granddad's old gas mask."

"I forgot we had that thing. Part of a U-boat rescue kit. I took it with me to college. Then I left it in my parents' attic. Then my mom gave it back to me. It's like a hot potato. Want it?"

Emily turned around in her car seat. "You took it to college. In case there was mustard gas in your dorm."

"Watch the road," I said.

"So. You were a real weirdo in college," said Zack.

"I was Goth."

"Like I said. Weirdo."

SHAME! It never gives up.

KATCHIE

At Waffles and Things, the mugs were sticky with syrup. The tables were also sticky, and the sugar packets looked like they had been carried around in a truck driver's pocket then put back into the plastic dispenser.

It was almost midnight and the shop was packed with people who had been out shagging at the dance clubs or watching baseball at one of the oceanfront bars. Sheila knew the waitress and they struck up a conversation. I sat and sipped my coffee. My hands and face were clean, though I could still feel the smoke at the back of my throat. Sheila had forced me into the shower and dragged me here to eat.

"I hate the taste of sperm," Sheila said when the waitress left.

"Pancakes not good?"

"Why do we have to deal with men's sperm all the time? And in our mouths? How can they expect it?"

"Not sperm, Sheila. You mean semen. Sperm doesn't taste like anything."

"Yes, it does."

"Tadpoles, maybe."

Sheila laughed. "It tastes like sour-apple sewage in an old sock."

"You don't have to eat it."

"Yes, you do."

"Troy doesn't make you, does he?" Troy had been her boyfriend since their first year at community college. She didn't seem to like him that much.

"It happens to all of us."

"What happens to all of us?"

"Coercion. Sexual violence."

"No, it doesn't, Sheila. That's just not true."

"What he did was, he made me give him a blow job. Wendell's penis looked like a mouse."

"They're not supposed to look like that."

"I know."

"They only look that way when they're broken."

"All the women in my AA group were molested by someone, a family member or a kid at college or whoever."

"That's impossible."

"Snow melts. Birds fly. Girls get molested."

"You molest a sleeping cobra. You molest a beehive. Not a little girl."

"Then think of a better word."

"I hate my parents."

"That's not a word."

Sheila reached into her purse and took out a bank envelope, handed it to me.

"Go back to New York," she said. "Keep going to AA."

I looked inside the envelope. A thousand bucks.

"If you stay here," she said, "you're going to kill someone."

Sheila dropped me off at home after midnight. I peeked into my mom's room. Gordon was there, sleeping beside my mom in the king-size bed. What had she learned about love, and what had she already forgotten? Were my mom and dad here to unlearn lessons? They certainly acted like it. Maybe what they knew got sucked back inside them like saliva. Not like blood—you can't get that to go back in.

My mom and brother were lying there, mouths open, breathing heavy. Vulnerable, like all people at night in the dark when they're sleeping. We gamble on the happy fact that most people are not psychotic.

SMOOSHED BUG

Katchie threw Jeff away in high school. She treated him like an old tube sock. Just left it on the floor with the lint and the used fabric softener sheets in the corner of the laundry room where she took his dick in her mouth. Mice think too much of themselves. People see them as self-hating. When really, mice are murderers.

She left Jeff behind and we went to college. Our parents drove us up to Brown at the beginning of our freshman year. We slept in one of the motels along the highway in Delaware. Mom and Dad each took a queen and Katchie got the cot. In the middle of the night Mom climbed into our cot. She was crying. She asked Katchie to hold her. Katchie didn't want to. But she felt she had no choice. That was a deadly feeling.

Mom burrowed against us in her nightgown. Mostly, and deeply, we wished she'd go away and leave us alone forever. Maybe even die. We're so sorry. These feelings aren't right. This was our mother. What kind of monster? Katchie couldn't find love inside. I'd like to know if you can come up with a scarier thought.

We didn't see Mom again that year until Thanksgiving. Mom changed herself completely the day before we came home. What the surgeon did to her, he traced around her ears with a scalpel. He stretched the skin, snipped off the extra bits, then sewed it back in place, at the sides of her cheeks. Her head was bandaged. The gauze was stained. New blood is red. Old blood is brown. She slept downstairs in the guest room. Dad wouldn't look at her.

An appliance repairman came by to fix the furnace. He caught sight of Mom as she shuffled down the hall. "Holy shit!"

"What happened to her?" he asked.

"A face-lift." Dad was casual.

"I ain't seen nothing like that since Vietnam."

Dad never, ever, EVER called a repairman. Unless he had to get a part and he couldn't find a supplier. Unless he could not, as a layman, get his hands on the part he needed.

Mom lost twenty pounds in a month. She had a new body to go with her new face. But still, my dad was under the car. Or against the wall, feeling his way along it with his eyes closed. He looked frightened of what his body wanted, or didn't want, and might do about this problem. My mom was fucking the floor but Dad didn't notice. It hurt to watch her beg, to throw her dignity away and for nothing. Maybe Dad had sex with her later after Katchie went to sleep.

Mom was back at it as soon as her incisions healed, rolling around, pounding her fists. In the violence of her performance she accidentally hit her head on a door frame. Then maybe her pain was real, but we couldn't tell. We didn't know how to help her. We didn't even want to.

That was a deadlier feeling.

DEAD GIRL AS HARRIET

World War I. My brother Walt was five feet, four inches and 124 pounds, almost as tiny as me, too scrawny for combat. He ordered supplies and filed papers. Never even made it across the Atlantic. A secretary at a VA hospital in D.C., he came to Charlottesville when he had leave. Walt hated weakness in a man. PTSD was the main thing he came across; boys got shipped home in pieces but still alive. Doctors called it "shell shock" then.

I was drinking too much. I'm not lying or hiding it. A few more years of staring into a telescope, and David found a new star. But he named it Wolf 25. Then he moved on to the moon. Naming craters.

"I don't want a crater," I told him. "I want a star."

"I work with a team," he said. "We can't name these things after our wives."

"You promised."

"You're ridiculous."

Walt gave me morphine tablets to take when I couldn't sleep, when I was pulling hairs from my head, when I was so nervous that my hands went after my own flesh. I didn't tell David about the pills. I used them sparingly.

I brightened for a spell when I finally had my first baby, Amelia. She was chubby and cream-colored like the inside of a candy. Then Walt was out of the army, away from spells and medicines. He sent me bottles of scotch and boxes of cheese. He was busy doing maritime law in Norfolk, but he saw me whenever he could.

I had a vision of taking Amelia out to sea, dropping her over the side of a ship like a barrel of wine. Not exactly a dream. A quick picture in my head and then it was gone. I lived in the Blue Ridge Mountains now, near the university.

Walt bought a cottage in Virginia Beach; I spent my summers there with Amelia, who was three and who liked to run away: up the road, down the beach, I had to search and herd, lasso her home. But I didn't throw her away.

"What's going on?" Walt asked. I slept all day with the curtains drawn; now six-year-old Amelia adrift in the house. Walt gave her beef sandwiches and malted milk.

It's hard to describe how a young girl holds her body without sounding creepy. How her body gets moved around by her brain. How her body holds her brain, how her brain holds her body. How a young girl holds her young body as she stands in the kitchen and leans against the refrigerator. She may as well be broiled as die of hunger.

David finished his book on meteors. I tried to stop letting my tongue run away from me. David had such moods and tempers. And a secretary at the lab.

Another baby, a flash of light. And then more darkness: "I'm happiest when I'm alone, and I'm never, ever alone." Postpartum depression. "Down in the dumps," we called it.

I snuck off to a hunting cabin that was in David's family. After Dooms, before Sherando. Off the winding road, up and over Afton Mountain in the blaze of fall. David kept my girls away from Walt, away from my family. They grew up knowing nothing of the Woods. I hated that.

How long has it been since I shot myself?

KATCHIE

The night train from Virginia to New York City took ten hours. I had a vague plan, and that plan was Phil. I knew he was back in New York, in his tidy bourgeois Brooklyn apartment, waiting for me to join him, though he didn't know it yet.

I got there just after dawn and sat at a coffee shop until I could call Ian. He was not an early riser. There were pay phones on every street corner in the '90s. Chewed gum in the change slots. After a few tries, Ian answered. Probably on the phone on his desk in his bunk room. He responded to my crisis as readily as a rescue unit. On his way.

He met me on Ludlow Street at a diner. It was empty except for the busboys, who were eating at a table in the back.

"You can stay as long as you want to in my apartment," he said. "It's not a problem."

He had the lease on a two-bedroom place. Bill, his best friend from Ireland, lived there. But that's not what I wanted to talk about.

I said, "You're telling me your new lover is even younger than me?"

Ian stirred his coffee. Clanked the cup.

"I didn't think you'd get this angry."

"Welcome to Katchie with feelings."

"I like her, actually."

Ian got up and walked the check to the register. Outside, a group of teenage girls was forming half circles on the sidewalk. About to fight.

We walked around the corner to his apartment. The street was lined with trucks for a street fair.

"I don't know why I can't stop crying," I told him.

"You left me, remember? I thought you were never coming back. Being a Virginian and all."

"I got totally clean. No booze, no pot, no nothing. For three months now."

"I wish I could do it."

Ian made the bedroom dark by nailing blankets over the windows. The noise of the playground behind the building seeped through the wool. He sat on the side of the bed and brushed the inside of my arm with his fingertips. I don't know how long he sat there with me. My fatigue felt like a plastic bag over my head. He was touching me when I slipped into sleep.

When I woke up, he was still there, sitting in the living room by himself. It was dark by then, nighttime. The only light in the room was coming from the TV. I went to the window and looked down into the street.

"How was it, then?" he asked. "At home with your parents?"

"My friend Sheila thinks I was sexually abused or something. By my dad maybe."

"That would make sense."

"I don't think so."

"Maybe you forgot."

"I think I'd remember something like that."

"Well, what do I know?" He came to the window and put his arms around me. He sweated freely during the summer and did nothing to hide it. The hair under his arms got very wet, and slick. "Let's go to bed."

Down in the street, a boy was carrying a huge teddy bear away from the street fair on Essex. His dad was walking next to him. The boy struggled; most of him was under the bear. I followed Ian into his room and we got in bed. I felt very close to him, my head on his chest.

"Why didn't you call me back when I was away?"

"Better not to."

"Because you don't love me?"

Ian smiled and used his tongue to get at a rear tooth, the place where the tooth should have been. I was thinking about AA meetings in New York City. What would they be like? My sober journey was just beginning, and Ian wouldn't be joining me. I was headed in a new direction. Was this healing?

He said, "You left your cutting kit under my bed."

My kit was an old vintage makeup case I got at a thrift store. It had a little mirror fixed into the satin lining, and a beautiful silver lock. I kept my blade, alcohol, bandages in there.

"I threw it out," he said.

"That's fine. I don't cut anymore."

This was true. It didn't mean much, because the cutting was sporadic, periodic. When the mood hit, before I stopped drinking in Virginia Beach, before I met Phil, I would dig into my foot with a razor blade. Ian knew about it, accepted it. He didn't approve of it. I won't say more about it here.

Ian saved my life, even if he was a slut. I was a slut, too. Every cell in my body knew that within a day or two I would be cementing myself to my future husband.

Part Three

DEAD GIRL

The submarine lies on its side, the bulk of it covered by the shifting sands of Diamond Shoals. Truitt has forgotten even the basics of engine repair. He can no longer distinguish between a submarine and a torpedo. The truth is, there is no difference. A torpedo is a miniature submarine, a self-propelled bomb. It only makes one run, either to blow up a target or miss and whiz off into the blue.

Bug finds Truitt in the stern, lying on the steel floor, kicking and rolling, bucking and screaming.

"What's wrong? What's going on?"

Truitt thrashes and moans and pushes a tiny baby out from his anus. At first Bug thinks it's a mouse, a friend for Innie or Outie, or the first of a litter of puppies. The creature is small, pale, and undefined. Truitt crawls away like he's trying to get away from a rattlesnake.

"Get that thing away from me!"

Bug takes the newborn and holds it to her chest, lets it suck on her pinkie finger. Star burns into the room.

"What do we have here?"

"It's a girl!" says Bug.

"Or a zombie," says Star. "Look! She's so pale. Like a burnt-out marshmallow. A pockmarked crater on a dead planet. She's decomposing."

"But she was just born!"

Truitt pulls himself to a torpedo hatch and burrows into the hole.

Bug peeks in. "Did you have sex with Phil?"

"Not that I can remember."

Star takes the baby and puts it down for a nap in an engine-room hammock. When she gets back, Truitt's at the periscope, turning it madly.

"Where do babies come from?" he barks at Bug. "Answer me!"

"Yours came out of your poo hole."

"No, babies don't come from your poo hole."

"Yours did."

"They come from a fracture in the ocean floor."

Star laughs. "Stop lying, Truitt."

"Nice of you to make an appearance, Star." His knees buckle. He's weak from childbirth, even though what he pushed out was no bigger than his fist.

"I want to hurt someone," he says.

"Hurt doesn't hurt," whispers Bug. "Not anymore."

Star blazes up and the whole submarine glows with white light.

"It's possible that this little turd is not even a baby. It could be a spy. Or a virus. Or a bomb. Have you considered that? We have a lot of enemies."

"We only have one enemy," says Bug.

"Dad?" asks Star.

"Phil," says Bug.

KATHERINE

When Phil asked me to marry him, I made a decision. Yes,
I'll get married. But I don't want kids. And I told him, even
before we got married, that I wanted a divorce. Or no, not that
I wanted a divorce. I said that if love stopped being voluntary,
I had a right to a divorce. Divorce would always need to be an
agreed-upon option, no strings attached. From the start.

We were living together in San Francisco by then. We flew
east for an engagement party at his parents' house in New Jersey.
They lived a half hour outside of New York. Phil's mom offered
me plate upon plate of traditional Greek food. I picked at and
rejected most of it. His older brother George gave me a look as
he passed through the kitchen in a barbecuing smock. *Eat my
mom's food.* George and Phil created NetWorth together. Started
it then, and it's still going strong. Their platforms are back end,
business to business. "B2B," as Phil says. Big bucks.

"Katchie," said George. "You changed your hair color again."

Phil defended me. "You have a problem with red hair?"

"No, I love it. She's doing okay? Katchie, you okay?"

"She's fine," said Phil. "She's taking a lot of yoga and writing
a screenplay."

"Good. What's it about?"

I answered for myself: "It's about a young woman who dies
and comes back as a swallow. She lives in a birdhouse. She's trying to send messages to her family, to tell them why she killed
herself, but—"

"Stop there. I'm an Adam Sandler guy. But keep at it. Stay
busy. I don't want Phil to get distracted."

"You don't want us to get married."

"Marriage is hard," said George. "It's hard work."

"It's hard work for you," Phil said. "Because you're a dick."

Phil walked away and George grabbed his arm.

"Hey," he said. "At least make her eat."

George knew a few things about me and Phil, but he didn't know everything. He didn't know that we spent most of our time in bed. I slept a lot, and when I wasn't sleeping, Phil and I were having unfinished sex, sex that never finished. It scratched at us when we finally got up to eat a meal, or bathe, brush our teeth. When we were out with friends, people who worked with Phil, it would spark suddenly when our legs touched beneath the table, forcing us to leave early and hurry home to bed.

If you think giants can't be handsome and even kind, you're wrong. They can also be helpful, wise, and forward-thinking. Phil talked me into seeing my first therapist. I met her in a New Age bookstore back when San Francisco was still New Age. Sara Jacobs, LCSW. We got to talking over a tarot card display. Sara was also a practicing witch.

Her office was a second-floor apartment at the end of the BART line in Orinda. There were two inner doors. Door number one led to the consulting room. I got a feeling Sara was living in the rooms behind door number two. Sara swore she wasn't.

The main giveaway was her pets, a dog and two cats. These pets sat in on our therapy sessions. The cats had no fur and tiny heads. The dog was an anxious French poodle, white and threadbare, with dark circles in the hair beneath his eyes.

Phil went with me to talk to Sara. He asked to go. I didn't know why. I thought he just wanted to meet her. When we sat down, he blurted out that I sometimes talked about hearing voices.

"They tell her dark things," he said.

Big deal, I thought.

"What kind of things?" asked Sara.

"Things about cutting off her hands and feet or having them chopped off by someone else. Then pretty soon she's saying she doesn't want to live."

"Is this true?" asked Sara.

"She has a personal guillotine."

"It's just in my head."

Phil turned to me. "Sara doesn't know you're suicidal?"

"I'm not suicidal."

"I agree," said Sara. "*Suicidal* is a strong word." She suggested I buy the movie *Gandhi*. I could watch it when I felt like swimming out.

"That's it?" said Phil. "That's all you've got?"

I decided to buy *The Matrix*. I heard Gandhi beat his wife.

"Her office smells bad," said Phil. We were taking BART home. "It's the pets. An unhappy setting."

"I agree."

"She lives there. She's lying about it."

"But why would she lie about something dumb like that?"

"Why do people lie about anything?"

Therapists can do and say whatever they want, really. Sara eventually told me my father was a pimp and my mother was a whore. She told me that my mother and father wanted to kill me. These suggestions comforted me at the time. I had no other therapy experience to give me a reference point.

I told Sara about my mom's family, because I know something about it. I know that my mom's dad, my grandfather Walt, tied his comb to the dresser so my grandmother Kitty wouldn't lose it. If that makes you heroic. He hit his kids—my mom and my uncle—with sticks and branches.

DEAD GIRL REGISTER: KITTY WOOD

Walt was old, almost fifty, when we met in 1935. I was half his age, poor, and plain (ugly). At least I thought so. And I said so. Maybe it settled with repeated use into the truth. But Katherine looks like me, and people call her a beauty.

My teeth were buck. I was "country," backward. Oh, and a racist. Walt married me anyhow. I moved into his house on Crane Crescent. We played bridge with his friends. We'd set up the card table in front of the fireplace on nights when we hosted.

I made toast and prunes for him every morning. Was rewarded nightly with the compliment of an erection between his pencil-thin legs. "Cundrums," I called them. To keep the sheets clean. Then it came time to put them away.

He wanted to have sexual intercourse every night. I wasn't crazy about intercourse. I didn't hate it, either. Maybe I did, maybe I hated it. I hated it half of the time. That's probably true. Within a year, I had a baby. Walt held baby Kate at night when he got home from work. He was enchanted, almost happy.

Baby Kate had cheerful blond curls and blue eyes. I was repulsed. I couldn't help it. I don't know what was wrong with me. I guess I had wanted a boy, or a doll. Three years later I got one, James Gordon Wood IV, or "Gee." I cared for both of my children the same way. By the book, Walt's book, which included enemas, even for babies. Walt feared stoppages.

When he came home, Kate was always the first in his lap, every time. But in his black moods, Walt didn't have a lap. Even Kate was locked out in the hall. She knocked and knocked on the bedroom door. All day Saturday like that. She went and found her brother Gee. She grabbed his fingers and pressed them backward. Not to break, just to bend.

She pulled her own hair out of her head in fisted clumps if I ever said no to her. I said yes and worked hard in the kitchen. And at the sewing machine. We didn't spend money on clothes or trips or cars. I only had a few nice dresses. I prayed for my children and enjoyed my scotch.

Walt lectured the family at dinner for years, little speeches on duty, honesty, and regularity. Clean water, airplanes, the telephone, laxatives. Laxatives, because sometimes a lecture isn't enough.

TRUITT

"You're shaking," said Sara. "You poor thing. What's wrong?"

Katchie asked Sara if she could lie down on the floor. Sara said that was fine. Not everyone gets a ladder. Not everyone gets the magic beans. We reach around up there and steal from whoever is dumb enough to believe us. I'm talking about bad hearts.

"My room was always freezing," Katchie told Sara. "I made a game out of it. Opened my windows in the winter and piled ten blankets on the bed."

"That's a lot of blankets," said Sara.

Where do you think oil comes from? Barnacle shells.

A shell is a home. A shell can explode.

"Dad gave me an old space heater," Katchie reported. "Red tin, rusty, with curly coils like fire. I used to sit in front of it for hours and burn pencils."

"Sounds like a fire hazard," said Sara.

"I'd wake up and see him standing there in his white T-shirt and boxers. Pull aside my blankets, all of them, no matter how many. He'd come under them. Gordon had a queen."

"You're the one he loved."

"He smelled like beer, or vodka. I don't know. Booze in his skin or his hair or on his face. He drank a lot. Every night."

A dead body inside of her living body, almost filling up the same exact space. The inner hull and the outer hull and the seawater going in and out between them. Katchie was a little girl from a perfect family and she randomly decided she wanted to hate her mom and dad for no apparent reason. She went around cutting her own flesh and pursuing doom because of a faulty gene.

"What did your dad do to you, though?" asked Sara, the first therapist.

No grown man would ever diddle a child!

"Nothing," said Katchie. "We snuggled."

"No harm in that," said Sara, the worst therapist.

"Exactly," said Katchie.

STAR

Truitt stands at the circuit board. He pulls and pushes dead buttons and levers.

He says, "I want to cut someone."

"Not *someone*," says Bug, who is sitting in Dead Girl's lap. Dead Girl is wearing a glamorous wool coat with a fur collar, a stylish hat, and elegant leather gloves. Weird, because it's sticky, hot, and airless in the dank cabin. Truitt still can't see Dead Girl. He thinks Bug is curled up alone on the steel bench.

"Admit it, Truitt," says Bug. "You want to cut *me*. Or the baby."

"Maybe Phil's the one I want to hurt. Do you ever think about that?"

"Phil's a good man."

"So he says."

"All men are good men," I remind them. "They will love you. But they will also hurt and reject you."

"Thank you, Star," says Truitt. "You can shut the fuck up now."

Dead Girl has been telling me that our boat needs to surface. The air is thin and fetid. The mice are dead, stiff, hidden away under the sink in the head. She says we can't wait another year, day, moment . . . however we measure our alleged units of time.

Truitt checks on the baby, asleep in the hammock. "A submarine captain approaches his target."

"Let her sleep," I tell him. But it's hard to stop Truitt when he sets his mind to something. He takes the baby into his arms. She doesn't wake up.

"This obviously isn't a real baby," he says, looking at her. No one responds.

"Remember that toy we had called Baby Alive?" he asks. "She came with a bottle and her mouth moved. She squirted pee when you squeezed her belly."

Bug sits paralyzed. "Don't hurt the baby."

"I'm not going to hurt her. I'm just pointing out that she's not a person. She's a doll and she runs on batteries."

"What?" said Bug. "What's a battery?"

"What's a battery? What kind of question is that?"

Things were leaving our heads. Lack of oxygen.

"Let's treat the baby with kindness," I said. "She's going to remember it when she's older."

"You're not listening," says Truitt. "This is not a real baby."

"She's here for a reason, whatever she is," says Bug. "We have to name her."

I brighten. The control room gets warmer. "How about we call her Star? Little Star? Dark Star?"

"For Christ's sake! Why would I name my baby after a ruined slut?"

I fizzle out in a split second. Even Truitt is surprised.

"We'll call her Live Girl," he mutters. "LG."

I light up again. A bright white spark.

"Elegy," I suggest.

We shake on it.

TRUITT

Katchie started to smell smoke in the air when she sat in Sara's office. Sara wouldn't admit she was smoking. She said it was the client before Katchie, who liked to smoke during his sessions.

"That makes sense," Phil said. "I wouldn't worry about it."

"She's lying," said Katchie. "You knew Sara was a liar. You called it."

"Wait!" said Phil. "Sara is helping you. I don't think she's a liar."

Sara showed up one day with a see-through mesh tote bag and left it on the floor by her chair. Katchie saw a box of Marlboro Lights in the bag.

"I yelled at Sara," Katchie told Phil when she got home. She was sobbing. "I don't know what came over me. I called her names. Now she hates me."

"Oh, come on, babe," said Phil. "It's not such a big thing."

Katchie was driving around in the clouds and she was looking to steal something from a giant. Money is good, sure, but it would be better to steal something that could generate an income of its own.

"Sara says I have no sense of reciprocity."

"Reciprocity isn't part of being a therapist," Phil said. "And getting yelled at is."

"I should have my head chopped off."

Phil has a good heart. Katchie's is bad. We've always known it. Phil knows it, too. Or he's coming around to it slowly. Which doesn't mean she doesn't try to be good. She just has better reasons to be bad. Plus, she can't help it.

Sara announced that she was moving her office to Berkeley.

The move would take a few weeks. She told Katchie to call her answering machine in a month; she'd leave a recording with her new address. Katchie called the machine a hundred times. Sara had disconnected the line.

Clothes, food, returned attention from an object of desire, things a girl must have. Water, movie tickets, headphones. A commemorative T-shirt from the world tour of a glam rock band. Private school, she went. Debutante, she was. Ivy League college, check.

Katchie was ghosted by her first therapist. Then what happened?

KATHERINE

My father didn't walk me down the aisle, which was grass. We did it outside. Uncle Gee arrived in a beat-up van. He's a beat-up van kind of uncle. He parked the van in the grass next to the barn, but it ended up being right where Phil and I planned to take our vows, where the view was best, off the hill over the pasture. Uncle Gee moved the van when we asked him to, but there was a huge puddle of motor oil in the grass. I leaned down and dipped my finger in it. The grass was matted like hair with blood.

Gee said, "That van's been leaking oil for a month."

He opened the side door; he had a case of motor oil sitting there. "I'll pour a couple liter bottles in before I leave. It'll get me to the hotel."

Uncle Gee, a very different man from my dad. But he was still a man.

I got married.

My face in his chest hair, resting there.

I got married.

Phil's white V-necked T-shirt. His cotton boxers, the flap wide open.

Frizzle frazzle, into the tub.

Bam! Bam! I took a BB gun and put holes in all the gas cans in Dad's garage. He stored them in a row on a shelf, like books of spells. Red metal cans, painted and repainted, labeled with his initials. Gasoline spurted out of the little holes. It was a liquid no color I knew, closer to green than blue, splashing the sand and dirt on the garage floor.

BUG

Truitt sits and cleans his rubber boots with a piece of steel wool.

"I have to clean these boots every day," he says. "Or they turn into reptiles."

"That's mold."

I'm sitting on the floor so I can keep an eye on the baby. The floor is made of folding panels that lift up. You're supposed to store things underneath. Tools, electronics, food, ammunition. It's very full at the start of a journey. But we went through our provisions long ago. Now the compartments hold the ship's logs, soggy notebooks where I write all my stories. The baby is tucked in there in a little bed I made. She wiggles around and starts to cry. Truitt leans down and scoops her up.

I hand him a blanket. It's an old T-shirt covered with grease stains. He wipes off wrenches and hammers with it. Truitt swaddles the baby, then holds her in his arms against his uniform, which is smelly and covered with dirt and muck. Truitt found a red metal oil can from the engine room. He inserts the nozzle into the baby's blackened mouth and squirts the finger pump.

"What's that you're feeding her?" I ask. "Oil?"

"No, it's milk."

"Looks like dirty oil to me. Did you drain it from our dead engine?"

Truitt ignores the question. I clap my hands together.

"Truitt! You love the baby!"

STAR

In college I spent a lot of my time with a boy named Matt. He taught me how to take photos. He gave me a camera. He taught me how to listen to music, how to hear the different instruments in a recording. He helped me buy my first leather jacket. He told me shameful things about himself, things he had never told anyone. We were drinking buddies who stood around in doorways at parties leaning into each other. We did a lot of kissing. We never had sex.

In New York, after college, I was still hanging around with Matt. He took me on dates with his new girlfriend, Ella. I'd ride along with them in the backseat. Most nights, after we dropped off Ella, he parked his Ford Fairmont downtown, and we drank forty-ouncers, listened to cassettes. Matt always had a new mix he wanted to share.

Why wasn't I his girlfriend? Was Ella prettier? She definitely took better care of herself. She shaved her legs and wore shoes that fit. She washed and brushed her hair.

Ella was in film school at NYU, so I gave her my birdhouse script to read. We were out at a bar with Matt and I asked Ella what she thought.

"It's good," she said. "Powerful. Funny in places. But it made me wonder."

"About what?"

"Were you ever raped?"

I was offended and totally thrown off. I didn't answer.

"Well?" Ella had smoky gray-blue eyes. "Were you ever raped, Katchie?"

"Me? No. Of course not."

"Really?"

Matt poured beer into Ella's empty glass, and then into mine. The two of them were sitting opposite me in the booth.

"Your screenplay makes me think you were."

"Maybe it's because I studied a lot of feminist theory." This was partly true. I had read a few books at Brown. I still had them in a box somewhere. I was getting sick of Ella.

Matt said, "You should have seen Katchie's art in college."

I made little dolls out of nylon stockings. I stuffed the stocking feet, sewed and painted them, hung them from miniature nooses on a clothesline. The dolls had no arms. I stitched up their vaginas. I stitched up their mouths. Xs for eyes.

I also staged a fake pediatrician's office in my apartment. Covered the walls of my bedroom with zebra wallpaper. Then posted xeroxed images of sexual atrocities. I scrawled weird notes all over it with red paint.

I stopped wearing tampons and pads during my period for three months in order to stain a stack of thrift store sheets with real blood. Then I draped the sheets over my bed and around my apartment.

"That was art," I said.

Ella laughed.

"That doesn't mean I was raped."

"Are you sure?"

I looked at Matt. Could he have chosen a pushier bitch?

"I only ask because I'm a rape survivor," said Ella. "I'm not trying to make you uncomfortable."

"I didn't know that."

"It's not a secret," said Ella. "It was in the newspaper."

What does it mean to love someone?

DEAD GIRL AS KITTY

I used to cut greens and flowers in Kate and Craig's yard. I lived right up the road, but my house didn't sit on any land. Kate and Craig owned a big property on Float Lake. Walt was dead by then. I made arrangements for my Episcopal church for the altar, where everyone could see them. It wasn't just about the flowers. I did pretty things with the leaves and branches.

I did some of my best work at Christmas, with the shiny, waxy green holly and its poisonous red berries. Katchie would sit and poke her fingers on its sharp points. Its spines. Its bones. She was an odd child.

I'm thinking about her mother Kate, my daughter. I guess you're wondering about what might have gone wrong there.

How many women trade their dreams for the love of one good man? They take a vow. They will only spread their legs for this one good man. If they don't trade their dreams, they can't keep his love.

Kate and Craig were never happy. Not even on their honeymoon in Puerto Vallarta in 1967. Kate got sun poisoning and swelled up like a tomato. Nothing but sun, way too much. A simple poison, the backside of something good. She lay alone in the dark hotel room in a lumpy bed. Craig sat in the bar and spoke Spanish with the staff.

All of this is hearsay. When Kate got home, she told me they stopped off in Atlanta to see Craig's mother. He cut a few days off the honeymoon without telling her. Kate woke up before daylight and heard whispering. She looked over and saw that her husband's mother had crawled into bed with them. Craig had his back turned and was holding his mother, was wrapped all around the old witch in his T-shirt and boxers. Kate pretended to be asleep.

I am, thankfully, dead. Dead, mind you! When our time comes, even our mothers can't snatch it away. Would you kill someone you love? It's been done. *Love!* That word!

Burn that word in the trash.

KATHERINE

When I was pregnant with Emily, Mom flew out to visit me and Phil in California. Phil met her at the airport and brought her back to our North Beach apartment. Every now and then I tried to make good food, which goes along with being a good woman. That day I made my first and last pad Thai. It was a lot of work, and it wasn't fun.

"Oh," said my mom when we sat down to eat. "I don't like Chinese food."

"Then have another bowl of ice cream."

"Don't be so pissy. I'll drink lemonade." She traveled with packets of Crystal Light.

"Here," she said, getting up from the table. She went off to look through her suitcase and came back with something in a brown paper bag. "I brought you a present."

She tossed a worn-out piece of military apparatus on the kitchen table. It was a German-issued escape set from World War II. It had a name stenciled with black letters on the canvas strap. *Craig Burns.*

Phil was interested. "Your dad was in World War Two?"

"No," I said. "He's just an enthusiast. He stenciled the name on. Labeling and monogramming is one of his hobbies."

Phil held up the mask to inspect it.

"It's called a rebreather," I told him.

Dad hid it in a secret compartment under the bookshelves in his office. I had marched around the house in it when my parents were out at parties. It was a quick way to suffocate yourself.

"Katchie's father won't speak to me," my mom said. "He's remarried."

Phil nodded. "I know."

"Use the mask in your birdhouse movie."

Mom got up and mixed herself a glass of lemonade. She scattered the tiny crystals all over the counter. I followed behind her with a paper towel. She stumbled as she made her way back to the table. She was only what I called "middle high."

"I've always wanted to make a movie," she said, plopping into a chair. "I've written a few ideas down. Mine would be mysteries, thrillers. I don't see the point of making any other kind of movie. Honestly, any other kind of movie would be a bore."

"No one is making a movie," I said.

Sunday afternoon, at the end of the visit, Phil helped my mom with her suitcase. The fog was rolling in and the temperature had dropped. The cab pulled up and Mom reached out for a hug. I held her, but I didn't want to.

"Why don't you love me, Katchie?"

I looked at Phil, but he looked away. What could he do? He didn't have any answers. All he had was a penis and a paycheck.

"Bye, Mom."

We loaded her into the cab. Then I hurried inside to my office, where my mother had slept on the foldout couch. I wanted to throw her empty Crystal Light packets in the trash and wipe up the makeup stains on my desk. Fish the half-eaten cookies out of the sheets. She always left a few things behind: panties, hairbrush, paperback novel.

I found her padded pillbox on the floor. Shocking that she forgot it. She must have had another bottle in her purse. The pillbox looked like something for sewing. It was the size of the palm of my hand, with embroidered flowers on it. I flushed all the pills down the toilet. Too risky to keep them in the apartment. I was careful then.

KATCHIE

I liked to touch the green, spongy, crumbling stuff that held my grandmother's flower arrangements together. It was at the heart of every bouquet. It only did that one thing. I put my fingers in places where they didn't belong. Sometimes they came out with a different smell.

Kitty lived so close to us. It was an easy walk up the feeder road that lined Atlantic Avenue, parallel to the ocean. But I never walked there, because Gordon and I only went when my parents were going out, and it was easy for them to drop us off.

My grandmother's house wasn't as grand as it should have been, if you listened to my mother talk. It was just a duplex in a courtyard of duplexes. A complex of duplexes; it didn't even have a proper name.

There were handfuls of broken glass on the feeder road. I have no idea where it came from. The glass was shattered into tiny glittering pieces. When I was at Kitty's house, I would hunt for broken glass along the road, then scoop it up and hide it, like treasure, in the hollow of a giant oak tree that grew between the buildings. The chopped glass didn't cut my hands. I suppose it could have.

DEAD GIRL

"Look at her," says Star. "She's hurting herself again. Katherine is huddled in the empty tub. She's digging into the dark place."

Legs pinned. Arms pinned. The feeling of the beard pushing through the skin. The sharp dark hairs.

"No, she's not," Truitt replies. "She has an itch there and she's taking care of it."

"She's got an itch there and she's taking care of it? You think that's what's going on?"

"Trust me."

"Trust you?"

"Yes."

"Truitt, you taped Bug's mouth for twenty-five years. Why would we trust you?"

"Was it twenty-five years?"

Bug laughs like this is funny. Oh, Bug.

The head smooshed into the pillow, the hand over the mouth, the back-and-forth.

"Tell them about how Truitt threw a glass at your head and it hit the wall behind you," says Star.

"That wasn't me who threw the glass. That was Dad."

Truitt is no longer in uniform. He's wearing a Hawaiian shirt and Birdwell Beach Britches.

The pleasure, the comfort, the heldness of Dad.

"Dad," says Bug. "My mom's husband."

"Be quiet!" Truitt whispers. "I hear something. Can you hear it?"

Truitt rushes around the control room. He pounds dead gauges and adjusts numb wires.

"MAKE ALL PREPARATIONS FOR SURFACING!"

I command that with my deepest male voice and throw in an Australian accent because why not?

"What the hell?" says Truitt. "Who's that?"

"Who does it sound like?" asks Bug.

"Like me at my own funeral."

"That's Dead Girl. She's our new captain."

"I don't think so."

Truitt grabs the radio handset and starts firing off commands.

"Bleed air! Empty ballast tanks! Blow negative. Dive!"

Bug holds the baby tight to her chest. The baby squirms and fusses.

"Stop resisting," I tell Truitt. "It's useless to resist."

"I don't recommend surfacing!" he shouts.

"Buoyancy tank one is already blown."

"How the hell did you do that?"

"Secure the ventilation. Shut bulkhead flappers."

Bug's eyes widen. "What does it mean?"

"Surfacing?" says Truitt. "It means prepare to die. The minute we reach the surface, we're going to die."

The freezing cold room. The coils of the heater with its chipped red paint.

"Oh my God," Bug cries. "We're gonna die!"

"So what?" says Star. "Dead means you can be born again. Let go."

"What does *let go* mean?"

"*Let go* means you're dead."

The ship lights up humming and shiny like it just came out of the yard.

"I know you'd feel better if you were wearing your scouting gear," says Star.

Truitt shrugs. "I'm not in charge."

"You're going to have to do the opposite of what you think is right," says Star. "Everything we know about love is wrong."

KATHERINE

I woke up in the middle of the night. Phil was snoring next to me in his T-shirt and boxers. I had no idea what time he got home. I went downstairs to the kitchen. Phil had scrambled eggs and burned a piece of toast. At first, I didn't cry very hard. I wanted Phil to hear me, though, so I upped the volume. He came down after a while, clomped down the aged wood stairs with the tread of a giant.

"My car is coming at five a.m.," he announced. I looked up at the kitchen clock. It was 2:15.

"Where are you going?"

"Sonoma County. Board meetings. I'll be back Thursday."

He handed me a paper towel and I blew my nose. Then he pulled a chair up close and sat down next to me. He took my hand and held it.

"What's wrong?"

"Let's do it. Let's get divorced."

Phil looked at me. He didn't know what to say. I don't blame him for that. He's a better person than I am. I stood up and went to the kitchen sink to splash cold water on my face. Phil came over and hugged me from behind. Then he kissed my neck.

"Are you hard?" I said. "Is that a boner?"

"I don't know why, but yes. I'm sorry."

"Either we get divorced or I'm going to kill myself," I said.

"Then we wouldn't need a divorce."

"Funny."

"We all saw this coming."

"Who is 'we all'?"

"We *all*. I don't know. Nance. My parents. Your friends from AA. You! You've been in a lot of psychic pain."

"Don't blame everything on me."

"Oh, come on, you've been talking about suicide since we met."

"Yeah, but I never tried."

I thought of Avery, Sheila's older sister, who broke her neck water-skiing on Float Lake. Jackie dove and dove to save her child. Phil kissed my lips, pressing a little, staying there a second, asking his question. Oil can. Baby bottle. I nudged his chest gently and turned away.

"Get some sleep before your flight."

"You're not coming up?"

When we went water-skiing, I got water up my ass. Float Lake water. Float Lake is nature's enema.

BUG

Surfacing, how does it go? You try to rise up slowly. You have to. Otherwise, the pressure is too much. But we don't take it slow. We never do anything right. We rise up quickly in the water. I can feel the pressure on my ears. Sound gets heavy, thumping, then flat.

Star buzzes a bright blue light and warms up the control room.

"If we're coming up," I ask her, "where are we coming from? Who is the *we* who is coming?"

"Don't worry about that. This is a miracle!"

We stand in the control room and watch the tachometer.

Fifty feet, forty feet, thirty. Truitt sits at the captain's table writing in one of my logs. An alarm bell clangs loudly. He snaps his head, gets up, and paces around the periscope housing. I sneak a look at what he wrote. *Air pressure change extreme. Head pains for crew.* He's right. My head *does* hurt. The baby is howling and covering her ears. We pass twenty feet, then ten.

"Lookouts to the bridge," Dead Girl commands with deep calm. Star flits around all over the place, reflecting off the walls, the machines, the floor, sparks everywhere. All colors of light at once.

"We made it!" she shouts. "Let's get the fuck out of here!"

Truitt scrambles over and attacks the latches on the conning tower. He tries to open the hatch, but the dogs are stuck, rusted and sealed by corrosion.

Star dances around.

"Good-bye, engine! Good-bye, midships! Good-bye, compressed air reservoir. Good-bye, indicator buoy. Good-bye, telegraph. Good-bye, periscope. Good-bye, mess. Good-bye, gun. Good-bye, battery—"

"If you know so much about the submarine," Truitt screams, "come open the fucking hatch!"

Part Four

KATHERINE

Gordon called me from Colorado two weeks after Emily was born.

"I got your photos," he said. "Your baby's ugly."

"All newborns are simian," I told him. "She'll be cute by the time you meet her."

"She'll be in college."

"No, she won't."

"And Emily? That's not even a family name. Phil has an Emily in his family? It doesn't sound Greek."

"Nope. Her middle name isn't Wood, either. Or Burns. She's got nothing to do with all that."

"Mom wants to fly to San Francisco. She wants to meet the baby."

"I'm not ready for that."

Over the next few weeks, Gordon and I called each other constantly. He asked about every little detail concerning the baby. Then he would call my mother and pass on the news. My father wasn't interested. Did I love them? Did I not love them? Did I want them to be part of my child's life?

I decided to try, and Gordon flew out. Phil greeted him in the driveway while I watched from the window. Gordon was impressed when he got out of the taxi. We owned a house in Pacific Heights. Phil's company was doing well.

Phil was wearing a Giants T-shirt and torn jeans. He was my family now—my husband, my baby's father. Phil is tall, very tall.

He has soft black hair and brown eyes. He's got a muscular body and he's a good athlete. Phil beats everyone at everything. Tennis, basketball, baseball, business. When he doesn't win, he's a good sport about it, because he knows he'll win next time. But look who he married! A serial killer in a nursing bra.

I watched from the window as Phil gave my brother a handshake. The handshake turned into a hug. Then Phil gave Gordon the news. Gordon looked up at the house, and I hid behind a curtain. Emily was in my arms, sleeping. She'd been crying for two hours before that and I was afraid to put her down, afraid she might wake up. My arms were tired and sore.

Phil handed Gordon his Amex card, as instructed. We were sending him to the Quartz, a swanky hotel downtown. They have an indoor pool.

"Don't worry, he's not mad at you," Phil said when he came inside.

"Yes, he is."

"I told him you have postpartum depression. That you've been up and down. But that you'll go to his hotel tomorrow morning and work things out."

"Did you tell him to call me Katherine now? Did you tell him I never want to be called Katchie again? Did you?"

"Yes, for fuck's sake. I told him everything you wanted."

The next morning, I walked to the Quartz with Emily in the stroller. I was hoping she'd fall asleep, but she didn't. I went up to Gordon's room. He was still in his pajamas, enjoying a room service breakfast.

"Hello, Katherine."

"Sorry."

I set up a portable play grid on the bed and we stuck Emily under it. She wiggled around, made some cute noises.

"This encourages her to move her eyes."

"Sweet," said Gordon.

"I think she's maybe fucked-up. Her eyes cross all the time. She can't lift her head when she's on her stomach."

"She's eleven weeks old."

"She's stuck on the basics."

I went to the minibar and got a Sprite.

"Are you still in AA?"

"Uh, yeah, dum-dum. You'd know if I left the club."

"It's been six years. Don't you get to a place where you don't need AA?"

"Read a book about it or something."

Emily grunted and turned red in the face.

"Is she okay?" asked Gordon.

"She's pooping."

Emily took forever to finish, and when she did, the stuff had exploded up the back of her polka-dotted onesie. I undressed her, wiped her down, and wrestled her into a new diaper. I was good at packing a diaper bag. I had a fresh outfit for her. I put the dirty diaper in the hallway in an ice bucket.

"Are you going to let Mom and Dad meet Emily before the end of 2002? Or is it gonna be in 2022?"

"I don't know. Mom keeps sending me texts."

"Since when does Mom text? She never texts me."

"Texting is better for me. I don't like talking to her."

"You're a horrible daughter."

I stared at him. "You think so?"

"Yes," said Gordon. "You're going to regret it. When Mom and Dad are gone. The way you treat them. All of us. It's shameful."

"It's like we grew up in different homes, Gordon. Why are you so hard on me?"

"Tell me what happened. Did Dad molest you?"

"*Molest*. I hate that word. You molest a pile of dirt. You molest a beehive."

"Well? Did he?"

"I don't even know for sure."

"Aren't you still in therapy?"

"I'll probably never know. I'll probably never be sure. The truth is gone."

"No, the truth is *not* gone. Reality exists."

"Not for me."

"There's a reality that everyone agrees on. You need to accept that."

"I accept that no one believes me."

"Believes you about what? What happened? What did Mom and Dad do to you, Katchie?"

"Don't call me Katchie."

I locked myself in the bathroom with the baby. Before I clicked the lock, Gordon was pounding on the door.

"How can I believe you when you have no proof?"

He kept up the banging, but I wouldn't open. Emily was crying now. I stuck her on my boob and she latched on, dug in. My world brightened. The nursing high was the best thing about having a baby.

TRUITT

Katherine took herself to the gynecologist in the city. After Dr. Miner retracted the speculum, she said, "You look great!"

"Yeah, right."

"No, really. You do. Some women look like a truck drove through it."

Katherine grabbed on to the sides of the examination table. "Check my anus, too, please. It's been bothering me."

Anus. Bug and I were both laughing.

"Bothering you how?"

"Itching. Burning."

The gynecologist looked inside our wrack seaweed with a penlight, but I couldn't see. She got her finger in there, which hurt. I liked that. Katherine left out the detail that she'd been picking at it again like an enraged crab. She'd get a few days away from it and would start feeling a little better. Then I would pull her back in.

"There's nothing wrong with you," said the gentle-fingered doctor. "I don't even see a hemorrhoid."

"Nothing?" asked Katherine. "Sometimes it bleeds."

"I can give you a steroid cream."

A steroid cream? Fuck you.

DEAD GIRL

Craig Burns drove up to New York on a sizzling day, midweek, July. All the way from Virginia. Katherine got home from a prenatal yoga class and he was sitting there in his car with the window open. He found a spot right in front of her apartment building on Eighth Avenue. As Katherine crossed the street, she saw empty peanut shells everywhere, scattered across the pavement. Her father got out of the car.

"Look at my goddamn parking spot," he said. "A goddamn stroke of lightning."

He had a paper bag of whole peanuts in his hand. He brought them in the taxi, and into the therapist's office. It was 2005. Katherine and Phil had just moved to New York City, and she was pregnant with Zack. She had another new therapist, Barb, who wanted Katherine to confront her dad directly. The goal was to take pressure off Katherine's psyche, because Katherine was abnormally worried about her pregnancy. Katherine worried so much, she could barely leave the apartment.

"So, Mr. Burns. Katherine says you called her 'Anode.' Her pet name for you was 'Cathode.' Together when you were physically connected in her bed you formed a complete battery circuit?"

Craig sat there on the couch in Barb's office. He was wiring up the battery, but with Barb there asking questions, something shifted, and the old pole wasn't there. Katherine felt no pull.

"That was our special thing," said Craig. "I remember. Between us. It was nice. We snuggled, and she charged my battery for the day. It was snuggling, father and daughter, something sweet. Are you implying otherwise?"

"You said she was negative and you were positive. That she charged your battery."

"Technically, *anode* can also be positive, in an electrolytic battery cell."

"But the metaphor, Mr. Burns."

Craig stood up in the woman's office. Like he was going to leave. Or hurt someone. Barb asked him to sit down.

"I can talk standing up."

"You got into your daughter's bed at night."

"No, it was in the morning."

"She said it was in the dark."

"Mornings are dark. Early mornings."

In a family of privilege, there are often as many as four bedrooms in a house. Everyone has a private room. What happens after bedtime? If a light is on, then carbon is burning somewhere, maybe a piece of coal, a cup of oil. Or maybe it's nuclear; maybe it's an explosion of particles. Better to turn out the lights. Better to lie in the dark, so nothing burns. In a family, which is a safe place. In a bed, which is a dreaming space.

Katherine and Craig walked out together from Barb's office into the streets of New York City.

"Oh my God," said Katherine. "It's so hot."

She could smell the tar melting between the seams on Columbus Avenue.

"Well," said Craig. "That was a waste of time."

He left within the hour to drive home. The next week, when Katherine went back, and the week after, Barb tried to talk about the visit with her dad. Katherine couldn't find anything else to say.

"He was threatening me," said Barb. "Did you notice that? Like, don't get too close. Don't ask that next question. Or else."

"It doesn't matter."

"He's scary," said Barb. "Your dad is a very frightening person."

"If I had the chance to do it all over again, I would," Craig told Barb. "I'd do everything exactly the same."

KATHERINE

Mom got wind of my confrontation with Dad and Barb, probably from Gordon. She demanded to drive up and talk to me about it. "But not with that awful woman, your shrink. Dad said she wasn't any good."

I made my mother stay at a hotel. (Was this healing?) She came over after I dropped Emily at preschool and we sat together in my living room. Phil had decorated our two-bedroom Chelsea apartment with modern, spare décor. His assistant at Net-Worth had picked out most of it. We had a wall of windows with a nice view uptown. Mom brought her own cup of coffee. White Styrofoam, with pink lipstick kisses on the rim.

"Your dad called me," Mom said. "Which never happens. He said you accused him of something serious."

"I think so. Yes, I did." I wasn't so sure of myself. I had no proof. The truth is gone. "It was incest probably. I'm not sure."

"Well," she said. "It takes two to tango."

I stared into her taut, surgically enhanced face and said nothing. My mom has blue eyes.

"You were a very seductive little girl."

Mom pulled out a packet of Splenda and dumped the contents into what was left of her coffee.

I was numb as a melon.

"Did Gordon tell you his plan to leave Colorado?" she said. "He's moving back to Virginia Beach."

I took her out to lunch. While we ate, Mom talked about her new husband, Ron, a retired nuclear submarine commander. A navy admiral. Ironic, since my dad's heart had always been the heart of a submariner. (Who got stuck in sales.) Dad didn't care much about nuclear submarines, though, or the Cold War or Ron's military clearance. Dad loved the U-boat and the U-boat only. The German menace.

Mom mentioned the love letters that Dad had sent to me at Camp Riverbow every summer. "I read them all, you know."

"Oh," I said.

"Not once," said my mom. "In all the years we were together. Your father never wrote me a love letter. You had baskets of them." She shook her head. *"Bastard."*

Katchie Burns. Me. The ten-year-old slut. I told Mom I had to cut our visit short. I felt sick and exhausted.

"I need to lie down," I said.

"I thought you had to get Emily from school? I thought I was going with you?"

"I can get her by myself. She likes napping with me. She watches her shows."

"And what about tonight? I can come over and help with dinner."

"Too sick," I told her.

"I'll call you later," she said. "Maybe you'll feel better."

At the corner when we said good-bye, I found it hard to move, hard to get back to my apartment. I hung on to a wall at the corner. I wanted Phil to come home. I needed his warm body, his smell, his mouth and his words and his reassurances. From that moment on, I would try to do whatever he said, whatever he wanted. Officer on duty. Giant. Husband. Family. Home.

It worked for a while, maybe ten years. I guess that kind of thing can't go on forever.

Part Five

TRUITT

Katherine marched into Dr. Goodman's office and Elegy trailed in behind her. Elegy was tall enough now to reach up and knock Dr. Goodman's coffee cup from the edge of his desk. It fell against her ballet costume. Dr. Goodman's cup was empty. Nothing spilled. He squatted down to pick it up and didn't even see that Elegy was standing there in her green tutu.

Katherine blurted out that she was bleeding from her *poo hole.*

"BLEEDING!" Katherine sat down on the couch. Undetected, Elegy climbed onto her lap. "And I'm having panic attacks. Usually in the shower."

"Does Phil know about this?"

"He doesn't care."

"You told him? Phil knows your anus is bleeding?"

"Oh my God! Do NOT use the word *anus.* I should maybe go to a mental hospital."

I wanted to stop Katherine from saying these things but I couldn't.

"You mean a psych ward at a hospital?" he asked. "Inpatient? A treatment center?"

"I mean the loony bin. Phil doesn't care. I wake up. I tell him I'm going to kill myself. He eats a bowl of cornflakes and goes to work."

"Is this maybe like the boy who cried wolf?"

"I don't know, Dr. Goodman. Is it? Do I look like a boy?"

Dr. Goodman sat there like a dazed cat, or a chocolate chip cookie. He would never ever EVER have guessed that Katherine was mutilating herself. And yet, she reported it.

"Anyway, the gynecologist says she can't find anything wrong. It itches. I scratch it. Then it hurts more, and I scratch it more. Maybe it's a problem. Maybe I have a serious problem."

There once was a cow named Milky White. One morning, Milky White gave no milk and the poor woman who owned her felt confused, scared, and, frankly, desperate. You see, this cow was all the woman had. She and Jack were practically starving.

"What shall I do now?" said the poor woman to no one.

Elegy stretched out on Dr. Goodman's couch. She put her head in Katherine's lap and fell asleep while Katherine sat there blabbing at her therapist. Elegy got bigger, exponentially, as she napped. Rosy cheeks, chubby thighs. During that one session, her two front teeth got loose, fell out, and grew back as permanent.

BUG

Truitt bangs his head on the hatch cover, straining, screaming, furious. Big rivulets of brown blood congeal on his forehead and neck. He's been working on the hatch wheel for such a long time, his efforts have become a kind of performance. But the hatch and its dogs are sealed with rust.

"I want to draw something," says Elegy. She's sitting at the captain's desk watching Truitt struggle.

"What do you want to draw?" I ask her.

"Something pretty. A horse. Do you have any paper?"

"Try this." Star hands Elegy an old folded-up letter on Camp Riverbow stationery. "I found it in the first-aid kit."

(JUNE, 1983)

Dear Mom & Dad,

My tent is OK. But there is a slut (exuse me) who wears blue maskara & all. But it's nice to hear her talk about how nasty & bad she is & think "Gee, I'm a nice little girl." I am the straightest girl in camp it seems! My counselor is 38 w/3 kids. See she's real weird. I don't like her. Got to go. I love you.

Love, Katchie

"This paper has writing on it," says Elegy. "I don't want it." She pushes the letter across the desk. Truitt starts kicking his tool bag, throwing things.

"Where's your all-knowing Dead Girl?" he shouts. "Why won't she help us? We can't bob around like this on the surface forever. We'll get bombed."

"Dead Girl hasn't gone anywhere," says Star. "I just got a message."

"I heard it, too," I say. "Same message she sent this morning."

"What was the message?"

"'*Leave Phil,*'" says Star. "'Leave him or die.'"

"But we love him."

I say this at the same exact time as the others: Star, Truitt, and Elegy, who looks exactly like me now. Elegy and I are the same age. We have the same soft voice, the same southern accent. Short brown hair. Big brown eyes. All arms and legs. Yellow overalls a size too small. Stained white T-shirt. Skinny. Loving.

"We can't leave Phil." Again, we speak as a group.

"You can and you must," says Dead Girl.

"Dead Girl!" says Truitt. "Where have you been?"

"It's time to go."

"We aren't strong enough." We all speak in unison again.

"Try," says Dead Girl.

"We don't know how to try."

The whole submarine fills with our voices, music, light, colors, magical symbols floating around in the air. Elegy gets up and dances beneath it all, twirling and laughing. I dance around with her in a circle holding hands.

"You're all stronger than you think," says Dead Girl. "You do know how to try. In fact, you try all the time."

"Everyone is strong," says Truitt. When his voice breaks off on its own, it sounds harsh and ugly. The lights and colors disappear. Elegy stomps her feet and I move away from her. She starts to cry.

"Everyone tries," he says crossly.

"No," says Dead Girl. "Not everyone tries."

Elegy comes up behind me and puts a hand on each of my shoulders.

"Ask him," she whispers.

"Truitt," I say. "Remember being in the bathtub after?"

Truitt walks over to us. I think he's going to punch me or knock me over, but Elegy steps out in front. Truitt kisses her forehead.

"You said you were going to draw horses." He talks to her gently. "But the next thing you know, you're imagining the black hair, the beard, the feeling of the beard pushing through the skin, and a scary giant hovering over your bed while you sleep."

"I didn't say that." Elegy doesn't fear Truitt.

"But am I right?"

She smiles.

"Everything we know about love is wrong."

KATHERINE

The lawyer's office building sat right next to a sewage-treatment plant. We met in the atrium, which felt like a mall. A small mall. Glass everywhere, shiny green reflective windows. Fountains and cheap marble. The lawyer told me that one time a drunk driver lost control of his car and drove right through the plate glass.

"He crashed into the lobby. And he wasn't hurt. Not a scratch. He got out and started to look at a road map."

I said, "He must have been pretty wasted."

"Drunks have guardian angels."

"Everyone has a guardian angel. Even lawyers."

The lawyer thought about this for a second.

"People die anyway," he said.

"And the angels cry harder than we do. When that happens."

"Do you believe that?"

"I try to."

We went upstairs. In the elevator, he said, "I see you wear a wallet chain."

I looked down at the silver chain that buckled onto the belt loop of my jeans, then drooped down and attached to a black leather wallet I wore in my back pocket.

"Chain wallet, actually." So off-brand for a suburban mom. I had only just started wearing it. Copied a guy, Jim, an ex-con, actually. A friend in recovery. Phil hated the wallet chain. So did my kids.

The lawyer stepped off the elevator. I followed him into his office, which felt like the catalog version of a lawyer's office, like a set on *Wheel of Fortune,* all put together already. But he appeared to be a good lawyer. He wore glasses. He had a receding hairline. According to his framed certificate, he went to A Law School.

"What's on your mind?"

"Everything good and everything bad that has ever happened to me is because I'm pretty. And now I'm old."

He looked at me. "You're still pretty. And don't worry. We'll take care of you."

I stared at my hands as he talked. He was explaining laws around alimony, custody, child support. I was crying most of the time, sick to my stomach with terror. Nance always tells me that feelings are liars. It's a confusing thing to say. But I find comfort in it.

"Tell me more about why you need a divorce lawyer."

"My husband thinks I'm crazy. He wants me to go to Arizona to a mental health place, a rehab center. I think he should go if he loves the idea so much. Why should I go?"

"Do you think you're crazy?"

"I think he's self-centered. Inconsiderate. Competitive, in the darkest sense of the word."

"What sense of the word is that?"

"Phil lives, I die. Phil thrives, I wither. Sexually demanding. A vampire."

The lawyer raised his eyebrows. "A vampire?"

"No, of course not. Phil's a great guy. I love him very much."

"I see," said the lawyer.

See, see. What does it mean to see? What does it mean to love someone?

"What do you see?" I asked him.

"I see what you're saying. I know what you mean."

"No, you don't. You're just being agreeable."

"Oh, I'm not agreeable. I'm a lawyer."

I asked for water, and the lawyer served it to me in a Homer Simpson coffee mug. The cup was stained and the water tasted like coffee, which made me want to throw up, and also, it made me want to die. I took his business card.

"Call me when you're ready."

TRUITT

I'm fast asleep in the captain's bunk with the curtains drawn. Star and Bug come to find me.

"I'm a bad person," says Bug. "A very, very bad person."

"No," I say. "You're not a bad person, Bug."

"I don't love my parents. In fact, I hate them. That means I'm bad. And crazy."

Star picks through my pile of tools: a wrench, a sledgehammer, the empty oil can, a bunch of dog-eared books and manuals, an ax, a straight-edge razor, scissors, a butcher knife, other sharp things. My hair is stiff and bloody, stuck to my forehead.

"We need a new plan," she says.

"Why did Dead Girl bring us all the way up?" asks Bug. "Then leave us floating here in the waves?"

"You know why," says Star. "She wants us to get divorced."

"From Phil?" I say. "Philip the Rock? Why would we do that? He's completely reliable, predictable, an excellent provider. You managed to trap him with your hot light. Maybe because of how much you like fucking. To me, this is normal and healthy."

"Yeah," says Star. "But what do you know about normal and healthy?"

I sit up in the bunk.

"Star. Why don't you put some clothes on?"

She shakes her head. Bug skitters through the darkness to the other side of the control room. Star shines red and illuminates the wall. I see myself asleep in the first mate's bunk. Or it's not me. It's Elegy.

"Look at her now," says Bug. "She looks exactly like Truitt."

"Don't be afraid," says Star.

"I'm not afraid," I tell her. "But I'm a little confused."

"Confusion is a form of fear," says Star.

"No," I say. "Confusion is a vomiting female monster with a vestigial penis. *Vestigial* means atrophied, no longer in use. When an organ is no longer needed, that means we're growing. Nature pushes us, and we evolve. Over vast fields of time. Consciousness catches up. And that's why we're here."

The girls stare at me.

"Who told you that?" asks Star.

"Everything Katherine does, everything she says, is part of her soul's desire to grow. But she can only make out shapes and presence, the outlines of love. She listens for echoes and bouncing sound waves."

Ping.

STAR

Katherine had the dumb idea of going to twelve-step meetings for sex and love addicts. Because she couldn't control her crabby pinchers. She found a meeting in New York City, lots of pretty women with long blond hair. But these women never talked about the important experiences, which are underwater, aquatic. None of them mentioned star matter, gushers, oil wells. No one noticed when Katherine's beating heart squirted blood thirty feet across the room.

She tried a different support group. This one was full of pale, pudgy men with shaking hands. Most of the men were there for their problem with porn and hookers. Sometimes we would see a woman at the porn-and-hooker meeting. But mostly it was men, and mostly they talked about torpedoes and depth charges, dives and drills and surfacing, engine grease and sardine cans. These men were sailors.

She took a bus into the city from New Jersey twice a week and walked over to the porn-and-hooker meeting from Port Authority. It was a quick walk, but not quick enough. In that neighborhood, the wind blew constantly. It rushed in from one river and headed across the island to the other. It rattled through Katherine's head as she passed through.

The meetings took place in an ornate Roman Catholic church with candles, statuaries, stained glass, and kneeling women. Homeless people slept on flattened boxes outside the entrance. The sex and love addicts sat in religious-education classrooms in metal chairs with attached desks. Taking notes was not allowed.

Katherine sat around for hours and hours and listened to all those pervy perpetrators. She got used to the concept that these men were not creeps or bad people. They weren't criminals, either. They were regular people who had become disorganized around their sexuality. Or maybe it was *me* who understood this concept. Maybe I saw the truth first, and gradually got Katherine to see it. I just know that there are three kinds of seeing inside a submarine. The periscope pokes up and down, rotates, but through a very narrow lens. Sonar travels wide and comes back with news of the enemy. And then there's what happens inside the boat.

We have different-colored lights for day and night. Blue means day, and white means night. Red means *I'm playing with you, Bug, so go to sleep.* Time is make-believe in a sub. There is no night. There is no day. Dark means danger. Even stars get scared.

I'm the one who stands at the door making jokes. I'm the one who draws your attention away from the little girl with a penis in her mouth. I'm a prostitute myself, but in a good way. Girls become women, women become hookers, and hookers make porn.

A pervy perpetrator got up to go to the bathroom at the meeting and I got up to go with him. Truitt stopped me.

"He's a perv!"

"He's not a perv," said Dead Girl. "He's a boy, a child. He's your grandfather, Walter. He's your father, Craig."

"No," said Truitt. "He's an unemployed waiter who jacks off to porn on his laptop all day."

That's nothing compared to incest. And yet, incest is natural. Not normal, and not right, not healthy or acceptable in any way. But natural, because it happens. That scrawny fetal mouselike thing hanging down between a man's legs. A tendency—no, a pull, *an obligation* to put it where it doesn't belong. Where it isn't wanted. Where it is wanted. Where it isn't wanted. Where it is wanted.

KATHERINE

When Phil took long trips to Asia, or Europe, or the Midwest, or the Northwest, WHEREVER HE WAS, I sometimes took the kids over to his parents' house for dinner. They lived in the same split-level ranch house he grew up in. Phil's room hadn't changed a bit. He had probably masturbated daily under that ribbed coverlet. Zack liked to lie there and read his dad's old yearbooks.

I struggled on and abstained, one day at a time, from digging into my own asshole. I got a keychain after thirty days, and a cake with candles. All the men at my pervert meeting clapped and congratulated me. A room full of Peeping Toms and date rapers.

This was the only twelve-step meeting in twenty-five years where I would or could let myself cry. I cried in front of the pedophiles. These were my people. The wankers with ugly shoes.

"Speech," said the pervs when they presented me with another coin. "Speech!"

"Well," I explained, "Mom was putting up a birdhouse in the side yard and she fell off the ladder and hit her head. Somehow this connects in my mind to Dr. Wickford, our pediatrician, and also to watching her roll around on the floor of the den in one of her meltdowns. I stood in the doorway, always the doorway. No bomb had fallen on Virginia Beach. No one was going hungry. But my mother didn't feel loved. She didn't think my father loved her, and probably he didn't. She didn't believe that I loved her, either. She asked me to love her more. How do you get your own child to love you more? Not by begging.

"This is just one version of the story. In this version, my mom was clothed. On the ladder with the birdhouse, she was wearing a head scarf, jeans, and a blue shirt. On the floor in the living room, rolling around and crying, she was wearing a nightgown and a quilted bathrobe that zipped up the front. Because often, so often, she was not clothed. What do you call that? Nude."

"That's shameless," said a compulsive wanker. "To be naked in front of your children."

"That's sexual abuse," said a flasher.

"It wasn't your mom being nude all the time around the house. That's not what fucked you up," said the child pornographer. "It's the way she always begged for love."

Phil's parents knew I went to meetings. But they didn't know what kind. They didn't know I was sick and crazy enough to . . . what did the wankers call it? Self-mutilate. Nick and Helen didn't know about that.

BUG

Truitt turns the hatch with all his strength for ten years. Or is it twenty minutes? He works on the hatch for a long time and then one day, presto! He gets it open. Seawater gushes in from above. Cold salty water crashes down heavy on my head and onto the steel floor.

I stand there in my nightgown. What is Phil going to do if I get out of the boat? He's going to stop loving us. And we are going to die. Truitt knows this, but he climbs right up the ladder, rung by rung. He climbs up into the light. Doesn't say a word. Just leaves.

Elegy shivers beside me, holding my hand. She's developed a skin problem, a crusty black covering. She's sticky and scabby, like a burnt marshmallow. A badly roasted marshmallow that caught fire. Like the tar on the road that fills cracks in the pavement. When tar melts in the sun, it gets gooey. You can scar it with your shoe. Semen on top of it. Semen dripping down it.

"Fuck!" Truitt screams into the open air. "Fuck! Fuck! Fuck! It stings!"

He laughs. He's very excited to be in the outside world.

"Your turn, Bug." Star sneaks into the control room. "Go up the ladder."

"It's not safe."

"The sun is the safest place, and the sky. There's safety in the sun, in how it moves across the sky."

"Sky?" asks Elegy. "What is sky?"

Star holds open her arms. "Come on. I'll show you."

Elegy moves past me to the ladder. Daylight pours down through the hatch, turning her into a silhouette. The light attacks my head and eyes and face. I can't see anything but sunlight. Star surrounds Elegy and turns into a spray of light.

"Stop!" I lurch forward but there's nothing to grab on to. Elegy slips up and away with Star. It's like the sky has swallowed them whole. The hatch cover slams down so hard, it shakes the submarine.

Out of the stale, dark damp and into the light. The pure, clean air. There's a leftover smell of fresh air, and sloshing water pooled up on the control room floor at my feet. Beyond that, just cold, blank darkness. A dripping sound.

I shout as loudly as I can. "Remember being in the bathtub after?"

Of course, no one can hear me now.

"Let go," says Dead Girl.

"Oh, great. You're still here."

"It's time to let go."

"But *let go* means you're dead."

"*Let go* means you can be born again."

KATHERINE

In the shower at 3:00 a.m. for no apparent reason, and I hurt myself again. Never on purpose with the ripping and tearing. Spider legs, they snuck up on me. I blanked out. When I came to, my fingers were down there, mad and frantic. I stopped myself. I washed my fingertips under the showerhead. Then I got out of the shower, dried myself off, lay down on the bed. I woke up an hour later wrapped in a towel, cold and shivering. I got dressed and put on my coat and hat and went outside. I walked the perimeter of our yard. I could hear the subtle rush of cars in the distance. Our street is closer to the highway than I like to admit.

I walked up Mountain Avenue. It goes straight uphill, getting steeper at the top, where a road runs along the ridge of the mountain, Overlook Street. During the winter, you can see the city skyline quite clearly. But Overlook is a tiny mountain, hardly deserving of the name.

My phone lit up. Only Sheila, texting from Virginia Beach. *Checking in.* At least Sheila loved me. It wasn't enough. I tried to remember the words to the Saint Francis Prayer, which I made Phil read aloud as part of our wedding vows. It's all about giving and not getting. Understanding and not trying to be understood. It's inhuman, completely unrealistic. I tried to pray.

I was halfway up the hill and losing my breath. I could be up on the ridge in less than five minutes if I walked fast. I texted Phil. *Where are you?* Into the green void. I called him, went straight to voice mail. I knew where he was. Why was I asking?

Phil was in Germany, having breakfast with a client. Mercedes. That was the client. Phil even bought a Mercedes sedan. At first, I was embarrassed by this. But then I grew to like the black leather. That's the deal in a submarine: You sleep when you aren't on duty, in order to save air. When you're asleep, you consume less oxygen.

Here's what I would have said if Phil had answered his phone. That I was never going to make a film about the girl who lives in a birdhouse. I was never going to make a film. Not one person in the world would cry over this. Except me. But my tears are toilet water.

Phil, I would have said, *are you mad at me?*

But Phil didn't answer. I walked back down the hill and went inside. The kids were both asleep. I sat on the bed and hatched a plan. I had a bottle of pills stashed in the toe of my ski boot in the attic. Just pain relievers and various opiates I had collected over the years. It wouldn't be enough. But I could get more.

The problem with taking pills was the possibility that I wouldn't actually die. Then it would count as a relapse, and I would lose my sobriety count. Sobriety. My precious life path. My great success. I didn't want to lose it in a botched suicide attempt. I had little to show for myself except a record of two decades without a drink or a drug. And the kids. I did that.

Once I was golden. Once I was bathed in gold. I went down to the kitchen and got a very sharp knife. It was just out of the box. Phil has a thing about buying new knives when the old ones get dull. He doesn't believe in sharpening knives. I tried him again and caught him on his cell phone.

"I have a knife in my hand."

"What do you mean?" asked Phil.

"I'm standing here in the kitchen by myself and I have a sharp knife. I want to cut someone."

"Don't cut yourself."

"I don't want to cut myself."

"Then why did you say you did?"

I was trying to tell Phil that I felt afraid. Afraid of what?

"You're not listening."

"It's early here."

"Forget it."

I hung up on Phil and he didn't call me back or text. I wasn't going to cut myself or anyone else. So why threaten? Phil ignored my insane ideas, and I learned to do the same. It's like I never thought or said them.

He was my dad. He made decisions about my life. He drove me around, fed me, paid for school, gave me a car. And I seduced him. I was too pretty. I looked like him. I manipulated him. I loved him. I was too trusting. I'm a bad person. I liked it! He made me feel special. I was warm, soft, sweet, beautiful. I had brown eyes and long, thin fingers. I am a cocksucker. Love will never find me.

TRUITT

When the engines start, I lash myself to the tower with my safety strap. I'm wedged between the periscope housing and the bridge bulwark. The entire submarine vibrates. Everywhere, a roaring sound. There's a strong smell of diesel exhaust. And then we're moving, flying, riding the waves at an incredible speed. Star and me, and Elegy, who's just a brighter version of Star, now shining from behind her. We tear through the sloppy waves, across the cheering sea. I have no idea where we're going. I'm not navigating! The sextant is down below in the control room with Bug. I have no instruments to measure the angles on the horizon. A passenger on my own ship.

We rise up and crash down on waves the size of bridges. Waves like walls, bulging with whales, seals, sharks, a giant squid, the ocean's aliens. The steel nose of the sub, the spray of the salt water, the fingers of sun, the thirst, the red skin, the hot skin, the waves, the tide, the tide, the skin, the sun. We skip across the surface like our wildest dreams.

We come close to the shore, where we see rippled wet horses on the beach. We see Katherine in the shower, her fingers in her own lost Atlantis, a drowned-world mystery, her fingers taking her into a private darkness. How many times has she done this? Her ribs are showing. Her head is tilted backward. There's an incision in her heart, but it keeps pumping. Pump pump. She doesn't know she's wounded.

Star hits me full in the face. Bright, blazing.

"Help her," says Star. "Make her stop."

"No," I say. "We are at war."

"With who? Phil?"

"No, honey, not Phil. We're fighting Katherine."

KATHERINE

I was a chubby toddler with curly brown hair and folds of soft, delicious fat on my legs. Zack was like that, too. Dad kept mentioning this when we met up at a grand hotel in Asheville, North Carolina. He came alone; Mrs. Pringle preferred golf to children.

We took a drive on the Blue Ridge Parkway to a folk art museum, where Zack and Em watched a man in knee breeches blow tubes out of melted glass. On the way home, winding down the mountain in a thunderstorm, Dad got his hands on three-year-old Zack.

Zack was in his car seat, all harnessed in, and Dad was sitting beside him. I turned a little in my seat and saw Dad's evil hands roving over Zack's legs. I turned all the way around and shoved the road map into my dad's face. It was torn and unfolded. He hates that.

"We're lost!" I screamed.

Emily was sitting on the other side of the car seat looking out the window. Dad couldn't reach her. But he had no interest. He had chosen Zack. That's how it works.

"It wasn't sexual touch," I said later to Phil.

"Of course not. We were sitting right there in the car with them."

We were at the airport. In Charlotte. Zack was strapped into his stroller, sweaty-haired, chocolate on his face. Our flight was delayed. Storms in the area.

"He didn't molest Zack." I yanked at Phil's shirt, his arm. I was getting out of control.

"No," he said. "All he did was grab the fat on Zack's thigh. Everyone does that. Zack's legs are fat and yummy. They're irresistible."

"Oh my God! Don't say that."

I was ready to cut my arm with a knife. Except I didn't have a knife. Airport security would have taken it away. But when I got home, when I got access to a knife. I wanted to. I would!

"We were right in the car with him," Phil said. "Nothing happened."

A car is a private space. Nothing is off-limits. And my dad's touch is greedy. I know his thumbs, the press of the bones in his hands. He grabs, grinds his way into the muscle with his fingers. Zack's little legs were like dough or sand or clay.

I didn't think I'd ever have kids. I didn't want to, that's for sure. Phil took my body. He put himself into it. He multiplied himself through my blood cells and organs. We made people! Zack and Em. We created a family.

I stopped talking to my dad after that. Zero contact. I did feel guilty, but I couldn't stand the thought that he was groping Zack. What if my father died when we weren't in contact? That was always on my mind. What if I was wrong, and he didn't cross the line with me? It's not like I remembered the details, in a concrete way. What did I remember? Was I making shit up?

"Why would you make up something like that?" Phil asked. "Children don't make that stuff up. It's not in their wheelhouse."

With one of my therapists—Garth? Judy? Randall?—we decided it didn't matter if sexual abuse had happened or not. Suppose I randomly decided to turn around and point THAT kind of finger at my own innocent, wonderful father. Maybe I came to this planet to hurt the people I love. That in itself was "crazy." We'd treat the crazy and not worry about the cause.

Crazy just a word. Words just disturbances.

Oh, who cares? For fuck's sake. He did it. To me. It happened.

BUG

We skirt along the ocean's surface for what seems like days. Boom boom BAM! Out of nowhere, an aircraft drops a bomb. It drops several bombs, I think, but only one hits. It cracks our pressure hull. I'm sitting in the dark control room. Do bombs look like thought balloons on a cartoon? Do they look like puckered lips? Bombs whistle down and then everything catches fire. Out of nowhere. Sudden wild flames and black smoke.

Another bomber buzzes over to finish the job. I can't see

the plane. But I can hear it. Who would bomb little girls? Oh, fighter jets of all kinds, male and female. They're everywhere, and they can be very self-hating. Nothing they do is on purpose. Most explosions are accidental. This doesn't mean they don't kill little girls. And knock out their hearing, vision, memory.

"It's over!" I shout. "Prepare to die."

The boat, the waves, the end. It all happens so fast. Tongue, eyelash, sea, lip, wind, sky, cloud, burning hands. It feels like life. We are finally alive. But only for a second! We make a false start, a mere approach. Then we sink. The sub heats up from the burning waves all around, its tanks empty of oil. The oil burns in the sea. Bugs can drown. Waves can burn. Blood, not oil. Blood! Not oil.

Guess who finally climbs down into the hatch to check on me?

"Get me out of here!" I scream.

"I have no authority anymore."

"Good!"

"Bring her up!" Star shouts.

"You're going to die. But don't worry. It won't hurt."

I hear pieces of the submarine creaking. Breaking apart. I catch fire at some point. Then I put myself out. I can't feel anything. My arms and legs are skinless in places. My hair is singed.

"What will happen to Zack and Em?"

"I have no idea," says Truitt.

"That's not comforting!"

"I'll take care of them." This is Dead Girl, weighing in at last. She appears in the control room as a woman. Old, steady, Kitty in the 1970s. Cat-eyed sunglasses, curly white hair. Saggy upper arms. She wears a sleeveless summer dress.

"Kitty!" I don't reach for a hug. Kitty's not a hugger.

Truitt stares. I guess he's never seen Dead Girl before. Only heard her. She doesn't often come in a body.

"The blame goes deep," says Kitty. "It goes so deep that the self has been destroyed. The blame killed the self."

This is something Kitty would never have said, or even understood. Dead Girl makes people weird.

"The blame killed the self? That sounds bad."

"We see it as a plus," says Kitty.

"We should never have surfaced," I say.

"Let go," says Kitty. "Then let go deeper. When you go inside, you find it. You take your last breath. And then another comes along, a miracle. After you die? You're still here."

I speak up. "If we let go, if Katherine really lets go . . ."

"Oh, that's done already," says Kitty. "Katherine no longer exists. All that's left is shame and blame. Not much to build on. We'll have to start over completely."

KATHERINE

"Horrible neck pain," I told the orthopedic specialist in Mendham.

He prescribed Percocet.

"Terrible cramps," I told my gynecologist in the city. Thank you, another bottle.

"Migraine headaches," I told the family doctor. They were eager to help me, these hardworking white-jacketed men and women. When you're sinking to the bottom, people who don't know you can really come in handy. People who love you, they're the ones who can say something and be heard. But they don't.

As for my friends, the women in town, acquaintances from the private school where we sent the kids, neighbors, the people in Phil's family and professional network—these people thought I was fringe, unstable. When someone asked how I was doing, it was: "Katherine is nuts. She's gone completely off the rails. I've heard they're getting divorced."

I knew they were saying things like this. I could listen in on conversations that happened miles away. If the God in us is the life in us . . . I was running out of both. Driving around town, taking care of my duties. It's a hell of a full-time job, parenting. It's a shit show. Everyone fucks it up.

Even my real friends, Nance and Sheila, were too busy to answer. *Pick up pick up pick up.*

I started to avoid everyone from AA and the pervs from the sex meetings. Those guys would have tried their best to help me, save me. Save me for what? Another night in a church basement?

One evening, after dinner and a cheesecake, I overheard Helen in the master bedroom at their house. Nick was back there with her. I could tell they were on the phone long-distance with Phil. They were reporting on my behavior, trying to decide if I was okay. After they hung up, I went in and sat down with them on their bed; the three of us lined up like we were saying prayers.

"So. You're spies now."

"We do what we have to," said Helen.

"Your son could also just come home once in a while and see for himself."

"He supports you!" Helen waved her finger in my face.

I got up and went to the door. I had to leave before I started to scream. I wouldn't come over here anymore. I would tell Phil as soon as he got back. His plane from Europe arrived in the morning.

Nick followed me into the hallway.

"Did you know my dad came here alone from Greece when he was twenty-seven? He worked for his third cousin down in Elizabeth, in shipping."

"Yes. You've told me that."

"He absolutely hated his boss. His cousin, Spiros. Took twenty years of bullshit. He was going to have a heart attack or kill the guy. My mother arranged for him and Spiros to meet with the priest at the church. The priest wanted Papu to fall backward into Spiros's arms."

"Oh," I said. "Like fake fainting? When you fall backward?"

"Yeah, that. Papu kept stopping himself with his back foot. Every single time. He kept trying, but he never let go. Spiros fired him a week later. Papu was so pissed, he went to the priest and cursed him out. The priest said Papu needed to learn to trust. So that became important to him."

"Trust?"

"Yeah."

I said, "Would you trust a toothless hitchhiker, a Vietnam vet in a ragged army coat?"

"I would. If I loved him. If he was my brother."

"But let's say he's not your brother. Let's say he's a random guy, down on his luck."

"He has a brother somewhere. And a father and a mother."

"Maybe not," I said. "Maybe he hated his mother and father. Maybe he killed them."

"We want you to trust us. To trust Phil." Nick emphasized his plea with his lips and his eyebrows. By spreading and crinkling them. I didn't answer.

It would be like drinking a warm baby bottle full of Fiorinal. Like guzzling a mommy bottle filled with milk and crushed Percocet. Mommy bottle, so different from a baby bottle. Love is the backside of hate.

STAR

We are having sex with Phil for the very last time. Katherine's hair is matted and damp. Her body so hot. Her cheeks flush. Her back and legs drip with sweat. Truitt tries to keep his head up, to breathe and tread water, grabbing at slabs of floating wood from the exploded sub. There is oil in the water, some of it on fire. He's choking, coughing in the moonless night.

"Do not trust Phil!" he splutters, flailing in the cold waves. "He wants you dead! He just doesn't know it."

Bug grabs on to whatever floats past: a bunk pad, a table leg, a pillowcase. She scrambles wildly in the cold water. Cloud. Wind. Salt spray. Head underwater. She shouts at Truitt.

"Remember being in the bathtub after?"

"Yes," yells Truitt. "I remember!"

The fighter jet comes back and circles the perimeter of the flaming wreckage. Its engine noise blocks out the sky. It drops a life raft, not a bomb. Truitt splashes over and scrambles in. I am already in the raft, waiting for him. Like I dropped down from the sky myself. Which is exactly what happened.

Bug slips around in the oily, burning water. The bomber drops life vests, and Bug swims to one. She tries to make her way over to the raft. The water is choppy, with giant white-capped waves. The current of the Gulf Stream carries the raft away.

The pilot passes by one more time, maybe considering his options. One in the water, two in the raft. Rough seas, hot sun. Enemies. He circles and assesses for about five minutes, then gives up and flies away.

Bug is alone in an endless expanse of black sea. The blackest sea we ever saw. Think of a childhood, any childhood.

KATHERINE

After Phil fell asleep, after we had sex (and it was good sex), a trooper showed up at the front door in his state police uniform. He rang the doorbell, so I jumped out of bed and said, "Oh my God, something has happened to Emily."

Phil said, "No, honey. What are you talking about?"

"The doorbell rang."

I was pulling up the shades and crying. My heart got so big, swollen, monstrous. It felt like all my small bones were breaking. The big bones wanted to break, too, but they couldn't. They had to carry my body into the next moment, which was when I realized there was no car in the driveway. There was no state trooper. I was dreaming. I was home with my husband in New

Jersey. Emily was asleep in her room. Good girl, she's a good girl.

The man was my father. He was my mother's husband. My bedroom floated on water like a dock. Like a raft. It had mirrored wallpaper. A purple rug. The giant came in through the door. I couldn't see him. But I could smell him.

Why had I stopped going to the perv recovery group? Those beautiful weirdos were showing me that it's possible to reduce shame. Eliminate shame? Probably not. Eradicate shame? I had doubts.

"Phil," I said. "I'm sorry. I'm so sorry."

He didn't answer. He was asleep again, tranquilized by his own orgasm. This was not unusual. But as I lay there, something cracked, sizzled, buzzed. A live wire in my head. I burned, smoked, emitted odor at my openings. I blew a fuse, shot red sparks through the blackness. The word *circuit* comes from *circle.* My marriage was the only thing holding me together.

Electricity travels in one direction. The wire that goes to the source cannot be used as the return. If any part of the circuit is broken, the current flow stops and the bulb won't light.

"I love you," I said to Phil. He didn't answer. I wanted to wake him up and ask him if he loved me, beg him to keep me, to forgive me for being so hard to handle, so out of range, so wicked, bad, and unworthy. But something stopped me. I want to call it a voice, but it wasn't a voice. It was an explosion. I reached for the pills.

Part Six

KATHERINE

When I got to Hope Haven—i.e., the MENTAL HOSPITAL—
I was assigned to a therapist named Gwynn. Gwynn wanted
me to meditate and write, using what she called a "trailhead."
Meaning, she got me started on the trail. It was supposed to lead
me into my own childhood.

I was waiting in Gwynn's office at Hope Haven on the red
couch, scratchy wool. The art on the walls was large-scale and
interesting, donated by an artist who went through their program. It was made of textiles, wool, quilted fabric, tassels and
canvas squares, buttons and zippers.

A cat came slinking through the open door. He was Hope
Haven's therapeutic pet. A scrawny thing with perfect triangular ears and gray stripes down his back. He sat next to me on
the sofa until I stroked him. Soon he was purring so loudly the
whole couch shook. I pushed him away with a gentle flip of my
hand. He came right back.

"You don't like Tiki?"

Gwynn had feathery white hair and an interesting, weath-
ered face. I had no idea how old she was. Maybe sixty. Maybe
eighty. She came in and leaned against the edge of her desk,
facing me.

"I don't like cats," I said.

"That's okay. Tiki has other friends."

Gwynn dressed simply, white button-down blouse and faded

jeans. She had a cowgirl biker vibe. I liked her twangy accent and her gold jewelry.

"Feelin' better?"

"Not really."

"Do you still want to die?"

"If I really wanted to die, I wouldn't have flown out here. I would have actually taken the pills."

"Were you just trying to scare your husband?"

"Maybe I'm just pushing things to their inevitable conclusion."

"With all your years in recovery, I'm surprised you keep that many pills around."

"How is this going to work exactly?"

"Same way it works on the outside. You dig in. Look for the truth. Then you look *at* the truth, once you find it. That's key. For thirty days."

"With other people?"

She nodded.

"You can say anything in here. If you hold back, we're wasting our time."

STAR

We move up and down on blue hills of water. White foamy spray everywhere. Beyond it the hot sun. Truitt bails water, scooping it up with his canister bottle and dumping it into the sea. His frantic efforts make no difference. Splashes from the swells pour in faster than he can bail.

Why are we still afloat? I can only guess it's Dead Girl's

magic. A seagull flies overhead and shrieks. Truitt tracks the gull as it rides the wind and disappears into the soupy gray air.

"We're not far from shore then," he says. "Maybe there's hope!"

"There's always hope."

Truitt's in uniform now. Khaki trousers and a red kerchief. His blond hair is freshly buzzed and his cheeks are sunburned. He's shiny with sweat.

"What's that you're hiding? You're hiding something."

"No, I'm not."

"I can see you've got something. You're sitting on it."

I get up and look. I act surprised.

"Oh! This old thing?"

"Bug's log," says Truitt. "Really? Couldn't you have grabbed a gauze bandage? A flare gun?"

"What about Bug?" I ask.

"Sharks probably got her. They go after the stragglers."

"Don't you care?"

Truitt shrugs. "I'm tired of her. I'm tired of everything about her."

"Don't you love her at all?"

He squints at me, shielding his eyes from the sun.

"Everyone knows that bugs drown. In fact, it's the best way to kill them."

"I wonder if Elegy is still alive."

"What's your point, Star?"

"Katherine wants the truth. I'm going to give it to her."

Truitt holds up the sextant. He must have grabbed it from the flames. Maybe a better choice than mine. He aims it at me.

"Not if I shoot you first."

We both laugh. We haven't laughed in so long. Maybe ever. We don't even know what's happening. We recognize the sound. I don't know from when. We're in sync with each other.

"What's happening?"

"I think we're blood dead," says Truitt. "I think this is what it feels like."

The swells toss the raft up, down, and sideways.

"We need to make land," he says. "Get to shore."

"Shore?"

"Phil. Family. New Jersey. Home."

"Oh, we don't need shore."

"Katherine needs love."

"Love is the sun's blood. And there's plenty of that out here."

"Trust me. We need to get to land."

"You said when we surfaced, we would die. But here we are."

"Are we alive?"

"I am. I don't know about you."

Truitt takes his canister bottle and holds it upside down. A few drops of seawater dribble out.

"I hate the surface. I hate it! Trapped by the sun, hot as hell, thirsty, miserable, baking, weak."

"I think it's wonderful. Look at this ocean. It's all ocean! Everywhere."

Truitt kicks at the filthy seawater in the bottom of the raft.

"We're lost," he says.

"You can't get into a tiny raft in a giant ocean and expect to stay in one place."

Truitt starts to weep.

"It's okay." I try to comfort him. "The currents carry everything to the same place eventually."

I surround him with light, but he doesn't want it. He covers his face with his hands.

"That's a fucking lie."

His chest heaves. I've had enough.

"No! no! no! no! no! Stop it!"

"Stop what?" he shouts through his snot and swollen lips.

"No more crying!"

He cries for five minutes while I watch. Then he gathers himself. He lifts up the sextant and holds it to the horizon. I can still see the sun, but I can't feel it. He throws the thing overboard.

"Poor Smooshed Bug!" he says.

"Poor baby! Poor, poor girl."

KATHERINE

I made it clear to everyone in my Hope Haven group that I didn't believe a word I was saying. But I said things anyway. Horrible things. Once I got started, I couldn't stop talking. People said whatever random shit they wanted. Many of them were on high doses of psychiatric meds. It was different from all those years of AA meetings. We were inside a treatment center. We were all certifiably insane. Thirteen humans. Various ages, genders, races. Listening to each other because there was absolutely nothing else required of us. Except the truth.

"Spill it," said Gwynn.

"What does the truth even look like? Who on this stinking earth would want to see it?"

"Love is information."

Zack was only seven the last time he saw my dad. In the car on the way home, I asked the kids if they thought my father was weird, and I warned them that if Grandpa ever touched them funny, they should tell me. Zack blurted out that my father had put his hands up his shirt at the dinner table. In the crowded restaurant. My dad was groping Zack with those same greedy hands, right there at the table with Phil and me sitting on either side of him.

We didn't see it happening, I told my group. *He's that sneaky.*

"Trust the process," said Gwynn when I wanted to retreat.

What I was doing was picking, pinching, and digging at my anus and rectal tissue so that it was always inflamed, swollen and bleeding. I convinced myself that it was a chronic medical condition as a result of the episiotomy I had when Zack was born, except I remember doing it in college. Back then, in my twenties, I was also a cutter. I used to have a little kit with straight razor blades in it. Rubbing alcohol. I would cut myself on my foot and pour alcohol over it.

"I'm glad you stopped doing that," said a member of my group. She was a tough-looking young woman with short black hair and tattoo sleeves up and down her arms. "I hope you can be gentle with yourself."

We walked together after the session, ended up in the meal hall drinking black coffee.

"You know what really hurts?" I was going for it. "On the inside? How much he fucking hated me. When we weren't in bed together."

She took a sip of her coffee. We stared at each other.

"You're talking about your husband?"

"I'm talking about my dad."

Her eyes filled with tears. I watched her and froze. Locked up. Left the scene. Left my body. Got numb. Got separated from my thinking.

"Are you okay?" she asked.

"I don't like it when people feel sorry for me."

"Oh," she said. "That's not what's happening."

I realized later I had forgotten her name. She must have told me. I was very foggy.

"The circuit board is complex," Gwynn explained. "Feelings go underground and surge out in a completely different form. They can be unrecognizable. You have some crossed wires. Sounds like you were dissociated. Dissociation. You've heard of that, right?"

A rope against poles. A clanging sound. That's what the wind does. No one believes me.

"I believe you," said Gwynn.

The head of a river. The tail of the same flow. Where it empties into the sea.

"Hopelessness is a form of shame," she told me. "It can burn out the circuit board."

I heard a buzzing, like a ringing, in my head. It almost felt like a headache. I closed my eyes.

"Hopelessness? You mean wanting to be dead?"

Later, lying awake in my single bed, I stared at the ceiling. I had a black-hole question eating through my center. It wasn't really a question; it was a realization. Something really scary. That I didn't know my inner world, not in a deep, full, true way.

I had always wanted to. And maybe I thought I did. But I hid things from myself. Important things.

I talked in group. I talked some more. The group was everything. The compulsive wankers, masturbators, the strippers and the barfers and the flashers and the pedophiles, the suicide attempters, the child abandoners. Wine tasters, kitesurfers, agented actors and galleried artists, handsomely compensated marketing executives and coolheaded traders. Convenience store workers, pizza makers. Refugees, terrorists, shopkeepers, welders. And me.

Hi, my name is Katherine and I live in New Jersey. The truth is gone.

BUG

She said she was blood dead. *Blood dead?* What does that mean?

It means I like being touched. A lot.

Shut up!

Who's there?

A father and a daughter ride bikes to the beach. There's tar in the sand. A bird feather coated in oil. Do you realize how many one-celled bacterial creatures had to die so oil could even exist? And you leave the lights on while you're sleeping. You burn it up maniacally, Katherine. Thoughtlessly.

Kill yourself!

Who said that?

If you're not going to kill yourself, at least cut off your hands and your feet.

Shut up!

All she's doing is crying. Inside her hull.

I'm a slutty child. And it's not just because my dad hits me with a wrench. Just kidding. He never hit me with a wrench. But he did rape me with one. Just kidding. He didn't rape me. Just once. Imagine how huge he must seem to a little bug, with a tiny heart, hiding in the dark, scared. No lock on the door.

Phil suffers. So did my dad. Men are made of earth and clay. Sand in an old shoe. He finds it hard to be alive. My father, too. Alive as himself, and alive as my mom's husband. He's a broker, so, for example, he finds an empty retail space in a new strip mall and then he goes out and finds a store owner who needs a space, maybe he reaches out to a national chain. And he matches a store owner with the people who build the strip mall and takes a cut of the—

"SHUT UP AND MEDITATE!"

It's not so unusual for a star to inhabit the core of a human being. In fact, it's quite normal. What we call *love*. Something needs to change in Katherine's marriage. Oozing tar.

"Look for the truth. Let's make this fast."

"Make what fast?"

"Pull down your pants."

No, he didn't rape me, but he did molest me.

Wait, these are jokes. My father didn't molest me. But he wasn't always nice.

Go clean yourself off.

KATHERINE

Gwynn told me I had inner children waiting for me, immature parts who were possibly at war with each other. Ideally, they'd be acting together, in my best interest, as a team. I remembered that Sheila did something like this years ago. Gwynn suggested that my inner children were already at the surface.

"Ripe," she said. "Eager to be known. I'll teach you how to find them."

Did I even want to?

I wandered down to the cafeteria and ate cold scrambled eggs from the buffet. I looked for my friends from my group, checked the lounge, the smoking courtyard, but I couldn't find anyone. I went to see Gwynn. Knocked on the door to her office.

"Come in."

She sat there in her comfy pleather armchair and looked at me. A wan sun, pale, peeked out from behind thick clouds, gray and purplish blue. The water all around us looked choppy, shark-infested, cold.

"What is it?" she asked.

Pebbles, wind, bushes, sand, wind, tongue, eyelash, sea, lip, wind, sea, sky, cloud, hand. What he put in my mouth. What he put in my whatnot. The love he had for me. The love I wanted, courted. I dragged my body to school in my Brownie uniform. Brownie comes before Girl Scout. So that's pretty young.

"I still don't believe it myself, what Dad did. He had a wrench and a flashlight. He was pointing them both at the torpedo hole. I saw him pull it out."

The sun. How it moves across the sky. The sun is a star.

I waited in the bed for him.

Flame. Shame. Estuary. Confluence.

I brought it on. I *liked* it. I am to blame.

I walked from my small group meeting to my room and then from my room to Gwynn's office. I slept, then I ate, then I went to a different small group meeting. This is a sandy path. These are clouds. This, the surface of the sea.

"I closed my heart to my mother when I was pretty young. Maybe thirteen. I didn't let her touch me. I didn't talk to her. I was alone, and by choice."

Words floated like crafty clouds around Gwynn's tiny office. Puffy clouds shaped like fingers. Gusts of wind.

"Phil has this terrible habit. He tells me one thing and then he does another. He bleeds me. I'm bleeding."

"Are you talking about Phil or your dad?"

"The very essence of Phil is coercion. Getting me to do what he wants."

"But you love him."

"*Love.* I burn that word in the trash."

I sat for a second, tried to clear my head. Boats on moorings, the anchors dug in soft white sand, beating wings, seagull screeches, the chug and purr of a tiny outboard motor. The slap of water against a dock.

"Anything else?" asked Gwynn.

Brown hair legs made me kiss it no hair there me so small so big made me bleeding inside me yes it hurt. Lips.

"He held me down the first couple of times. After that he didn't have to. Because he was handsome and he smelled good and he loved me. I had a pink bicycle with a basket that had flowers on it."

"Good," said Gwynn. "Keep going."

Do I matter? Is it my fault? Did I know he was doing it? Why didn't she stop him? What the hell was wrong with him?

"Should I keep doing this?"

"Doing what?"

"Living."

Dad's head, the head of a hooded priest. What moved him? The wind moved him. The sun is gone. Where did it go? Behind the clouds. What are clouds?

DEAD GIRL REGISTER: KATE BURNS

I stood next to the examination table. Katchie was lying there with her skinny legs open. Dr. Wickford was doing something to her, between her legs. I had only a limited understanding of what was happening. The limit was, I had no idea what the pediatrician was doing to Katchie. When he finally let her get up, my child fainted, collapsed against a filing cabinet and sliced her back. We left the office with a lollipop.

Hi, I'm Katchie's mother and I admit I had a harmless crush on Dr. Wickford. Did it start then, at his office? No, when did it start? I made out with Dr. Wickford—Wick—at a party at the house once, in the laundry room. Craig and I drank. We liked to throw parties.

Wick Wickford was the doctor to the posh set, Garden Club types, the Junior League. High society in Virginia Beach was equal to middle society in Richmond, but my friends and I didn't worry about Richmond, or (God forbid) Washington, and New York. Applicants to the Virginia Beach Garden Club were blackballed if they were born too "low."

Katchie wandered into the laundry room and caught me and Wick in a drunken, adult embrace. Because when you're a kid and your parents throw a party, you slink around and spy. You smell the perfume. I did the same when I was her age.

It meant nothing, me and Wick, drunk in the laundry room. It never went anywhere. The next morning, I crawled downstairs and drank leftover booze from the glasses. I took an accidental swig from a wineglass with cigarette butts afloat in it like U-boats. This kind of sneaking around, this living in the imagination, it's a disease. Fantasy is painful. Nothing is rational, nothing is right-size. A cigarette butt is a submarine, when in reality it ought to be a torpedo. But it's not moving, is it?

Katchie scraped her back at the doctor's office. That's all they recorded. Nothing about what was going on between her legs. Childhood is a leading disease.

KATHERINE

Gwynn gave me my phone back after twenty-three days. She felt I was ready to call people. I started with Nance.

"How are the kids?" she said. "Have you talked to them yet?"

"I thought I'd call you first, get an update. I'm scared to call the house."

"Why? They're dying to talk to you."

"I'm a charred marshmallow."

"That's a funny way to describe yourself."

"You know why I fell in love with Phil? In Virginia Beach when you first introduced us a million years ago?"

"Why?"

"He had a leather Dopp kit. And it was clean. There was no toothpaste stuck to the bottom of it."

"He's also kind, and generous. And smart and handsome and a good father."

The search for land, the line of earth, or rock, bush, sand, tree. Where branch tips meet the sky. Call it the horizon.

"Tell me what you're doing there. How are they helping you? What's their program?"

"My counselor says I have many inner children. Or inner parts."

"I've read about that kind of therapy. It's like you're in family therapy, but *you* are the entire family."

Like Nance, Phil asked questions. But he only half listened to the answers.

"I really love Gwynn," I said. "She's the best therapist I've ever had."

A rubber lifeboat dropped from the sky as a gesture of mercy.

"Why? What about her?"

"Maybe it's because I'm living here, seeing her twice a day. Once by myself. Once in a group with the other fuckups."

I waited for him to say *You're not a fuckup.*

"What are you doing?" he asked. "What's the treatment program?"

"You wouldn't understand it if I explained it to you."

"Why are you angry?"

"Sorry. I didn't mean to sound angry."

"When are you going to be ready to talk to Zack and Em?"

"When are you going to stop asking aggressive questions?"

"Jesus. They're not here anyway. They're with my parents. I'm leaving for the airport in a minute."

"Only monsters don't love their parents."

"Well, Zack and Em love you. I guess they're in the clear."

"While we're on the topic of reciprocation, I got a book about it from the library here. They have every self-help book in the universe."

"Are we on a topic?"

"Reciprocation. The idea is simple. If you've done something for someone, and the person thanks you, you should answer *I know you'd do the same for me.*"

"Okay." I could tell he wasn't interested.

"You make it clear that they owe you. And when people owe you, you have to give them a way to pay you back."

"You mean back and forth?"

"Yeah, like you scratch my back, I scratch yours."

"When are you coming home?"

"I have a week left. I think after another week of this I'll want to come home."

"No rush."

"I don't want to miss Nance's wedding celebration."

"Is that reciprocity?"

"*Reciprocation.* I didn't say *reciprocity.*"

"What's the fucking difference?"

That's what the wind does.

KATCHIE

I went to a high-rise building at Columbus Circle for a job interview. The job?

Whore.

Pandora, my friend at Eddie's Topless, told me about it. A woman with red hair interviewed me in one of the "session rooms." Just a regular place. Not like a hotel room, dumpier than that. Like the set of a TV show, the bedroom in an apartment on an after-school special. The coverlet was cheap and the bed was particleboard.

"This place isn't real." It wasn't the woman, the whore with the red hair. It was a larger voice, a beautiful chorus of males and females. They sounded kind, like they wanted to teach me and take care of me.

"You're creating this scene with your mind," they said. "Because of your unresolved childhood pain. And your unresolved childhood pain isn't real, either. It's all so funny."

The woman in the brothel started to laugh. I laughed with her.

"Can you hear those strange voices?" she asked.

"Yes. They come from the inside of my head."

"Pain isn't real," they said, again as a chorus. "It's just another flawed premise. Someone starts talking about it, explaining it, until you're sure it's true. If you stopped talking and thinking about pain, it would go away."

Dad's thing in my mouth, choking on it. Kissing Daddy's mouse. He put it in my mouth. It's in there now. It's all shoved in there. Forever, basically. Hairs and wrinkled skin. He's lying on top of me. He's . . . something is hurting. He sticks things places sometimes. Then he tells me to take a bath. He wants to touch some things. And lie down under stuff. Stuff in my face. And it hurts. Stuff white sticky stuffy stuff. Bloods.

I opened my eyes. Gwynn was sitting behind her desk, waiting patiently. I looked at the clock. How long had I been "gone"? She smiled.

"You dissociated again," she said.

"I haven't worked since I met Phil," I said. "Haven't earned a dime."

"You raised two children. That's work."

"I'm a whore."

"Most whores are good women. You're a good person."

"Everyone thinks they're a good person."

"You don't."

Inside her office, it was growing cloudy. A thousand different colors.

"Work from the known to the unknown. From the simple to the complex. Basic troubleshooting."

"I don't want to go home next week. Maybe I should extend."

"You'll be ready."

"I told you, Nance is getting married. They're throwing a party at some hotel on the Jersey Shore."

"I know," said Gwynn. "Phil's aunt."

"Right," I said. "I forget that sometimes. His father's youngest sister. Family."

Gwynn smiled. Seagulls making *M*s against a moody saltwater sky. Gales and high seas. A nor'easter was coming.

"Have you been doing the guided meditation I gave you?"

"Yes. I did it three times."

"Did you find any younger parts? Lost selves?"

I nodded and flipped through my spiral-bound notebook. Best to keep it simple and read it straight out.

"A girl, a teenybopper. Very cute, sunny disposition. A flirt. Outgoing. Maybe even a slut. I thought that was her name. *Slut.* But then she said she prefers to be called Star."

Gwynn smiled. "Better."

"She's relaxed. She's floating in a raft in the ocean."

"Did you talk to her?"

I blanked out. It was dark in my head. I had no answer.

"It's okay," said Gwynn. "Let's sit for a second. This work should be gentle. Just read what you have there."

"There's a boy. A bossy boy. Angry. His name is Truitt. A little soldier. A scout. He likes to try to get the girls around the neck, bang them into walls, hurt them. But Star can't be hurt. She's happy all the time. She can't feel anything but sexy love, excitement. Truitt's very responsible. He gets a lot done. But he's always in a rage. Star loves him. She's used to him. He's with Star in the raft."

It got darker in the office as we spoke. Gwynn's hair was blowing around. Paper was flying and the room listed from side to side. Every time we went sideways up a swell, all the furniture shifted to the other side of the room.

"Can you feel that?" I said.

"Feel what?"

"Nothing."

I read from my notebook.

"Another girl. Eight years old. She looks like a shrinking blue bug with twitching antennae, very sensitive, afraid of success, hiding, withdraws, hard to locate. I'm looking at her now."

"Where is she?"

"She's in a different boat, a motorboat. An older kid is there with her, driving the boat. This one is dressed in men's clothes. Jeans, a windbreaker, work boots. Short hair. Looks like me when I was twenty-one. Or like who I wanted to be. Rugged. Handsome."

"A young woman?"

"Hmmm. I don't think so. I'm going with young man. But it's also me."

"What's he doing? Where are they going?"

"They're in a motorboat way out in the ocean. A speedboat, you know. What do they call that? A cigarette boat."

"I know what kind of boat you mean," said Gwynn.

"It's red. And there's a storm brewing. The boat is fast. It's moving very quickly, making a beeline for the girls in the raft, who are still very far away. The cool dude with the boat . . . he rescued Smooshed Bug."

"Smooshed Bug?"

"That's the little one. They're looking for the others. They need to get to them fast. They're about to be drowned in the storm. The raft I told you about."

"This boat captain sounds like a good sort."

I took a few breaths.

"This is very trippy," I told Gwynn. "Like I'm on hallucinogens."

Gwynn came over and sat with me, took my hands into her

own, which were warm and soft and made me want to cry. I kept my eyes closed. I was too afraid to open them. We sat there and said nothing for what seemed like a very long time.

"Can you talk to the cool guy?" Gwynn asked me.

"He's busy driving the boat. He's wearing mirrored sunglasses. His hair is slicked back. He's smoking a cigarette. Strong, invulnerable."

"Talk to him, Katherine."

"What's your name?" I asked.

"I'm Elegy," he said.

"Who are you?" asked the bug. She was cute for a hardshelled, many-legged, upright, child-size bug. A bug that looked like a crab.

"I'm Katchie," I said. "Katherine."

Elegy cut the engines. Everything went calm and quiet for one split second.

"WHAT?" The bug almost fell out of the boat. "WHO?"

She started jumping up and down in the boat. She was wearing a big orange life jacket. Her hair was blowing around in the wind.

"You found me!"

STAR

We hold a false belief that feelings from our childhood are our feelings from childhood. Actually, we arrive with them from outer space. Everyone who was ever alive is still alive now and living within and around us. Even people we consider long dead. We made that word up, you know. *Dead.*

Yes, Katherine. It did happen. It happened. If it didn't happen, then why are you so split? Why have you been to one million trillion therapists? And none of them can fix you. Because of us! We are the shards. We are the fragmentation.

A version of me is still in the Stable, and she's still putting her lips around that erect penis that belongs to an assault. Everyone will agree that no child should ever have to do that. But every child who does that needed to. Nothing happens by accident. And it's not evil. If a child is involved, it's innocent.

In TV nature documentaries, scientists pull giant creatures out of the sea. The poor things have all kinds of parasites riding pillion on their hides. But barnacles have feelings, too. Barnacles live on whales and sea lions, on their skin, their hide, their fur. Barnacles are simple aquatic animals. They move and twist their bodies in the current. They fish with their feathery feet. They make love. I'm not saying they screamed when Dad scraped them off the bottom of his boat with a flat-nosed shovel. (DAD'S BOAT, not some little inflatable raft.)

If you don't like the word *parasite,* then let me put it another way. Spouses, marriage partners, they are often symbiotic. It's what happens when an individual stops swimming around. Take Phil, for example. With his body buried inside of yours, he doesn't have to feel his own feelings. Love! The sun's blood!

Truitt grabbed the ship's log from my hand.

"All right, Star! That's enough. I give in. I admit it. Dad did that shit."

Truitt started shaking all over. The papers in the notebook were rustling, flipping and flopping in his hand. He threw it over the side of the raft.

"Don't ever talk about it again."

I blasted him with some heat. "It's not your fault, Truitt."

"Oh yes, it is."

"No. It never was. *Let that be true.*"

"You can't just LET something be true," he screamed. "Truth either is or isn't."

"Then it is."

Part Seven

KATHERINE

Phil met me at the Newark airport in the baggage-claim area. He looked different when he made his way through the crowd. His muscles filled out his shirt; he had his hair buzzed short. His neck was thicker.

We hugged, got my bags, walked to the parking garage, talking small things. In the car I said, "I'm scared about this wedding party for Nance."

"You don't have to go."

He placed his hand over mine as he drove. I jerked my hand away.

"It's going to be hard to celebrate a wedding," I said. "With what's happening to us."

"What's happening to us?"

"Come on, Phil. Please don't act like everything is fine. That makes me feel crazy."

Phil turned on the radio. His mouth was hard, chin thrust forward. We drove without talking. I'll tell you the radio was offering up hit after hit of classic rock. You can plug in whatever exhausted songs you want. Dad's head. The head of a river. The head of a hooded priest. A roaring sound.

"Oh my God!" I turned off the radio. "I'm gonna have a heart attack."

"What's wrong?" The way Phil asked this . . . it made me want to put a needle in his eye.

"Want to hear a joke? I made it up at Hope Haven."

"Oh. At Comedy Camp?"

"When I was eleven, my dad hit me with a wrench."

Phil didn't respond. He kept his eyes on the road. I closed mine. The vultures and seagulls started to circle overhead. Elegy's boat motored forward into huge waves. Nor'easter waves.

"That's a joke?" said Phil. "That your dad hit you with a wrench?"

The speedboat was tilted at almost ninety degrees.

"I wouldn't call that a joke."

"Okay . . . he didn't hit me with a wrench."

The boat headed due west. Maybe to stay out ahead of the storm.

"But he did rape me with one."

"Jesus," said Phil. "Am I supposed to laugh?"

"No, not yet, it's still going. It's a dark joke. He didn't rape me with a wrench."

"Is that it? Is that the punch line?"

"Stop interrupting. This joke is all about timing."

The storm blocked out the sun. The storm brought the night. Bug and Elegy leaned into the darkness. According to Gwynn, these kids needed me, wanted my attention, would die without my love.

"He didn't rape me with a wrench, thank God. But he did rape me."

The boat sped, clipping along, over larger and larger waves. The outboard motor was roaring.

"I'm just kidding. He didn't rape me, but he did molest me."

I waited. Phil didn't seem eager for me to finish my joke.

"Just kidding. He didn't molest me. He did get mad a lot."

Bug and Elegy crouched and steadied themselves. It took all

their strength to stay upright in the oncoming gusts of wind. The sea was rising, getting more violent.

"Your dad got mad at you a lot," said Phil. "You've told me that."

"No, he never got mad. But he did make me do my homework. Can you believe that?"

Elegy's giant engine started to clear the surface of the water at the crest of every wave. It made a wild, frightening noise.

"Is that the end of the joke?" asked Phil. "Are you done?"

"It's starting to rain," I said.

"No, it's not."

"Open your mouth and drink the rain."

"Whatever that is," said Phil, "it's not a joke."

He dropped me off in town and drove into the city for a meeting. I found Zack at the bagel shop with his boy posse. Middle schoolers were streaming in with their crumpled dollar bills. Or filing out with bagels and chocolate milk. Zack met me in front and gave me a hug.

"Glad you're home," he said. "I love you more than anything."

His friends came out and he gave me a look. *Off you go.*

I nursed both my children until they were a year old. I fed them from my body, my breasts. It felt good, and it felt necessary. When my infants were sucking, I was happy. It's because of the milk that I couldn't kill myself. The milk is sacred. Four bottles of pills versus Zack and Em. The heart is a gushing idiot.

STAR

Bug went nuts when she saw us. She pointed and whooped and did a little jig in the boat. The boat did its own dance, flirting with the sea, trying to get close to our raft without capsizing us. It was daylight now on the ocean. Huge black clouds loomed over mountainous waves. Bug threw the end of a rope to the raft, but Truitt let it fall into the sea.

"Fuck healing," he said. "I'm giving myself to the sharks." He could barely balance himself in the raft, which was tilting and dipping in the roll. I sunned myself in the no-sun. Pleased, relieved. And then I was in the motorboat, in the same position, on the bow cushions, spread-eagle and sweet on myself.

"Truitt!" Bug screamed. "Grab the rope!" She pulled the rope back into the speedboat. Then she gathered up her strength and threw it again. Truitt hesitated, and the rope bounced off the side of the raft into the water. He laughed as it sank away. Bug pulled the rope back and thought about it.

"Jump, then!" she said. Then she was chanting. "Jump! Jump! Do it do it do it do it!"

Truitt leapt off the side of the boat. He came up, spat out some water. Splashed around. The empty raft disappeared over the top of a wave. Truitt paddled after it, went under, came back up in the froth.

"I can swim!" he said. "I never knew I could swim."

He frolicked around almost casually. "Where are the fucking sharks?"

Everyone looked disappointed when they didn't come.

KATHERINE

I fell into bed with my jacket and shoes still on. Weird to be back in the castle after thirty days in a rehab center, surrounded by fuckups and losers. Those people never judged me. The house was very neat, everything in our bedroom in perfect order. Even the pillowcases matched. I never bothered with that.

"Katherine," said Bug.

"Yes?" I replied.

"I need you."

It still felt very new, and very weird, to connect to my inner self this way. Bug stared at me with her round brown eyes. Her antennae searched the air. Everyone was listening. The waves threw the boat in every possible direction. The girls held on to whatever was available: seat, steering wheel, cup holder. I saw Truitt in the water, spluttering, barely staying afloat. When he went under, he was way under, but he managed to get his mouth and chin above the surface again, then his whole head.

"What's the feeling you're having, Truitt?"

According to Gwynn, this was always the right question.

"Ashamed," said Truitt. "I'm deeply ashamed."

"Thank God!" said Star. "Was that so hard?"

The boat slid down a wave right on top of Truitt's head.

"Cut the engines!" screamed Bug.

Elegy shut everything down. Then he reached over and pulled Truitt into the boat. It was night again, pitch-black dark. Dark and light were switching places, back and forth, without warning.

"Look at you now," Star said to Elegy. "So handsome!"

Three red flares shot up from where Star stood, straight into the air. They didn't stop there. They shot to the outer rim of the sky.

Bug wasn't in the same mood. "I'm worried about the storm!"

"Oh, don't worry about the storm," said Star. "We always survive."

"I'm not worried for us. I'm worried for her." Bug pointed at me.

"Okay, Bug," I said. "What do you need?"

"We need calm. We need gentleness. Warm hands. Someone to listen who won't lie."

"Phil doesn't lie," I told her.

"You know he does."

"Maybe, but I can't prove it."

"He looks good on paper," Star added. "But we're not safe."

Elegy turned the key again and again, but nothing happened. "The engine's flooded."

Soaking wet and sitting in the bow, Truitt was trying to get his wet boots off.

"Truitt," I said. "What are you feeling?"

"We're not safe!" he said. "Do something!"

Do something? I didn't know what to do. So I called Emily.

"Mama! You're back! Welcome home!"

"What's your plan?"

"Just finished lacrosse practice. Can I go over to Tucker's house after? Stay for dinner?"

"That's fine," I said. "I'm going to sleep now."

"It's only five-thirty!"

"Wake me up when you get home? I want a kiss and a hug from my strawberry girl."

"I'm so glad you're home. I love you."

What happened next? I got in the shower. The hot water pouring down on my wet hair. My face. My skin. There was no feeling. I felt nothing. I lost track of the boat. The storm had finally swallowed it whole. Luckily, it was a fake storm, where everything is a trick. The boat is a toy boat, attached to a machine. The machine moves the boat up and down and sideways on a little stand. A prop guy stands off-camera and throws water from a bucket. Or he uses a special hose, made for theater.

I got out of the shower and collapsed, wrapped in a towel, on my bed. The girls came into view again, waterlogged, shivering, their lips blue. Elegy was smoking a cigarette. He held the steering wheel with one hand.

"Katherine. You need to come at this with an open heart." He calmly dragged on his cigarette. "Or any kind of heart."

"Take mine!" said Star.

Elegy looked at her. "You don't got one, honey. An animal needs to have a backbone to have a heart. Frogs, toads, lizards, snakes."

Bug moved closer, smooshed up against Elegy's body.

"I have a backbone!"

"You don't." Elegy shook his head. "Which is too bad. Houseflies and snails have hearts. Sometimes it's just a simple tube."

"You loved it, Katherine!" said Truitt. "Dad took you to lunch, and you sat across the table from him. Every part of you wanted to be touched. You knew how it would feel in your

hands. You already knew what to do with it." He spat in the
bottom of the boat. "Your mother's husband."

I got out of bed and went into the bathroom, lay down on
the marble floor. The itch predicting the sore. I'd bleed, but
only from one place and only a little. The storm was back, full
throttle. Did I have a heart? Had I ever felt love?

A huge wave came over the bow and almost knocked Truitt
off his seat. He choked on seawater. "We don't like sluts!"

I started to dig into myself with my fingers. Bug spoke next,
her face half under a wave. "We don't deal kindly with sluts!"

"Get up," said Elegy quietly. He knew it would make no difference. "Stop doing that."

"I have to," I said. "I can't help it."

"If we knew you were going to keep hurting yourself," said
Star, "we would have stayed in the submarine."

"What submarine?"

"The one you sank a month ago."

"What kind of submarine?"

"Military," said Truitt. "Because why would you need
a submarine if you weren't going to attack someone from
underneath?"

"Let me explain how you draw a horse," said Bug. "You do
it with circles. Two circles for—"

"Oh my God, Bug. Shut up!" Truitt punched at the air.
"Don't listen to Bug! First, she starts to explain how to draw
horses and the next thing you know, we're back in the Stable in
Gloucester, and Dad's putting his thing inside her!"

"Truitt's right," I told them. "I couldn't wait for his next visit
to my room."

Elegy suddenly got up and stripped down to his black Calvin

Kleins. He dove off the side of the boat and disappeared under the waves. He had the end of a rope in his hand. The rope was attached to a cleat on the port side of the boat. It went taut. He reappeared a minute later in the foamy water.

"Pull me in!"

Truitt dragged him over with the rope. From the water, Elegy flung a gruesome, bloody object over the side of the boat. Then he climbed up the stern ladder and flopped down in the skipper's seat. He hoisted the bloody thing into his lap. It was huge, the size of a pumpkin, and throbbing.

"Is that a heart?" Bug spoke from a bench cushion in the stern. Disgusted, unwilling to get any closer.

"Katherine, do you remember Millie?" Truitt asked.

"Yes. I remember Millie."

"Remember that day in the raft?"

"The day I sliced my feet up and got stitches?"

The heart started pumping harder, spraying like a hose. Blood went everywhere, but it just made more.

"Elegy," I said. "The boat is going to flip any second."

"It only takes a second," Elegy said. "And a second is the duration of a heartbeat. There's a little spark plug in the upper chamber. It sends electrical signals through the heart muscle, making it contract, or pump."

"Maybe I can fix things with Phil," I said. "We can learn to communicate better. Make it safe."

"It's never going to happen," said Star. "Prepare to die."

BUG

Truitt tied the heart to the end of the anchor line and tossed it over the side of the boat.

Down it sank like a hot stone. We looked at each other, all of us covered with blood and in shock, as if we had never seen a heart before. Had we?

The sinking heart hit the sandy ocean floor. It kept going, burning through all the earth's layers, straight down to its hard nickel core. The line pulled tight and the boat was still. The ocean surface was black with light bubbling up from beneath the waves, golden bubbles. Star started to vibrate, pulsing, heating up the boat and the water, the sky all around. She climbed into Elegy's lap.

"We're almost ashore," she said. And she was right! We had dropped anchor just beyond the break, and we could see the monstrous storm-driven waves pounding onto the beach five or six hundred feet away.

None of us cheered, smiled, or even said anything. What was there to say? We could never make land. Star was stroking Elegy's arm, the inner part, pale and soft. I took Truitt's arm and copied Star, stroking sweetly. Truitt slapped me away.

"That time in the raft," said Elegy. "With Millie when we were seven. Millie saw you crying. She kissed your face. She held you until you stopped crying. Millie rowed you back to the dock and helped you out of the raft. You climbed up a wooden ladder nailed to the bulkhead. Something your dad had built. He built it for you and your brother. To be nice. The barnacles did not slice your feet. Did not shred your feet. Your feet never—"

"That's enough," said Katherine. I had almost forgotten about her. "My dad never built a ladder."

Truitt pointed to something floating in the water. It was too far off to identify.

"What is that?"

"Don't change the subject," said Katherine. "That's a falsified story, Elegy. You're rewriting my life. You think you can fix me that way?"

The floating thing came closer slowly, as if magnetized, pulled toward the boat with an invisible cord. I jumped up. "It's a dead body! Grab it!"

Decomposing, discolored, bloated. A girl, her hair matted with seaweed and chunks of salt.

"Who is it? Do we know her?"

Another corpse floated by, and another. All girls, all face-down and naked.

"Let's see her face."

The flotilla of dead girls washed in from seaward. They looked like kelp from a distance. Waves swelled up underneath us, then rose, moved ahead, and broke with a crazed roar, crashing and tumbling, one after another, before hitting the shore.

"Pull one in!" I screamed.

Truitt shook his head.

"These girls have been dead for a long time. I'm sure the faces have been eaten away."

I leaned over the side of the boat and grabbed one of the dead bodies by its hair. I was using strength I didn't know I had. Truitt flipped the dead girl around. Katherine turned away, but Truitt wasn't having it.

"Look at her face!"

DEAD GIRL REGISTER: KATHERINE BURNS

It was me, the dead version. Bloated gray-blue face. Skinny waterlogged body with shark-bitten limbs. My current hair, a short wedge. Soccer-mom stylish and dyed black to cover the gray. Black like the oil that flowed in my old heart. The blackest smoke you ever saw.

"Speech!" said Bug.

"All right," I said. "Let's start with this. I learned it early. Seduce, and dream of rejection."

"Electrons flow," Truitt said, "only if they have somewhere to go. And if a voltage pushes them." He looked over at Elegy, who nodded in agreement.

"Stop interrupting her," said Bug.

"My dad had sex with me," I said. "And that's natural. It's not normal. It's not *right*. But it's natural. Because it happens. People do it. Some fathers force their own children into sexual acts. This is a human truth. These men are not *perverts* or *criminals;* it's not that simple. At the sex-addict meetings, I learned this. Different understandings about these men became true. Giants who have sex with children are often overgrown victims themselves. We all end up in the waves together."

"Katherine," asked Truitt, "do you remember Dickie Mueller?"

"Yes, I loved him in elementary school."

"Dickie Mueller loved you, too."

"Is this another rewrite?"

"Of course it is," said Star. "Go ahead, Truitt."

"Dickie loved you the same way you loved him, and don't kid yourself that he didn't. He could see the love in your eyes.

It kept him going. He waited for you at the water fountain at school. Pretending to drink. When you came up, he stepped aside. *Katchie,* he was thinking. *I love you. I will always love you. Take my love. It's all yours."*

"I didn't know that."

"Are you sure you didn't know that?"

"We were little kids. Both of us."

Truitt let go of the corpse and it rammed the side of the boat, started nudging and bumping against it. The rest of the floating bodies did the same thing, until the boat was set to capsize.

"Can we rewrite the cutting kit?" I asked. "The razor blades and the bandaged feet? I wish that had never happened."

"That's up to you," said Star. The dead bodies turned into an oil slick, miles wide, stretching off into the distant ribbon of darkening sea. And then they were bodies again. Then they were oil. I picked myself up from the cold tile floor of my master bathroom. What was I doing there?

I got dressed and dried my hair. The hot air from the hair dryer felt good against my face. Star sent light showering into the dark night and the ocean around the boat. All at once the girls had dry hair, were cozy and warmed up and smiling.

"Come close," I said to them. "Let me hold you."

KATHERINE

Nance's high school friends were the first to arrive at the hotel for the party. Promptly at six-thirty, all in a bunch. They took turns hugging the new bride. Nance looked ten years younger than her friends. Her husband Jack was blond and handsome, like a Swedish prince. Pastor Jerry showed up next with all kinds of sweet things to say to my kids and to Phil. I felt like I barely knew my husband.

"Phil and I are getting divorced," I told Pastor Jerry. We were sitting alone at one of the lavishly set banquet tables. Most of the guests were gathered around the two bars.

"Does he know yet?"

"I don't want to hurt him anymore."

Jerry took a slug of his rum and Coke.

"I'd like to personally invite you to church on Sunday. You might find my sermon of interest. I'm exploring the Garden of Eden, the serpent, the origin of shame."

I stared into Jerry's glasses. "A man swam up and I married him."

He stared back at me without blinking. His eyes were filmy and bloodshot.

"You're familiar with the story of the Garden of Eden?"

"Shame is a spirit," I told him. "It settles down on human beings. Uses them. We are hosts to it, like a virus."

"I don't know about that." The skin on his cheeks was red, spider-veined. He looked like he drank too much.

"Family is a vector," I told him. "For shame. We carry it forward. It survives the death of each human host. Then lives on in our genes."

"I'm going to talk about Adam and Eve," said Jerry with a snorty laugh. "Genesis. Not GENES."

It's hard to come up into the sunlight. It's hard to say *I'm leaving.* Crabs at war in a bucket. The underwater menace. I hate it when Phil goes down on me in the dark. I hate it when he goes down on me in broad daylight. I hate it when he goes down on me at all. I hate the taste, the smell in his mouth afterward. I hate the oil, the tar, the bitumen. Get sunk in shallow water or don't get sunk at all.

I excused myself, snuck away to the Ladies Lounge of the grand oceanfront hotel in Spring Lake, New Jersey. Built: 1905. I spoke to myself aloud, talking straight into the mirror.

"I forgive you," I said. "I love you."

The bathroom acoustics plumped up my proclamation, gave it more power. A woman appeared in the bathroom in old-fashioned clothes. She was pale, and small, bony in a long-sleeved dress with a tight waist and buttons up the front. Victorian. I could see her reflection quite clearly in the mirror.

"That's right," she said. "You're only human. Can't be more than human. Or less."

Too afraid to look sideways and face the voice—was it a ghost?—I froze. She fixed her eyes on me in the mirror. They were green with flecks of gold in them.

"Who are you?" I asked.

"Olive Wood. Your great-grandmother."

"Are you dead?"

"No such thing as dead. You were just explaining it yourself. I'm here inside you. Or with you. I want you to get it through your head that it wasn't your fault."

"Yes, it was. I brought it on by being a slut."

She came up so close to me that I could smell the fish on her breath.

"Stop holding on to that."

"I must have liked it," I said. "I loved him. I didn't want it to stop."

"Don't be afraid to let go."

"Why would I be afraid to let go?"

"Because everyone is."

DEAD GIRL AS HETTIE

We gathered at the sea's sucking edge and stood where our feet would stay dry. Meanwhile, the storm's rain and wind soaked us to the skin.

"Do storms slow down gradually or all of a sudden?" asked Harriet.

"They don't slow down," said Kitty. "They pass through."

"Wrong!" I said. "They rage until they dissolve, exhausted."

"Either way," said Kitty. "This storm isn't done. Let's get the lifeboat!"

I gripped her arm. "No. Katherine can wait overnight. Come to shore in the morning."

"She won't last the night," said Harriet. "If something happens to Katherine, it happens to all of us."

"That's true," I said. "But you can't take a lifeboat into waves this size. It will flip immediately."

"Put Katherine back," said Harriet. "Return her to the submarine."

"I'll return her," said Kate. "I can take her down."

I turned to stare at Kate. I had forgotten she was there. Empty orange bottles in a suitcase in the attic. Fiorinal, Percocet, Vicodin, Valium.

"You've got some nerve," I said.

"Weren't you guys paying attention?" Olive was suddenly there with us again. She held on to her hat with both hands.

The ocean's bluster wanted to blow it off. "Katherine is ready to let go."

"Great news," I said. "All hands!"

Harriet, Olive, and Kitty grabbed on to the keel of a heavy wooden lifeboat. We had discovered it in the dunes, leaning against the side of a lifesaving cottage. The cottage and the equipment belonged to the hotel. The lifesaving boat was heavy and the four of us could barely lift it. We wore ridiculously restrictive clothes, shirts buttoned all the way up to our chins, tight-fitting sleeves, long skirts sewn from heavy fabric, hats, belts. We were dressed for the opposite of saving lives.

I shouted to Kate. "Come help us!"

Kate didn't hear me. The wind was vicious.

"We need your help!" I shouted. "Kate! Help us with the boat!"

Kate was wandering on the beach with her back turned. She kneeled down in the sand. She was after the tiny yellow crabs, exactly the color of the sand, with eyes like pinheads stuck to the outside of their heads. Ten, maybe twenty of these creatures were brushing camouflaged over the beach. Sand fiddlers. Hole dwellers. Skittish and cowardly.

Kate didn't try to catch them. She tracked their movements in and out of their burrows, little holes. They scurried away from the water's edge, where gushes and gashes of black-brown oil were washing onto the sand.

We steadied the boat at the edge of the churning surf and pushed the lifeboat into the waves. Our skirts and dresses were wet, weighing us down, but we all somehow managed to jump into the boat. We rowed backward into the roar.

BUG

Here's a rewrite for Katherine. I screamed as loud as I could. My mom ran to the bedroom. She opened the door and saw what was happening. She pulled my dad off me. She yelled at him. She beat him up. She pulled the hair from his head. She ran to the kitchen and got the butcher knife and threatened to cut off his balls. But then she relented and beat him around the face with a high-heeled shoe. Still, we didn't know if he was alive or dead.

She came to me, bathed me, wrapped me in a dry towel. Saw the blood. Didn't flinch. She never called me a whore. Why would she?

The next day, she gathered up a suitcase for the three of us— me, Gordon, Mom—and she left my dad forever. A few weeks later, in our new apartment, when Gordon and I were eating breakfast, she said, "I'm sorry I've been so shameless about shitting. Obviously, there's nothing shameful about shitting, not in itself. But when you use it to let your children know that your life is out of control, that's another matter. I'm going to get help."

That same week, Mom went to a therapist and was actually honest. She told the therapist everything that was going on. Mom admitted that she was abusing laxatives. She told the therapist, "I'm also addicted to opiates. Pills. I'm a pillhead and I'm tired of being sick. I'm exhausted. I simply won't tolerate it anymore!"

To put it simply, Mom had a spiritual awakening.

"Ignore my body," she told us when she got home from her

therapy session. "Don't let it scare you. I don't want or need you to pay attention to me."

Gordon and I looked at each other and wept with relief. Mom was going to heal! After that, she never took pills again. She owned her body, was fully in it, awake and present every day. She took care of us.

KATHERINE

"Mama," said Emily. "What are you doing in here? Talking to yourself?"

"More like listening." I looked down at my dress. A puddle left a wet mark where I leaned against the lip of the ceramic sink.

"Don't worry about it. You can't see it."

Em dragged me out of the bathroom and took me to sit with Sheila, who had arrived late with her third husband, all the way from Virginia Beach. Sheila and Nance had gotten closer over the years, maybe from their involvement in the life-coaching scene. AA, EST, rebirthing, Church for Psychics.

Sheila entertained our table with photos of her Bernese mountain dog. Emily sat right next to her, squeezed in tight, totally enraptured. I loved her freckled hands, the smell of straw-berries, all that Emily was at sixteen. I tried, for her sake, to act normal. *Normal.*

My gene path comes straight down the line from General Wood. I grew up staring at his framed daguerreotype, Hettie by his side. I flipped through a book of collected love letters he and Hettie exchanged during the Civil War. We saw his army uniform on display at the Museum of the Confederacy in Richmond. There was an ancient bloodstain on his pants from the Battle of Gettysburg. I could harvest DNA from the wool.

What would I find? The faulty gene. The die-early gene. The evil-slave-owner, whoremongering, card-playing, fake-Christian, white-trash gene. I carried it in my eggs. It's too late. I already passed it down to Emily and Zack. Luckily, Phil's genes also make up half their package.

I looked around the banquet room. Phil's family stretched out in front of me at big round tables like illustrated characters in a book of fairy tales. The Greek gene, the heroic gene, ancient and courageous.

"Look, Mom!" Emily thrust Sheila's phone in my face. "Aunt Sheila got a new puppy."

A waiter came over to fill my wineglass from his bottle.

"No, thank you," Sheila said. "This whole table is on the water wagon!"

She was right. Every glass on the table was turned over except mine. I noticed a little mouse was sitting next to it, nibbling at the spilled bread crumbs. Imagine how huge we must seem to a little mouse, with his tiny heart, lying in the bed in the dark scared. No lock on the door. Is he coming? Can I clean myself off? Am I dead? Am I alive? What is this burning? When will he touch me? Will it be too late? Will I still be alive? Am I alive now? Is he inside me?

The mouse looked up at me, then collapsed.

"You see it!" said Truitt.

I reached over and lifted the mouse, cupped him in my hand.

"He's dead."

I laid the dead mouse down on the butter plate.

"Either he took some poison, or someone poisoned him."

"No," said Truitt. "We ran out of air."

Bug stared at me with great love and devotion.

"Do you remember the submarine?"

"Did we have little mice?" I asked her. "Did they breathe for us?"

Bug nodded and clapped her hands together. Emily reached over me to return Sheila's cell phone.

"You okay, Mom?"

I nodded. Sure. I'm fine. Just losing my fucking mind. Was this healing?

"Who's the bigger dog in the background?" Emily asked. "Rosie?"

"No," said Sheila. "Rosie passed away. That's Daisy."

Her husband said, "We name our dogs after flowers. Zinnia, Pansy, Marigold, Rosie. They're our children. Since we don't have the real thing."

"Dogs aren't kids," I said. Everyone looked at me, then went back to scrolling through the photos. The waiter came back to the table and passed plates around. Fish, chicken, and julienned vegetables. Hot rolls and roasted potatoes, stacked pats of butter.

TRUITT

Phil's parents got up from Nance's table to socialize, and Emily dragged us over to steal their seats. We sat down next to Nance and she pulled Katherine close for a hug. Nance was flushed, a little drunk. Phil was seated on the other side of Jack, the groom. Emily dropped into the chair next to him. I've told you, Phil's a much better person than Katherine. That's obvious to anyone. On the inside. And outside? Who can we compare him to? Honestly, it has to be our father.

Craig, Dad. What about his genes? I don't know much about them. He never talked about his parents. All he talked about was Japan, Germany, combustion engines, maritime flora, coastal native trees, and the bulkhead that protected our yard from Float Lake. That was his family.

I pulled the diamond studs out of Katherine's ears and put them in the water glass. They sank down through the ice.

"What the hell are you doing?" Nance reached in with a spoon and pulled them out like false teeth. "You're going to lose them."

I put the earrings back in, tightened the backings.

"Do you and Jack have good sex?"

"Umm . . . Yes? We just got married."

Here's what a barnacle looks like: a tiny Band-Aid-colored squishy thing, shaped like a shrimp. The female glues herself upside down by her head to a boat bottom. The male swims up and latches on, fuses with her. He's no longer a separate entity.

"Last night Phil and I took our clothes off and tried to fuck. He was slurping at my nipples, lying on top of me. I could hear his saliva cells replicating in his mouth. He put his hand between my legs."

"That's what he's supposed to do."

I took a chocolate from a bowl on the table. The candy was round with a white chocolate cream filling. I bit into it. It tasted like sour-apple sewage in an old sock.

"Sex can't always be exciting," Nance said. "You and Phil have been married for a long time."

Nance found Jack in a fairy tale. When it's time to get hitched, you know it. The spark must be strong enough to jump across the gap between the spark plug electrodes. Even barnacles can figure this out.

"Katherine," I said. "Tell Nance how you feel."

"I'm in a lot of pain," Katherine said.

Nance looked concerned. She really does love Katherine, even if Katherine can't feel it.

"What kind of pain?" she asked.

"Angina, chest pain, discomfort, like pressure or a squeezing in the chest."

"Here?" Nance cupped her palms and pressed them in the center of her chest between her breasts.

"I was lying there like a corpse," I told her.

She and Katherine exchanged a long look.

"I don't know what to say, honey."

I scraped my chair back and got up from the table. "I don't want to ruin your party."

Nance pulled me back down.

"All marriages have rough patches."

I could feel my face getting red. My heart was pounding. My voice twisted up and around itself and came out of my throat with spikes in it.

"We're getting a divorce."

"Phil is sitting right there," Nance said. "With Emily. They can hear you."

"Let me tell you what crabs can do. If a limb is trapped, if a limb is injured, a crab can let it go, just let it drop away. A swimming leg, a walking leg, crushed by a rock. Self-amputation! The performance of surgery upon oneself."

Nance had a frightened expression on her face.

"What are you talking about?"

"The limb drops away! Takes two seconds. Plus, the leg grows back. Takes three years."

DEAD GIRL AS KATHERINE

Zack was over at a table with his teenage cousins telling a story. At the exact same time, the rescue party was getting clobbered in the high surf that separated them from the girls in the speedboat. Harriet and Kitty faced backward with their oars, trying desperately to push out and over the incoming waves.

Everyone at Zack's table started to laugh at something he said. He looked over at me, and I crooked my finger. *Come here.*

He got up and walked very slowly to where I was waiting for him.

"Did you have dessert, darling?"

"Not yet."

Phil was eating his second piece of cake.

"Hon, get up and let Zack sit down."

"I'm waiting for my drink." Phil's mouth was full of blue frosting.

"Oh, come on. I want Zack to sit down."

Phil kept on with his cake. Emily gave up her seat instead, and then flitted away. Kitty lost her grip on the oar. The ocean grabbed it right out of her hands, yanked it from the oarlock.

Then it took Harriet's oar as well. Like a toy, the nose of the lifeboat pushed into a huge wave and flipped. Maybe fifty feet from shore. Everyone in it tumbled out and lurched, tried to swim for the beach. The waves threw them under and pounded them into the darkness, crushed them to the ocean floor.

Emily came back to the table with cocktails. Plastic swords through dyed cherries. She stood behind Jack and smiled. She had no idea how much danger she was in, standing there with a drink in each hand. The four women tumbled and flipped. Swept under, kept down by the swirling sea. Hettie, Kitty, Olive, Harriet. I stood up.

"Emily? Who did you get those drinks for?"

The table started to shake. The whole thing was quaking—glasses, ice cubes, the silver forks and spoons, the butter plates, the flower vase, the saucers and cups and wineglasses.

"Not for you," said Emily.

Everyone laughed, even Nance, even Jack. (Jack didn't know why he was laughing.) The overturned lifeboat tumbled and flipped, eventually reaching the beach. Black oil and tar had congealed on its hull. The same sticky brown foam was washing up onshore. My skin was on fire. I was bulging from my bones. Oil all over the beach. The crabs got drowned in their holes. The black water came in with the tide.

"I am your mother," I said to Zack and Emily. "Do you know what that means?"

They stared in horror.

"I'll tell you what it doesn't mean."

I walked straight into the ocean. Someone had to. The water was so very cold. It was March, a winter storm in the mid-Atlantic. My socks were wet now, and my feet felt wooden as I stepped farther into the waves. The bottom felt gooey beneath my toes. There was poison in the water. You could smell the oil. *Ping.*

The current sucked and slapped at my legs. Chunks of tar and oily blobs, no name for them. Dark brown, congealed, a gusher. I was shivering. My hands stung. My legs and arms went numb. My clothes were heavy enough to weigh me down, to sink me.

What common features hold us together? The dead and the living? Some of us move through the world like ice-cream cones, others like the human hand. Some are shaped like trombones. Others develop their gifts and interests like farm outbuildings, where the tools are kept and the hens lay eggs. Umbrellas, carburetors, the human heart. Plants, trees, vines, a fetus in the womb.

KATHERINE

"Stop that!" said Star. Elegy was seated at the command center in the boat. Messing with the key. Trying the engine. Over and over. It was dark. The ocean was black; the sky starless, moonless, endless.

"The boat will explode with all this gas in the water!"

"That's not gas," said Elegy. "It's oil."

"Whatever," said Star. "It's flammable."

"That's how we get rid of it," said Elegy. "We burn it."

"Let's get you into a hot bath," said Phil, taking me by the elbow.

"What the hell are you doing here?"

"You're exhausted."

I did feel exhausted. But I didn't appreciate Phil's patronizing attitude.

"I'm not tired," I told him. "Leave me alone."

"I'm worried you'll hurt yourself."

We were in our hotel suite. I wasn't sure how we got there. I saw my clothes, soaked in a sandy pile, on the floor near the bed.

"I'm not who you think I am," I told Phil. "In fact, there are parts of me that you don't even know. And they don't like you. They know you lie whenever you want to get your way. You scare them."

He shook his head. "What the fuck are you talking about?"

"Just go back to the party."

Phil didn't argue. He left. I got into the bathtub and let the water run. It was a deep porcelain tub with water jets, fake gold fixtures. Hettie came and sat on the side. The others crowded into the bathroom behind her. I tried to cover my naked body, but they all just laughed. Kate stepped up and pushed Hettie out of the way. She had an oversize ziplock bag full of pills, which she emptied into the bathtub.

"Just drink it all up," she said, "and you won't be here anymore."

"Ha," said Harriet. "You wish."

"There's more where these came from," said my mom. She was wearing a yellow silk blouse and paisley pants, orange-and-purple arabesques. Her stomach looked hugely fat, grotesque, giant, ready to burst.

"Your mother wants to kill you." Harriet had a square face like mine, with a wide, strong jaw.

"That's why I never visit her."

"Well, we don't like her, either. But she's one of us."

"I don't want to live anymore."

Harriet threw her head back and laughed. I could see she was missing teeth, and most of the surviving teeth were brown.

"You have to be extremely careful. Underwater, everything rots, even steel. Everything loses its inner strength. Its structural integrity. The whole thing might collapse."

"Katchie," Mom said. "Do you love me?"

Everyone waited for me to answer. I wanted to say *no*. I couldn't say *yes*. I put my head under the water. If I couldn't see my mother, then maybe she couldn't see me, either. Down we all went, quickly, to swim around. The site was intact, preserved. A rare find at 115 feet. The conning tower poked sideways out of the sand like the arm of a corpse. It had one finger left, the attack periscope, mostly corroded and eaten away by salt water. The rest of the boat was in good shape. Even its deck gun was still attached.

How do you move around a submarine? Front to back, of course. The boat was flooded, submerged, sunk. The water was cold and murky. Nothing working, nothing moving but the fish and the sharks that had made a home inside the hull. Amberjack, hammerhead, baitfish, crabs.

"Listen," said Olive. Bubbles surrounded her mouth. "We need to tell you something." She moved her lips violently like a silent movie star. The others watched with pale underwater faces. Their long braids and hair floated up above their heads.

Harriet grabbed Olive's dress sleeve. "Mama," she said. "Be careful."

"It would have been brutal for you to wake up to the truth

about your dad. Luckily, you didn't wake up to it all at once. The whole truth has dawned on you very gradually since the first time it happened."

Ping. I hadn't been breathing for quite a while and I panicked. I thrashed around in the water. Hettie grabbed me by the wrists to calm me down.

"Stand fast," she said. "We're surfacing."

We came up again, into the brightly floodlit hotel bathroom. The air was steamy, the mirrors obscured. I gasped for air.

"I didn't forget," I said. "I never knew it happened."

I got up out of the tub and grabbed a towel. My head felt light. I was dizzy. Maybe the water was too hot. I started to wobble and faint, but Harriet caught me from behind. The others crowded around to help her steady me.

"Acceptance means you let go," they sang. Their voices had fused into a sweet, smooth chorus. "*Let go* means you're dead."

I crawled into the stiff and stinky hotel bed. The voices followed me.

"*Dead* means you can be born again."

It sounded like their sweet tones were being run through a rainbow vocoder.

"Was it my fault?"

"Always already dead, my love."

"That's not an answer."

"We were with you when he was hurting you. We kept you alive."

"You were? You did?"

I put a pillow over my head. But the chocolate syrup voices poured themselves into the nooks and crannies, sticky and sweet, sealing me in.

"Yes, my girl. We were there with you then. And we're here with you now. You can sleep."

DEAD GIRL AS KATHERINE

I woke up at 6:00 a.m. Phil was snoring next to me. The kids were crashed out on the two queen beds in the other room. I got up and found my cell phone in the darkness.

"Hey, Gordon," I whispered.

"Katchie!" He was groggy, half asleep. "What time is it there?"

"It's almost dawn. Why is your phone on?"

"Long story. Is everything okay?"

"Remember your rock tumbler? How you used to sleep with it by your bedside?"

"Umm. Yes?"

"That was probably the best Christmas present anyone ever got in our family."

"I still have it," he said. "In a box in my storage space. What's new? How are the kids? Mom and Dad are always asking about them. Jesus Christ, it's been at least three years!"

No submarine has space to take prisoners on board. Captains must prioritize their own crew. Which means tough luck for torpedoed survivors. And who is a crew? A family. We're all trapped in one. Then we go out and create a new family, join it with the first.

"I used to steal your polished rocks," I told him. "The prettiest ones."

"Yeah, I know."

"I'm sorry."

Little rocks grinding together in sand. When the tumbler had done its magic, maybe after a few days of grinding, they looked like the rocks in a gift shop. Smooth, shiny, and polished. Touchable and soft, even though they were still hard. I took them, threw them away on the road between our house and the bus stop.

Kids will find their comfort. Gordon rubbed rocks; I stole them. Also, I talked to stuffed animals. Only one of them was real to me: Robby the Raccoon. I beat him senseless on the bedpost of my canopy bed. Threw him out of the window and then went down and walked barefoot over pine needles and gravel to assess his injuries. When I got him back to my room, I cried and begged. *Forgive me.*

Here's a rewrite. Dad fell on his knees in the grass and apologized for wanting me. He ran inside and fucked my mother in a fever of love, which wasn't exclusive, or twisted, or tainted by anger and his childhood pain. He never desired me, as I was a child, and his daughter. I served a different love purpose in his life. I'm not mad at him, or my mom. I don't blame them. I don't blame Gordon. I forgive them. And I forgive myself. That's the magical thing.

"Katchie?" said Gordon. "You're talking gibberish."

"I must have dozed off," I told him.

When I hung up with Gordon and tried to sneak out of the room, Phil came after me. He must have been awake already from my phone call. He caught up just as I got on the elevator.

"Where are you going?"

The elevator bank had mirrored walls all around. I could see Phil from the front, the back, and both sides. He was in a fighting stance: T-shirt and jeans, hunkered down, taking control, the boss. The elevator door opened; I got on. So did Phil. He zipped up his jeans.

"I can't be with you anymore," I told him. "Not even for another hour. It isn't good for me. For my mental health."

"Why not?"

"We're not safe with you."

"Who's *we*?"

"Lord, it is time," said Bug.

We got off the elevator and walked into the lobby. The carpeting was thick and dirty, maroon with a looping floral print. The giant TV was playing a cooking show.

"You're going to break up our family," said Phil. "That's fucking selfish."

I answered with something Kitty had said.

"There is no self. The blame killed the self."

I pushed through the glass hotel doors into the parking lot and Phil trailed behind me, not in a rush. Outside, a small strip of parking spaces, the beach, and the gaping Atlantic. The air smelled of salt and seaweed. The cloudless sky was turning a paler black, layered with grayish blue and a hint of orange. The rising sun edged the horizon.

Here's a rewrite. Phil understood and knew exactly what I needed. He even read a few books about abuse survivors and codependency. He learned about symptoms of PTSD, especially dissociation. He became "trauma-informed."

When we were having sex, and I left my body . . . when I crawled away from Phil after he orgasmed, when I receded into the dark, and curled up into a ball at the foot of the bed. When I was crying as we were fucking, Phil was very gentle and patient. He realized that sometimes it's not a good idea to have sex. He accepted that "sex" and "not sex" were two different sides of the same loving relationship.

He said to himself, *Phil, don't push for sex right now with your wife. There will be plenty more opportunities. She's not herself tonight. In fact, right now she seems more like a wounded child than an adult woman. Think about it. Would you ever have sex with a child?*

Out on the beach, the surf had calmed. The waves rolled in gently with soft white curls. Dead girls started floating in, washing toward the beach. As soon as the corpses crossed the break, they turned into muscular white horses. The horses shook their manes and cantered out of the sea, sure-footed in the froth. They thundered onto the slick wet sand and galloped down the beach, shoulder-to-shoulder in perfect rhythm. Hundreds of them. They seemed to know where they were going.

"What are you looking at?" asked Phil.

I took a deep breath of sea air, a swig. The last breath. When you go there, you find it.

"I'm letting go."

I trembled from the thunder of hooves. The ground shook. I thought the hotel might crumble to its foundations with Phil's whole family inside of it. And my children, Zack and Em.

Phil didn't feel it.

"The kids want to see you at breakfast," he said. "They'll go crazy with worry if you're not there when they wake up."

"You're thinking of our kids ten years ago. They don't need me that way anymore."

But my other kids certainly did. They were standing in the

boat, lined up at attention, as if they were ready to walk the plank. But there was no plank. An unexpected swell came up from under the waves, from out to sea, an outlier, a giant.

"Oh God," screamed Truitt. "The anchor will never hold."

I had never heard that much fear in Truitt's voice. The wave moved through and the anchor didn't give; it held. But the boat broke apart and splintered. Everyone went overboard. Everyone went under. Everyone. The boat's bits and pieces knocked around in the water. I knew what I had to do. I walked toward my car and hit the key fob. The lights blinked and the car made a muffled beeping noise.

"You're actually going to get in your car?" Phil asked. "And just drive away?"

I got in, closed the door, and started the engine, while he watched in disbelief. Finally, he banged on the window. When I opened it, he leaned down and pressed his entire face toward mine. Under the skin, his face was exploding with rage. His face was just a lid, a Tupperware top on an active volcano.

"If you drive out of this parking lot right now," he said, "I'm never taking you back. Do you get that? Never! You drive away now, and our marriage is over."

"Phil. This is terrifying. But I need to do the opposite of what I think is right."

"That's a dumb idea."

"Everything I know about love is wrong."

I reversed with a lurch and screeched out of the parking lot. Bug, Truitt, and Star emerged from the surf like gods and goddesses. A glowing gold, as if someone had painted them. Each on the back of a snorting beast. Herded, stampeded, carried down the beach in the clarity the storm had left behind.

Elegy wasn't with them. I checked my rearview mirror, and I saw his face there, overlaid on mine. His eyes. My courage. I also saw Phil in the rearview mirror. He stood there, stunned, as I pulled onto Ocean Avenue. I drove about five blocks parallel to the beach before the tears came. When they came, they came so violently that they forced me off the road. I parked on the shoulder and sobbed.

The sky was bright orange now, the sun a liquid red. The white horses were still on the run, but they had gone so far down the beach that I could barely see them. My girls had ridden off, or they had been ridden off. The herd was still running. It might run forever. Once I was golden. Once I was bathed in gold.

"Keep going," said Dead Girl. A chiming reminder, an exhortation. Birthday cakes in the coffin. Widow's weeds in the wedding trousseau.

"But where am I going?"

"We'll take care of that," they said. "Go!"

Dear Mom & Dad,

Hi! My tent is OK But there is a ~~fat~~ slut (exuse me) who wears blue maskara & all But its nice to hear her talk about how nasty & bad she is & think "Gee I'm a nice little girl" I am the straightest girl in camp it seems! My counselor is 38 w/3 kids See she's real weird I don't like her

Got to go

O LOVE YOU

LOVE.

Katchie

NOTES

My process while writing *The Daughter Ship* included a practice called "cut-ups." I sampled bits of text from fairy tales, operating manuals, encyclopedias, textbooks, internet chat rooms, war novels, and other sources. I wove these appropriated text fragments into *The Daughter Ship*. I've cited the embedded, often adapted passages in the order in which they appear in the book.

PART ONE

11 "He bit into her belly": Matt Soniak, "The Horrors of Anglerfish Mating," *Mental Floss,* July 22, 2014, https://www.mentalfloss.com /article/57800/horrors-anglerfish-mating. Soniak writes: "Once the male finds a suitable mate, he bites into her belly and latches on until his body fuses with hers."

40 "Take that! . . . And that!": This scolding comes from a lively and irreverent retelling of "Jack and the Beanstalk." Joseph Jacobs, *Jack and the Beanstalk* (1890; New York: H. Z. Walck, 1975), 10.

52 "It lies in a slanting position . . . The lower end is the part that beats": *World Book Encyclopedia* (1973), s.v. "heart."

61 "The blood in our circulatory system is always under pressure": *World Book Encyclopedia,* s.v. "heart."

68 "June 23, 1895": "General Agent Pender Killed," *Daily Concord Standard,* April 23, 1897. My great-grandfather's actual obituary. I've changed his name here, and wherever else he appears, wholly reimagined, in *The Daughter Ship.*

74 "No doubt it's a surprising fact" and "We will now consider a little more in detail": Charles Darwin, *The Origin of Species* (New York: Signet Classics, 2003). *The Origin of Species* softens its radical conclu-

sions with apologetic introductory clauses: "It is scarcely possible to avoid"; "Further we must suppose." I imitated this "rhetorical hesitancy" in some places and used direct quotes here.

PART TWO

94 "An oil leak would be a basic engine problem, and would produce excessive smoke that is gray, not black": Walter E. Billiet, *Small Gas Engines & Power Transmission Systems* (Englewood Cliffs, N.J.: Prentice Hall Direct, 1982), 36.

95 "Open-heart surgery is a technique for repairing a damaged heart. The surgeon first opens the patient's chest": *World Book Encyclopedia,* s.v. "heart."

95 "Oil has been found . . . but lighter than water": Hershell H. Nixon and Joan L. Nixon, *Oil and Gas* (New York: Harcourt Brace Jovanovich, 1977), 10. A LET ME READ book stamped by an elementary school library in Odessa, Texas.

112 "Like a tall stack of jelly sandwiches": Nixon and Nixon, *Oil and Gas,* 29. In the original, this passage describes the creation of oil, not shame: ". . . the layers at the bottom were squashed by the weight of those on top. Some of the 'jelly' was squeezed out."

116 "some are smaller than the head of a pin": Nixon and Nixon, *Oil and Gas,* 14.

123 "Middle of the night somewhere in the Atlantic": Jeffrey Knight, "What are the most dreadful or haunting sounds?," Quora, September 5, 2017, https://www.quora.com/What-are-the-most-dreadful-or-haunting-sounds. Knight, a former submariner, responded to this question on Quora. He continued: ". . . at 200 ft. All very quiet in sonar then we hear what sounds like a faint baby crying. . . . It gets louder and changes to what sounds like a woman being brutally murdered. Screams and shrieks then it stopped. . . ."

134 "She may as well be broiled as die of hunger": Jacobs, *Jack and the Beanstalk,* 14.

PART FIVE

182 "Milky White": Jacobs, *Jack and the Beanstalk,* 108. "Milky White. The best milker in the parish and prime beef to boot."

197 "I'm wedged between the periscope housing and the bridge bul-

wark": Lothar-Günther Buchheim, *The Boat* (New York: Dell, 1988), 246. This book was indispensable as a research aid, since I have never lived or worked on a U-boat.

PART SIX

227 "Work from the known to the unknown. From the simple to the complex": Billiet, *Small Gas Engines & Power Transmission Systems,* 36.

231 "riding pillion": Rebecca Stott, *Darwin and the Barnacle* (New York: W. W. Norton, 2003), 99.

PART SEVEN

241 "Frogs, toads, lizards, snakes": *World Book Encyclopedia,* s.v. "heart."

257 "The spark must be strong enough to jump across the gap between the spark plug electrodes": Billiet, *Small Gas Engines & Power Transmission Systems,* 36.

260 "What common features hold [the family] together?": Stott, *Darwin and the Barnacle,* xxi.

A NOTE ABOUT THE AUTHOR

Boo Trundle is a writer, artist, and performer whose work has appeared across various platforms and publications, including *The Brooklyn Rail,* McSweeney's Internet Tendency, and NPR's *The Moth.* She has released three albums of original music with Big Deal Records. She lives in New Jersey. *The Daughter Ship* is her first novel.

A NOTE ON THE TYPE

This book was set in Bembo, a typeface based on an old-style Roman face that was used for Cardinal Pietro Bembo's tract *De Aetna* in 1495. Bembo was cut by Francesco Griffo (1450–1518) in the early sixteenth century for Italian Renaissance printer and publisher Aldus Manutius (1449–1515). The Lanston Monotype Company of Philadelphia brought the well-proportioned letterforms of Bembo to the United States in the 1930s.

Typeset by Scribe, Philadelphia, Pennsylvania

Printed and bound by LSC Communications Harrisonburg, Virginia

Designed by Jo Anne Metsch